SUDDEN EXPOSURE

Also by Susan Dunlap

A JILL SMITH MYSTERY

SUSAN DUNLAP

SUDDEN EXPOSURE

Delacorte Press

Published by
Delacorte Press
Bantam Doubleday Dell Publishing Group, Inc.
1540 Broadway
New York, New York 10036

ISBN 0-385-31025-0 (HC)

Manufactured in the United States of America
Published simultaneously in Canada
Book design by: Susan Maksuta

To Jill Moyer-Okray,
wise woman, good friend

I am indebted to the Berkeley Police Department and particularly Sergeant Steve Odom, Brenda Logan, and all those who put on the Community/Police Awareness Academy, a fascinating class on how the police department works,

to Sergeant Kay Lantow, who is always there with help and answers,

to Officer Teri Rein, for sharing her patrol shift,

to Sergeant Mike Holland and Albany Officer Karan Alveraz, for always being willing to help,

and to Officer Abbie Cohen, for her generosity, her insight, and her friendship from beginning to end.

To Ron Wright, thanks for his tales of chess.

When writing I am reminded again what a wonderful resource our public libraries are. I have relied on the research librarians at the Berkeley Main Library, and am grateful to Oakland librarian Barbara Bibel for her special efforts.

And to my superb editor, Jackie Cantor, a writer's dream.

CHAPTER 1

IF YOU CAN'T ENJOY the peculiarities of your fellow citizens, you'd better not live in Berkeley. Certainly you should not be a police officer there.

I love Berkeley, and the "Only in Berkeley" events that pop up as a regular feature in the press.

Like the daffodils already in bloom, some of our protests are annuals, and some, like the flowering plum blossoms, are perennials. And some—I've exhausted my knowledge of horticulture —flash and are gone.

The nudity movement should have fallen into that last category. And would have if the regents of the University of California had been governed by common sense and the understanding of one rule of life:

Winter follows fall.

Maybe the regents were pressured. Maybe they panicked. Whatever. The result was that nudity became a Berkeley cause célèbre.

During the spring and summer a college junior known as Naked Guy bared all for campus strolls. An article made *The Daily Californian*. Campus police asked Naked Guy to cover himself. But nothing is forever, and soon Naked Guy was naked

1

again. News coverage increased in inverse relationship to that of Naked Guy. In September, after undergraduates returned to campus, and the California Golden Bears trotted toward the scrimmage line, a coalition of Golden *Bares* formed a line of their own in Sproul Plaza. It was hard to say which team garnered greater support. In the theater, Berkeley Repertory Company rehearsed. On the plaza, the X-plicit Players performed— to an audience with no no-shows.

The New York Times reviewed.

October arrived. Rain loomed. Cold tail winds threatened. It looked like the nudity movement would be quashed with the blanket of winter, that Naked Guy had flashed and would fade . . . into oblivion.

Until the regents of the University of California made the one move that could save his campaign. They expelled him.

He who seemed dead, lived.

Hallelujah!

On campus a new crop of undergraduates demonstrated, clothing their protest in the dour garb of the first amendment and freedom of assembly.

The regents bristled.

And we citizens of Berkeley settled in to watch the show. In the world of protest we've seen it all (and most of us have done part of it). We are the sophisticates of the field. When a nude undergraduate trots purposefully across campus as if he's been too rushed to remember everything, most of us sip our *caffè lattes* and grin. And when the body he has offended is the stodgy regents, we lift our cups in salute.

But we in the police department, the guys on the Crowd Management Team in particular, grinned less enthusiastically when the conflict shifted from UC-Berkeley to Berkeley proper. Still, it wasn't our problem. In the city of Berkeley, it was illegal to be lewd but not to be nude.

But some eyes were offended. To their rescue came the Nudity Ordinance. To the City Council Nudity Ordinance hearing came the X-plicit Players, playing explicitly on the council steps. As the meeting began, nine council members sat in a semicircle before the audience. Facing them in the first row, holding a BAN NUDITY banner, were four protesters in skirts and blouses, shirts and slacks. And one pro-nudity advocate wearing a turquoise headband.

Audience statements began. One after another—ten citizens, chosen by lot—approached the podium. A man in a suit spoke on earthquake preparedness. A man in shirtsleeves protested freeway widening. And opposing the nudity ordinance was a man with a bright blue fanny pack on his tanned fanny. He, it turned out, was to be the interpreter for a Spanish speaker attired in an earring.

Cameras flashed. Audience members flashed. As the council discussion wore on, clothes in the audience came off.

But in the end, ends were to be covered, legally. The defeated lupines might beat their breasts, but not bare them. Berkeleyans were to be clothed except when breast-feeding or on stage. Complained the X-plicit Players, "We don't want the police to make ultimate determinations of whether something's obscene or art."

It was a stand with which we on the force concurred.

Alas, unauthorized offshoots had sprung from the X-plicit Players like sprouts from a potato. Performances began popping up all over town. For their successors, the Bare Buns Brigade, all of life was a stage.

But all reviews were not raves. And when the audience booed, they called us.

Had I still been in Homicide–Felony Assault Detail, I might still be chuckling. But Detective Jeffrey Lee Brucker had flown in from a two-year plum assignment in Sacramento, landed in Homicide, and bounced me back to patrol. Brucker resented being sent back to Berkeley; I resented having him. We both were trying to keep our mouths shut and not appear petty. But when I had stood in my old office and emptied the contents of all but my bottom two desk drawers—all that would fit—into a box, I felt a flush of anger rising, and waves of sadness damping it down.

I'd spent years in the department battling the lingering sexism: I am the only woman in the Berkeley Police Department ever to make it to Homicide Detail. Then there was my reputation as someone a little too cozy with the counterculture, more "Berkeley" than cop. In Homicide it doesn't pay to be macho; it pays to be smart, and trusted. I could have kept on the promotion track, headed to be Chief of Police. But I'd opted to stay in Homicide, because I was making a difference, answering the only question that could ease a survivor's grief—who was the killer—and getting that killer off the street in my city.

Now I was out of Homicide, *and* off the promotion track. I was treading water. Or maybe just flailing my arms.

After a week of patrol, grappling with the dispatch codes I'd long forgotten, battling the uniform into which breasts and hips fit like a fat guy in a coach seat, I still felt disoriented. Getting back in uniform was like donning a costume that covered my body and masked my face.

Now as 6 Adam 19 (team 6, swing shift, patrol officer 19), I back-burnered one of the calls I'd come to hate—a minor complaint from an outraged prima donna athlete ready to complain to the mayor if I didn't hustle my buns to her house—and headed to an impromptu al fresco stage in the Berkeley Hills, to lower the curtain on the Bare Buns Brigade. To Rose Walk, to be exact. One of the pathways that bisect long residential blocks, Rose Walk begins at Euclid with a curved Florentine staircase. From there a path leads to a wide cement circle with a big-globed streetlight. Theater in the round. With the spotlight provided by the city. It was, of course, more than the Bare Buns brigands could resist.

"Six Adam nineteen, your ten-twenty?" the dispatcher's voice came over the radio.

I grabbed my crib sheet off the seat. I felt like a foreign tourist, frantically paging through *Police-Talk Made Easy*. I was thinking of writing the codes on my wrist. Ten-twenty? Ah, my *loca-*

tion. "Euclid and Buena Vista. I'll be at the, uh, ten-nine-seven in a minute." The *scene* was only a block away.

"Ten-four."

"Ten-four." Whew!

Adam 2's car was at the bottom of the stairs on Euclid, blue and yellow pulsar lights still blinking at the street. 6 Adam 2—Howard—had left the pulsars on to alert me, and more importantly, any other backup units we might have to call. The solo patrol officer's safety comes from the dispatcher and backups knowing where he is—always.

I pulled up behind and swung out of my car. My protective vest felt like an iron lung. I had to keep my arms clear of the gun on one hip, the baton on the other. A foot-long flashlight dangled from the back of the belt. The whole ensemble weighed in at twenty-five pounds. I moved like I had stepped into someone else's body.

As I walked up the Florentine staircase, the glow of the streetlight accented the pink azaleas and the deep purple flowering plum trees, and cast delicate shadows on the grass. And on four men. One—Howard—was in uniform, towering over the others. And they, facing him, backs to me, were standing shoulder to shoulder, the light dancing off their doughy white derrieres. All men are not created equal—in size, shape, in texture, firmness . . . But perhaps I was assessing the result of their misdemeanor with greater than necessary thoroughness. Howard from his own vantage point was struggling against a grin.

Most of the residents on Rose Walk watched the performance from the box seats of their living room windows. But two couples stood at the edge of the lamp's glow holding up wineglasses in a bemused salute.

It was the demonstrators who were shifting uneasily under red velvet horns, a Statue of Liberty crown, or a bulldog Halloween Mask. The three seemed baffled, as if their script had been yanked away, their mission aborted. They were here to offend the bourgeoisie, not to entertain them.

"Let 'em go, Officer," one of the wine drinkers was saying when I arrived at the circle.

"When they're dressed they can leave," Howard said, never taking his eyes from the trio.

"No way," the red-horned blond said, "this is freedom of assembly."

"Come on," a woman with a glass of red said, "it's March. These cherubs are already covered with goose bumps."

"They have to be clothed with *clothes*. City law," Howard snapped. His wide lips pressed together and his lantern jaw jutted forward. The Nudity Ordinance was a silly law. It made a fad into a crime, and us into the bad guys. Howard, the department's King of Sting, the Prince of Panache, the Emir of the Attenuated Gag, just hated being turned into a Toady of the Tush. I wouldn't have been surprised to see him redden with fury, or humiliation. "Nakedness is a misdemeanor," he growled.

"Misdemeanor!" The masked one took a step toward Howard. "What kind of repressive, Victorian society is this?"

"Yeah," the blond seconded. "If we want to have the cops on our tails every step we take, we might as well live in Trenton."

I grew up in Jersey. Abandoning Berkeley for Trenton seemed rather a high price to pay for the privilege of mooning the world. In Trenton, the police wouldn't haul a nudist in for indecent exposure, they'd assume he'd been robbed.

Howard shook his head. "Okay, gentlemen, last chance. Cover up and you can leave."

"Hey, man, we've got our rights. Like there's still the first amendment, you know. Even in Berkeley."

"The district attorney will be glad to discuss that with you."

Howard nodded at me: the signal to move in.

The blond stared. The dark-haired guy yanked off his Statue of Liberty crown, threw it in the air, and shrieked. Suddenly, bulldog mask lunged at the two spectators standing together, grabbed the woman, and threw her to the ground.

She screamed, as her husband jumped between them. Glasses

hit the ground. There was a crush of bodies slamming into each other.

"Hold it!" yelled the first backup, running up the path. I aimed my knee at the back of one nudist's knees and grabbed his shoulders to pull him down. But he twisted away.

"Hold it right there," Howard yelled.

Horns and Crown held. Bulldog shoved Howard hard, and he went sailing into a rhododendron.

"Stay where you are! Don't move!" the backup, Leonard, yelled.

Bulldog didn't stay. He leapt at me, grabbed my hair, and spun me around.

When I got my feet under me, he was halfway up the path. I glanced at Howard and Leonard and the suspects. Howard was back on his feet. "I'll take him!" I yelled. It sounded like a statement but Howard had the final say.

Howard hesitated just a moment—an eternity in this situation. There was amused disbelief in his voice when he yelled, "Right. Go get him. I'll get you backup."

Did Howard think I couldn't handle this? Howard, the man with whom I swam every morning, and shared a bed—not unathletically—at night? He could explain later. I wasn't about to let this kid tell his friends how he'd grabbed a cop by her ponytail, spun her around, and then left her in the dust—not and hear it from Howard, and Leonard, and everyone else. I ran after the kid, up onto Rose Street, a steep, narrow, patch-paved lane, sided on the south by a wall, on the north by houses hanging down the hillside. It ends abruptly at the base of a cement overhang of La Loma Street that now swings out over the top of Rose.

But it does have streetlights. And in the glow, halfway up, I could see the nudist huffing hurriedly up the steep street, the globes of the streetlights shining on the globes of his buttocks and his head. The guy was entirely bald.

I followed, huffing a lot harder than him. "Po-lice!" I yelled, "Stop where you are!"

He stopped, looked around, and resumed pace.

It was a real low-speed chase, this. The night was clear but cold. The cold wouldn't bother him now. There are detriments to being naked, but by the time I was halfway up the street I envied him. *He* wasn't sweating under a wool uniform. *He* wasn't carrying half the hardware in Berkeley on a belt, or a radio on his shoulder spitting out calls too soft to hear. I pushed off harder with each step; my legs were moving like lead. Sweat dripped over my eyes. I wiped it away and looked ahead.

The nudist was gone!

He couldn't have gotten up over the railing onto La Loma; there hadn't been time. Hiding under the roadway, that's where he had to be. I pulled my flashlight free. The railing up above would come in handy to anchor the cuffs. I could hear sirens coming up La Loma. I shone the light under the overhang and shouted, "Come . . . out . . . now. Hands where . . . I can see them.

But he wasn't there.

I stood staring, the sweat running down my spine and pasting my hair to my neck.

"Adam nineteen, do you need more backup?"

"No," I said in disgust. Not when I'd lost the suspect.

"Ten-four." The radio growled and went silent. Leaves rustled.

But it wasn't *rustling*, exactly. It wasn't leaves; and it wasn't overhead. I fanned the light before me, on the steep hillside. The nudist stood out in a thicket of ivy, like the only ornament on the Christmas tree, a hundred feet down, two thirds of the way through a steep slide to Shasta Road below.

"Oh, shit!" I pushed the mike button. "Adam nineteen. Top of Rose by La Loma. Suspect going down through the ivy to Shasta. Send me backup." I didn't wait for a reply. I hit the ivy feet first, half running, half sliding, on the muddy ground and wet leaves. Like surfing or skiing, or one of those cold, slippery sports in which your best hope is you don't break some body part you might want to use again. A thick live oak branch came

■ SUDDEN EXPOSURE ■

at me—or me at it. I ducked, too late. It scraped my head, caught at my hair. Twigs poked up from the ivy, catching on my pants, snapping the baton against my leg. And poison oak, it was all around. I had envied the unencumbered nudist as he sprinted up Rose Street. No more. By the time he got down to Shasta Road, his legs would look like they'd been graffitied. And in another day or two he'd have good reason to be nude.

The slope eased. He was off to my right, disappearing behind thick trunks of redwoods and reappearing in open patches, the full moon his spotlight. He was fifty yards ahead now, but I was closing on him. My thighs ached, but my breath was coming easier now. I longed to reach the street and run. I could almost feel my arm stretching out, my hand grabbing his scalp and smacking him to the ground.

He was almost at the street. I slowed, watching as he leapt from atop the railroad ties that blocked the end of the path. I'd driven Shasta Road on patrol: *I* knew the ties were there: and so had the suspect.

"Northbound on Shasta," I gasped into the mike.

I leapt off from the ties onto Shasta, and chased north after him. Damn it, where was the backup unit? The suspect was running like a satyr. He reached the fork at Tamalpais and, without a break in stride, headed down.

"Tam . . . al . . . pie . . . is," I panted.

Now that he was on the macadam, it was a different story. Berkeley, the Preserver of Potholes, was hard on bare feet. In another hundred yards I'd have him—*if* he didn't disappear in the peninsula of redwoods eighty yards ahead where the street looped back on itself. Or in the wooded backyards across the street. Or worst of all, on Tamalpais Path, a long, steep, very dark staircase that would toss him out in the wooded back of one of the city's biggest parks. Not only would *I* not find him down there; the entire force could be looking and miss him.

I had to get him before that. My legs ached, my lungs burned. I was closing in. In another fifty yards—

His right side gleamed red.

Taillights, gleaming off him.

Van backing out.

The van was going to hit him. Or he'd smack into it.

"Watch out, you fool!" I yelled.

The van accelerated, coming at him. He skirted right. Brakes screeched. The horn blew. Kept blowing. The driver must have smacked forward into the steering wheel.

"Oh . . . . shit!" I skidded to a stop at the passenger side. The noise stopped. The driver was sitting up now.

The nudist looked back once, the streetlight shone off his face veiled by shadow, and disappeared into the dark.

I hesitated, knowing I had no choice but unwilling to admit it. Losing a suspect is hardly a headline event. But it galled me to lose this one when I was so close. Particularly him. I'd hear about this plenty when I got back to the station. Guys on patrol would be lined up with comments. My ribs would be sore from the poking.

But I couldn't ignore a possibly injured citizen in the van. I sighed, coming around to the driver's side of the van. "Are you okay?"

"No I am not okay! What the hell do you think you're doing, banging into me!" She was out of the van and glaring at me before she seemed to notice my uniform. "Oh, you're the cop. Well, it's damned well about time you got here."

Bryn Wiley, our own prima donna athlete!

"Wait a minute here!" I snapped at her. "You almost killed a man just now. You backed into the middle of a police chase—"

"Look, I'm Bryn Wiley and—"

"Right. And I'd expect more awareness from a woman used to diving off the high board." But I wouldn't expect a bit more from *you*, I could have added. "The guy you almost hit, you saw him in your mirror, right? Did you recognize him?"

"What? Are you crazy?"

"Answer the question, please."

Her sharp features were drawn into a fist of a face. It was the expression she'd had when I'd finished taking her statement four days earlier. But now her blue eyes flickered with amusement. "The guy behind my van," she said, grinning, "was he *au naturel?*"

I shrugged, vainly trying to cover all those emotions a police officer is not supposed to show when dealing with one of the city's prominent citizens. Motioning Bryn Wiley to pull her van back in the driveway, I called the dispatcher with the disposition on my chase, made sure there was no need to rush back to Rose Walk or the station, and arranged for Patrol to bring my car here. Already two backup cars were converging from the ends of Tamalpais. As I waved them off, I could hear the dispatcher notifying the others they could disregard her initial call.

The nudist, of course, was long gone. No point grumbling about him, or the whole burlesque of a chase. Not when I had a real problem: Bryn Wiley.

She was going to be trouble. The only question was how much.

CHAPTER 2

B<small>RYN</small> <small>WILEY</small> <small>WAS</small> <small>AS</small> close to a hero as you get in Berkeley. Normally we shepherd our passions into justice, the environment, and politically abstruse causes. Sports fandom is a quirk at best tolerated by your friends. You can get away with attending the occasional Warriors or A's game, or your first love, the Cal Bears. As long as you don't take it too seriously, or are sheepish about your déclassé obsession.

But with Bryn Wiley all rules had been broken. The days she had dived in the Olympics twelve years ago, the police could have put an OUT TO LUNCH sign on the station door. No one in town was far enough from their televisions to assault, batter, or break and enter. Bryn Wiley was an Olympian, Berkeley-style. She had come within an inch of being tossed out of Cal for leading demonstrations against sexual inequity in funding college sports. She was hardly a favorite with the Olympic Committee; by the time she reached the Games, they'd already given her two warnings. But when she heard the announcer mention the *men's* team and the *girls'* team, she headed straight for a microphone and became the focus of every reporter there. She shrugged off those warnings; she never minced her words or worried about their fallout.

They don't call them men's teams and girls' teams anymore. Bryn Wiley didn't bring back a medal, but more endearing in Berkeley, she came home with her principles unfurled.

Back in the Olympics she hadn't been one of the well-tanned Californians whose skin boasts of hours spent in the pool year-round. Her hair was not blond but chestnut brown, her face almost delicate, and her body lean rather than muscular, and there was always an air of potential fragility about her. It may have come from her scoliosis, as the commentators suggested every time she climbed to the diving platform. The curvature of the spine was in her lower back, almost invisible even to the cameras that focused on her buttocks at every opportunity. "Up-nostril Close and too damned Personal," Bryn had commented afterward. But she hadn't denied the accompanying story of an early coach of hers who had insisted on a regimen of breast-stroke and jogging that overstressed her back and sacroiliac joint and laid her up for a year. Sheepishly she had admitted how hard it had been at fourteen not to know if the spikes of pain down her leg or the numbness in her foot would ever heal, and then to worry that every training lap she'd run, every dive, would bring them back. She had never been to a high school dance or football game; she had only studied and trained. And still it had been a miracle, the commentators concluded, that she had made it to the Olympics.

When the interviews were over, she had walked to the end of the high platform, turned, and balanced on her toes with her heels poised in air frighteningly far above the water. Without pause she had dived back, creating a stunning arch of somersaults and twists, then snapped her body blade-straight and cut into the water without a splash. She'd climbed out of the water, her face aglow with triumph. A photographer had captured her expression an instant later, revealing how very much she had been willing to risk for her principles.

Later, she had lent her fame to the quest for safe exercise, insisting that no one should have to go through what she did. She was always in the news, volunteering at swimming programs, pushing for water therapy classes and subsidized access of the poor to municipal pools, focusing on, as she put it, the "fitness of body, fitness of life." Or as others put it, promoting her own fitness center: The Girls' Team.

In the twelve years since the Olympics, her chestnut hair and startlingly blue eyes had become a familiar sight on television and at city events. I'd admired the smooth, confident way she moved. I wondered if all those years of training had given her such control over her body that no movement was random. Cloaked in her commitment, bejeweled by her fame, she faced the cameras with aplomb.

But tonight the woman who stood at the door was no exemplar of poise. She paused, hands on hips, and glared at me. "I called you two hours ago!"

"Forty-five minutes at most. But let's not take any more of your time than we have to now."

Ignoring my comment, she insisted, "I've been cooling my heels for a hundred and twenty minutes."

I only wished I'd been cooling anything. Sweat was still running down my forehead. My undershirt was soaked through and the protective vest had created its own private steam room around my breasts. I made a show of opening my notebook. "About your vehicle . . . ?"

"*Vehicles. Plural.* First my van, now my car windows! I expect you to— Look here." She strode over to her blue Volvo wagon.

I walked down to the dirt driveway and around the damaged car. There were three holes in the driver's window and two in what was left in the passenger's. Shattered glass lay on the floor and the seat, and on the ground beyond the passenger side, decorating the gray-brown leaves like Christmas tinsel. I pulled my flashlight free and shone the light around the floor, between the seats, inside the other door. No bullet. I checked the ground outside. No bullet or casing; but in such a woodsy area they could be anywhere. "Did you hear shots? Anything that could have been shots? When did you last see the car intact?"

She stared mutely at the bullet holes. Her jaw quivered and

for a moment I thought she was going to cry. But the tough don't cry; they bark. When she turned back to me, it was with fangs bared. "Last time, with the van, you did this same thing— a cursory glance, a couple useless questions. If you'd had your lab analyze the brick, you could have—"

"This isn't the O. J. trial." Bricks are too porous for prints.

"Is lab service in Berkeley reserved for the rich?"

"Rich?" I said, glancing pointedly at her house here in the hills. In Berkeley, wealth is not so much a sign of accomplishment as a suggestion you've sold out—politically or spiritually.

She winced. "I'm hardly rich."

Wiley was five years younger than I and owned a house in the hills. More to the point, she had never deviated from her goal. If I'd done that, instead of opting to stay in Homicide because I was so sure I was making a difference, I'd have taken the sergeant's test and been rotated back to patrol as a *sergeant*, not bumped from Homicide by a guy with better connections. As it was, I'd gotten tossed back here as a *patrol officer* responding to calls from a woman with better connections.

"Let's discuss this in the light," I said, motioning her toward her house.

It was a Mediterranean villa with a living room windowed on three sides, a house meant to bask in the sun and open its portals to the warm breezes of evening. Here, it might as well have been in a cave. Branch upon redwood branch thatched a dark ceiling over it, and the steep, wooded hillside behind clasped the damp to its back.

By the time I had breached the threshold, Bryn was halfway across the living room, a cathedral-ceilinged rectangle of hard surfaces, cold colors, and the bitter smell of Japanese green tea. How perfect for the diver who had never given herself slack. There was no warming fireplace—it must have been removed— and in its place was the skeleton of a confessional booth. Paint gone, wood bare, outer walls missing. But the center seat where a priest had sat was intact. So was the left side grating through which sins had been whispered, and the kneeling bench awaiting guilty knees. On its right flank the kneeler was gone, replaced by a seat with a provocative statue of the Hindu god, Shiva, clasping his voluptuous consort. It was quite the display of kitsch. I had to restrain myself from chuckling.

My face must have betrayed me, for Bryn looked at me and smiled. "That was my reaction. Ellen swore the thing would make the room—"

"Ellen?"

"Ellen Waller, my cousin. She works for me. I can't afford anyone else," she said pointedly. "Anyway, Ellen insisted this *thing* was the perfect accent piece, a touch of devil-may-care. I'm a diver, what do I know about decorating, right? But a huge piece like that in a living room this size: it's like dropping a pound of curry in your stew!" She shook her head. "Ellen spotted it at the flea market. She stripped off five coats of paint and spent a week sawing away walls and sanding posts. So what could I do? I could hardly call out the Goodwill. Besides, they probably don't have a big market for used confessionals." She grinned and caught my eye, inviting me to laugh with her, her recent outburst forgotten.

I'd seen her do this push-pull with fans. It was amazingly effective. The pull of her intimacy was so great that when she pushed them away, they weren't insulted, but just tried harder.

She glanced at the empty priest's seat. But instead of grabbing a cushion and settling there, she raked strewn newspaper sections off the sofa till there was space and sat, motioning me to the other couch.

I propped myself on one of the padded sofa arms so my gun and flashlight and baton could hang freely. "So," I said, "do you have any idea who shot at your car?"

"Not an *idea*. I *know*. The asshole opened up the great con job of the century two blocks away from The Girls' Team. You know The Girls' Team." It was a statement, not a question.

"It's a block below Telegraph, built on the parking lot next to the Berkeley City Club, right?"

"*Over* the parking lot. I saved all but two parking spots when I built there, so I wouldn't harm the neighborhood. I planted trees around the building, full-grown and damned expensive trees. The deck has window boxes with flowers growing all year. I went out of my way to create the best health club in town. My StairMasters are the safest, my Exercycles have seats tilted to preserve the riders' lumbar curves. I've got cold dunking pools to use after workouts, a sauna, a snack bar with healthy food and Peet's Coffee. I've put my entire self into the Team."

I couldn't help but be impressed. Bryn Wiley had that effect. She could be a pain in the ass, but there was no doubting her commitment. "So," I said, "what is this con job of the century a block away?"

"The name 'Heat Exchange' mean anything to you?" She spat out the words. Any resemblance to the shaken victim I'd met outside was gone.

"Tell me."

"The biggest fraud on the Avenue."

That was saying a fair amount.

"Sam Johnson—you do know him?" Her hands curled into fists—tight, symmetrical weapons on arms poised to strike.

"Of course."

"He's opened a so-called health club!"

"What?" Sam Johnson was the least likely individual to operate a health club. I couldn't imagine him even having stepped inside one. Johnson was an old-time radical. If he saw a StairMaster, he'd probably take those endless steps to nowhere as a metaphor on capitalism. "Sam Johnson?"

"Yeah. Even when I realized the place was right on the Avenue, two blocks from the Team, and a whole lot more convenient for people coming from Cal, I still laughed. Who would waste their money on a fitness center run by a man who . . . who—"

"Thinks a Nautilus machine is something for mollusks?" I said.

"Yeah"—she grinned at me—"exactly. But when I heard about that ripoff, fraudulent, self-delusionary sham— At first I couldn't believe it was real. Then I realized just how much trouble I was in. The guy really knows Berkeley."

"How so?"

"Oh, you haven't heard about The Heat Exchange's gimmick? Well, here it is: Deep in their hearts, old lefties think working out is hedonistic, yuppie, politically incorrect. But they don't want their butts to sag, right? To the rescue comes Sam Johnson, saying: 'Pin up your ponytail, wear your *"U.S. Out of Wherever"* T-shirt proudly, and pedal your ass off on The Heat Exchange's stationary bike, because—ta-da!—the friction you create can be converted into heat and that heat will cut the utility bills of the deserving poor who live on the floors below. Then you can feel downright smug about yourself.' It's just too good to be true, right?"

It sounded good to me.

"And it would be good. *If* it worked. But if the poor get one erg of energy from that club, I'll eat my foot. And in the meantime, Johnson, who knows not a whit about exercise, will be injuring people right and left." She was leaning toward me, her pale, angular face aglow with conviction, those startlingly blue eyes of hers open wide. This was no act.

I almost felt cruel saying, "Wait a minute. Why won't the energy conversion work?"

"Because the machines you use in a fitness center don't create energy, they consume it. Take the treadmill: You don't move the belt as you walk, the belt goes electrically and you race to keep up with it. You *can* get a manual treadmill, but it's a pain to operate. Johnson's got both. Which do you think his people are going to use?"

"But the Exercycles, you do pedal those."

"Right, *if* you just pedal like you would on a bike riding on an endless straightaway. But should you use the hill program, or any one that changes the level of intensity—and that's the only thing that makes the Exercycle tolerable, believe me—every change within that program takes a jolt of electricity. And you know he's not telling club members 'only the hard, boring machines help the poor.' "

"Still, if someone wanted to—"

"Sure, you could use the bare-bones equipment. But, even the most noble-spirited person isn't going to pedal full out on a machine that doesn't tell you how you're doing. You're going to slow down without even realizing it." She nodded in agreement with herself. "Look, what Sam Johnson has created is the perfect vehicle to fool yourself. If *wanting* created change, no one would even have pimples."

I smiled. "So why not get a disgruntled customer to subpoena Johnson's electric bills?"

"He's too smart to give guarantees. He'll say if there's no excess electricity, people aren't working hard enough." She shrugged as if to say the implications were obvious.

But the corollaries weren't clear at all. "Bryn, if he's doing so well, why is he battering your vehicles?"

She let out a sigh of disgust. "Because I am the only one screaming 'The emperor has no clothes.' "

In the dining room, a board creaked. I turned just in time to see a woman eye me nervously and scurry into the kitchen. She looked eerily like Bryn Wiley. "Who is that?"

"What?" Bryn glanced quickly toward the dining room, and then back at me. "Ellen."

"Your cousin?"

She nodded.

There was a remarkable resemblance: similar height, similar coloring, that same suggestion of fragility. But in Cousin Ellen it was more pronounced, as if she were the child who got fed second. Or maybe she just looked older. Her hair seemed duller than Bryn's shiny chestnut, her sharp features taut not with outrage but nervousness. "She lives here?"

"Like I said, Ellen works for me."

I nodded. "And she lives in?"

"Yes."

"Did she hear the shots? Would you get her?"

She sat a moment, as if she suspected I'd staged the diversion to derail her complaint. Then she jolted up and walked into the kitchen.

The sofa arm wasn't meant for a chair; I shifted, trying to find a more comfortable position. I glanced around the colorless room, looking for any personal item. A white-on-white glassed collage hung behind the sofa. But there were no photos of Bryn with diving greats, no shots of her twisting high above the water, no awards or trophies. Not even a snapshot of her cutting the ribbon for The Girls' Team. An amazing lack of self-congratulation. On my office wall in Homicide I used to keep news articles about every case I closed. When leads dried up in new cases, and the pressure of too many felony assault cases got to me, I'd look at those yellowed news stories and remember the relatives who no longer wondered, the dead whose death hadn't been forgotten.

In a moment Bryn was back. "Ellen's gone."

"Gone? Gone where?"

"I don't know. It's not like this is a mansion. She's not here. She must have gone for a walk."

Or fled at the sight of the police. "At midnight?"

"She walks a lot. Anytime. Walking's her outlet. We're a good pair: She doesn't drive and I never let anyone drive my car. Christ, now *I* can't even drive it! Look, what's the point of paying for police if your car can get shot in your own driveway?"

"Bryn, if someone wants to shoot out your window bad enough, a hundred police officers aren't going to stop them. You know that," I said. "You must have asked Ellen about the shots. Did she hear them?"

"No. I don't think so."

"Did she see anyone suspicious?"

"She didn't say so." Bryn's face hardened. "Look, it doesn't matter who she saw. How many times do I have to tell you, Sam Johnson's the one you need to get after. The man's a danger to society . . . with that ripoff club of his. He's . . . he's . . ." She sputtered. Then she stopped and stared at me in bewilderment. "I just don't understand . . . How can people—my own *Team* members—go over there? They'll get injured; I told them that. How can they do that to themselves?"

"And to you?" I said softly.

"How can they let themselves be deluded . . . I just don't understand it."

For the first time, I truly felt for Bryn Wiley. She *didn't* understand. She didn't even realize why she was upset: not because of their poor reasoning but because she had been rejected. "You've made the Team the best fitness center around."

She shook her head slowly and again looked right at me, beseeching me to understand. "I don't have a husband or even a lover. I spend my nights with sports medicine journals and equipment catalogues. I've given my life to the Team; it *is* the best. How can people . . ." She slumped back against the doorway.

Her eyes had faded to the color of worn denim and her wonderful cheekbones only made her look weary. I had the eerie sense that I was seeing the reflection of Ellen Waller, or, more accurately, seeing beneath the tough outer layer that Bryn had molded and Ellen apparently had failed to grow.

I tried for other suspects, but in Bryn's mind there were none.

I asked to look through the house. But a survey of the bedrooms didn't yield much. There was a small room with a scarred dresser and a futon covered by a black on white print comforter, and one larger room filled with an array of white wicker furniture. The bedspread was in the same design as the lesser room's, but in bright primary colors. Even in home decoration, it seemed, Bryn reminded her cousin of her lesser place.

"The ID tech should be out in an hour or two. It depends how many calls were ahead of mine. But he won't have to disturb you. You may just see him flashing his light around your car." I moved back out the door. "Get an alarm on your car. Park the van in a safe place. If you've got a cellular phone, keep it with you. Hire a guard for The Girls' Team for a month. I'll be talking with Sam Johnson."

"Is that all?" she demanded. She inhaled, her face the picture of contempt. "That's nothing! If you're too lazy to do more than that, then get out of my way!" She paused, took a breath, then tossed the bomb: "I'm giving a press conference Saturday, and I'm telling you if this isn't settled by then, I'll settle it myself. Don't tell me how dangerous Sam Johnson is; I don't care. I'll expose the bastard." She slammed the door.

I walked down the steps into welcome cool air. Her last threat unnerved me more than I'd have expected. I handle my share of frustrated complainants, but Bryn Wiley was in a class by herself. She was like Aesop's fabled lion holding out a paw with a thorn in it. And when I'd reached out to pluck out the burr, she'd taken a swipe at me. If I accused her of that, she'd deny it, because—and this was the scary part—it was so natural to her, I doubt she realized it.

How many people had she clawed over the years? At her press conference, how many of them would be waiting for a shot at her?

CHAPTER 3

IT WAS CLOSE TO midnight when I left. Branches of giant redwoods muted the light on Tamalpais Road. I pulled my flashlight out of its loop and aimed it at the ground, but it was like pouring skim milk into a cup of cocoa—it made only a momentary difference. The ground was still muddy from the rains. Maybe Raksen would find a bullet casing I had missed, or an incriminating footprint, and take a mold. But footprint molds are only useful after the fact. Footprints aren't like mug shots. You don't circulate the likeness of an 11B sole and wait for calls from everyone who saw it. Chances were the suspect had been shod in Adidas, or Nikes, or a pair of Teva sandals like half of California.

Suddenly I realized how tired I was, less from the chase than the strain of dealing with Bryn Wiley. She was an exasperating woman. But there was something seductive, too, about her utter commitment. Knowing who you are and where you're going had always intrigued me. I had grown up never believing I would be an adult, much less one with a focus. My marriage had been based on that focus, as if Nat Smith's absorption with Irish literature would be purpose enough for both of us. I had even stumbled into the police test—one of six civil service exams. I'd taken

25

the job because I thought it would be different, fun, and because
Nat and I needed the money. That I would care about the work
as much as I did hadn't occurred to me.

What I was sure of now was that, if I didn't come up with the
suspect in this case, it would be a snowy day in Berkeley before I
ever got out of patrol, much less back to Homicide Detail.

The wind had calmed down. The air was still but for a tickle
now and then, hauling in the light, clean scent of redwood.
Houses stood dark, cars tucked in garages or cozied up to or
over the curb. Below the white glow of Oakland, the festive
string of lights scooping and peaking across the bay bridge, the
fog-muted glow from San Francisco was dazzling. But here the
silence was thick as the fog. I could have been in the forest. That
was a big part of the lure of this neighborhood—one minute you
were "in the Sierras," the next downing a latte at Peet's. It was
what made people sink half a million dollars into a house on a
hillside that could become a valley in half a shaking minute. It
was what made Ellen Waller feel safe strolling at midnight, if
indeed that was what she was doing, cloaked in the silence of the
redwoods, the fog held up by the tall spikes of the houses.

Or more accurately the tall spikes of the *house*, the one between Bryn Wiley's and the path where I'd lost the nudist. Black
snag-toothed walls cut the night. The lighter fogged sky shone
through the supports where the roof used to be. The place could
have been a villa for Dracula, but chances were it was merely
under construction. Probably an earthquake casualty.

Beyond it, in the shadows across the street, a dog howled. I
jumped. A duet of barks pulled the scene back into the familiar.

"Nora! Ocean! Quiet!" The man calling his dogs could have
walked out of Dracula's castle. He was tall, gaunt, hunched over,
dressed haphazardly in black pants that flapped as he hurried
across the lawn to the dogs, and a navy blue zippered jacket. But
there was something familiar about him. "Nora!" he warned—
just loud enough to be heard, just intent enough to be taken
seriously. No color, no emotion.

By the Dracula house, a dog panted.

"Pablo! Come here! Dogs! Here!"

The three canines—one medium-sized mongrel and two very large dark ones—arrived as I did beside their owner. I put out a hand to be sniffed—not exactly regulation behavior, but I always assume the best with dogs. One of the big dogs leapt at me, panting for attention. I scratched his chest and behind his ears. The other two inched backward warily. I looked questioningly at their gaunt, gray owner, but he made no excuses for his unsocial pets. He stepped back warily in line with the two dogs, letting his hand pass above them before he dropped it to his side. The dogs seemed to relax under the awning of his protection.

In Berkeley there is a subculture of solitary walkers—not amiable strollers or determined striders, but loners who walk because they must. Some get out with the dawn after another fitful night; some make their way midday warning off the world with their too old, too drab, or too clashing garb; some choose the safety of night. In a city known for its nonconformity they are the community of the noncommuning. But I hadn't been on patrol in Beat Two long enough to know if this man was one of them. Why did he seem familiar?

"Is this Nora, Ocean, or Paul?" I asked, rubbing the big, thick-coated black dog behind the ears.

"Nora, Ocean, and *Pablo*. This is Ocean."

"Radio dogs?"

He didn't reply.

"You've given them radio code names," I explained, wishing I hadn't veered into this conversational detour.

"Yes." His tone wasn't so much impatient as wary. I hoped his unease was not for fear of me finding dogs Adam through Mary in the house. Four's the limit of the law. But if the neighbors weren't complaining, I wasn't asking. "Do you live here?"

"You're standing on my walkway." There was no change in his pale, narrow face, no hint either of accusation or of playfulness in his voice, but something about him made me think that later, in the safety of solitude when he recalled that comment, it would be with a wry smile.

I glanced up at his windows, ones that overlooked the street and the path between his house and the construction site. "I'm Detec— *Officer* Smith." When he didn't respond, I said, "And you are?"

"Karl Pironnen."

Aha! One of the local papers had done an article on Sam Johnson a couple years ago. Of course, it had included the Golden State Bank demonstrations. The robbery itself had failed; the robbers, not exactly the elite of their trade, were caught before they made it to the getaway car. The cash involved had been less than the two could have earned for a week of real work. And the only casualty was Pironnen's brother, a bystander who had died not of gunshots, but from hitting his head as he stumbled off the curb. The event had been a Mouse That Roared affair, from its inept conception and sloppy handling to the elephantine official reaction. It was that latter issue that rang a bell for Sam Johnson and catapulted him to prominence as he organized protest after protest, decrying the government's misappropriation of time and money—an issue with which 99 percent of the populace couldn't disagree. Classic Sam Johnson.

When asked about the robbery, Karl Pironnen had said he'd never met Johnson. He was surprised the reporter knew his brother's name.

Dan. I was surprised I remembered it. I found my voice a little softer as I asked Pironnen, "Have you seen anyone near Bryn Wiley's house tonight?"

"Besides the naked runner and you?"

I almost laughed before I realized that he hadn't meant to be funny. I wouldn't even have been surprised if he didn't know who Bryn was. What I had here was the antithesis of Bryn Wiley, a man with no innate or acquired charm and a wish only to be left alone. "Was there anyone near Bryn's house besides us?" I asked.

"No."

"Did you hear a shot or backfire a couple of hours ago?"

"I was out. With the dogs."

"What about the naked runner? Where did he go?"

"Down the path."

"Into Codornices Park?"

He shook his head. "Under the construction house."

"*Under* it?"

"Yes."

My patrol car was down the street where Howard or one of
the other patrol officers had deposited it. I got in, shut the door,
and called in for a CORPUS check on Pironnen, Johnson, and
Ellen Waller, and for two backups. No priors on Pironnen,
nothing on Waller, and—big surprise—the only thing on Sam
Johnson was a complaint about him shooting tin cans in the
waterfront park. It was a surprisingly rightist, fifties kind of
hobby for a committed anarchist. I would have been amused had
it not reminded me that Johnson was a practiced shot, certainly
good enough to take out Bryn Wiley's windows. I upped the
request for backups to four.

It was Howard who arrived as the top-side backup, blue eyes
intent, but a grin trying doggedly to make it onto his mouth.
Howard was pondering the nudist and his cold, uncomfortable
hour under the house.

Failing to suppress my own grin, I put a finger to his lips. All
searches are serious. Any call could go any way. Cops die not
only in shootouts with drug dealers but in innocuous car stops.
You have to be ready all the time. It's exhausting, but easy to get
psyched by the intensity. And Howard— Once we got going,
he'd be all business. But now the grin had taken full control and
softly, softly he was humming the old Limeliters' song that
ended: ". . . when the cold, cold tailwinds blow."

We'd both been on patrol years ago, way before we'd become
an item; we'd hashed over each other's cases; but we'd never
worked together like this. I loved hitting the lights and sirens,
giving chase (or at least I *had* until the nudist—I'd have to re-

think that tomorrow), and cruising around town after midnight when the streets belonged to me.

Howard hadn't been far away when I called. Beat 2—here—was his.

"Not much chance the bare sprinter is still under the house. Still . . ." I said.

"If he's there, he's ours." Howard grinned. He'd hated to give up Narcotics Detail, where there were dealers still loose, and stings of his still unstung. But at six feet six with curly red hair, blue eyes, and a lantern chin, he was hardly a candidate for undercover work any longer. Unlike me, he had opted for the sergeant's exam, rotated back onto patrol, and was prepared to work his way back to Narcotics Detail when a spot opened for a detective sergeant.

"So, Jill, you think you can ID this guy?" He was grinning.

"Sure, if it's from the back and he's moving. Course here, he'd be under the house for an hour cooling his . . . heels." I kept my voice down to a whisper. But back in the station I knew no one was toning down their comments on my inaugural patrol chase. "Adam one and Adam eighteen are coming up the path from Codornices Park; Adam seven will be up here. As soon as they check in, we'll move."

Again Howard nodded. One officer always has to be in charge. I was the one who'd called for backup; this operation was mine. Murakawa—Adam one—would call when he and eighteen arrived at the bottom of the steps in the park. I'd give them another three minutes to make their way up the flights of cement steps.

We think of this area as in the hills, but it's really part of the canyon system, with sudden, sharp, steep walls. We assume it's tamer than bare canyons because those walls are padded with trees and brush, and houses that thumb their chimneys at earthquakes, cracked and hobbled houses like the one we were headed for.

The radio crackled. "Adam one, with eighteen, ten ninety-seven." Murakawa, and whoever was eighteen tonight, had arrived at the bottom. Levine—seven—pulled up behind us. He'd watch the street.

"Let's go." We'd keep the channel clear, to be used only if essential, so the radios on our shoulders wouldn't broadcast our arrival. When we were next to the open basement I yelled, "Police! Get your hands where we can see them and walk out! Do you hear me?"

No response.

"Answer me!"

Still nothing. I wasn't surprised.

With the smallest of movements, I motioned Howard to take the staircase. Before my hand was still, he was on the steps. I would go through the mud on the far side of the yard, outside the hurricane fence, looking for a way in. The house stood like an upended shoe box—precarious for a hillside dwelling. When I turned the corner and started down, the light of my flash revealed interior walls that ended abruptly, doors open into nothingness, rooms bare to the night. In the basement, corners were held up by beams, and between them two-by-fours crisscrossed in ways more quixotic than supportive. Had the earthquake led to all this? I didn't want to think that; we Californians never do. I preferred to imagine that the earthquake was a minor excuse for a major rehabilitation the owner had had in mind anyway.

Howard's flashlight beam was slicing in from the far side. "Po-lice! Walk out slowly. Keep your hands where we can see them."

I waited, then repeated his call. Both of us worked the territory with our lights, psychologically pinning the suspect in his hidey-hole. The place was a jumble of buckets and cans, piles of wood, troughs and barrows, wooden horses, saws, tools, machines the size of ride-on lawn mowers.

I moved along the fence, looking for an entry hole. Howard would go no farther down now, keeping watch on the basement till I signaled him. The ground was mushy, and the covering of dead leaves, ivy, and redwood burrs had me hanging on to the fence and bracing my knees as if I were skiing.

I was almost at the bottom when I found the hole. Murakawa and Sapolu—eighteen—were at the other corner. Lanky, easygoing Murakawa had assisted me more than once when I'd been in Homicide Detail. Sapolu, I'd only worked with once. I signaled them over and pointed to the hole.

They nodded.

I'd expected to see the thick, diamond-crossed wires of the hurricane fence raggedly rolled back from the support pole. I'd pictured a trespasser doggedly pulling them loose, folding them back, leaving the smallest possible opening he could get through. But this hole was invitingly big. And it had been cut with clippers. Obviously the work of someone with time and plans of permanency. Had my nudist perched here other nights? Or was this someone else's nest? The hole was far enough down that the workmen up top would have no reason to notice it. But for a transient on the lookout for a spot to sleep, it was like a flashing Vacancy sign.

"Kids?" Murakawa whispered, hand shielding his mike.

I shrugged. Some kids might not care if their deed was discovered, but those kids wouldn't be likely to do such a tidy job. And this wouldn't be the work of the homeless; they'd be the last ones to draw attention to their find. The hole just didn't make sense.

I climbed through into the yard, unsnapped my holster, and shifted my flashlight to my left hand. I motioned Murakawa to the walkway side and Sapolu to cover the bottom. Into the mike, I said, "Coming up," and started through the weeds and clutter.

"Po-lice! Come out; keep your hands where we can see them."

Not a leaf fluttered in the dead air. Murakawa and I moved quickly, mowing the ground with our beams. Clutter was everywhere, but no pile was large enough to conceal a person. Halfway up, Murakawa motioned me to a bunch of rain-wrinkled newspapers wadded together with a sheet of clear orange plastic —a poncho the police department gives to the homeless. It's the shower cap of the rain gear world, but it keeps them drier than they'd be otherwise, and as was clear here, for them it was not an added responsibility of possession.

I stopped a few feet from the house and fanned the light. From this angle the building looked like it was hanging from the edge of the hill by its fingernails, its rump sagging down wearily over the empty space beneath. Boards were propped below like legs of a flimsy folding stool.

Under the house, I could hear a pair of feet slam to the ground. "Stop where you are!" a male voice shouted. "I've got a gun!"

CHAPTER 4

I DROPPED TO THE ground. Murakawa ducked behind a wheelbarrow—concealment, maybe, but hardly protection. I pulled out my automatic, slipped my finger into ready position, and belly-crawled till I was behind two rows of paint cans. Hardly protection, either. "Police! We have the house surrounded. Put your hands on top of your head! Walk out now!"

Silence.

"Lights!"

All three of us sprayed our beams. Murakawa and Howard's were trained on the ground, and mine was aimed higher, in the hope of temporarily blinding the suspect. It hit hair, wiry brown hair. The rest of the suspect was hidden behind a work bench piled with cans.

"Hands in the air! Now! Move it!"

"Cops?"

"Correct. Berkeley Police."

"What the hell are you doing here? Goddamn, fucking pigs."

I recognized that voice. Not some unknown nudist, but Sam Johnson, Bryn Wiley's chief suspected assailant! Hiding under her next-door neighbor's house! I couldn't believe it! Was he huddled in there *with* the nudist? Or was this the subterranean shooting post from which he'd taken out Bryn Wiley's car windows?

"Who's in there with you, Sam?"

"No one's here. No one's got business to be here. Least of all you pigs."

Sam Johnson, notorious Berkeley anarchist, had been a regular at the People's Park demonstrations over the years. Now his hands moved resignedly over his head, and he walked slowly—regulation slowly—out in front of the can-piled workbench.

Johnson looked like hope gone sour. He was only forty-five or so, but they'd been hard years. Deep lines furrowed his brow and creased his cheeks. Barely taller than my five feet six, he had the sunken-chested physique of one who would rather suffocate than enter a health club. Spiritually he was an unregenerate radical. Sartorially, he resembled an aging Young Republican, in yellow oxford cloth shirt, green crew neck sweater, and, his one concession to the movement, jeans. And of course, loafers. Even in the dirt under the house the man was wearing loafers. In his way Sam Johnson was the anarchist of the anarchists.

By now the front of my uniform was smeared with dirt and smelled of soot and some mixture of oil-based chemicals, but Sam Johnson looked like he'd just stepped out of an alumni meeting.

There was a time when I would have second-guessed his plans, but now, looking at his drooping shoulders, the nervous movement of his eyes, I wondered how he felt knowing that his decades of work "against oppression" hadn't made that much of a difference. Did it leave him weary, angry, bitter, or desperate?

I couldn't recall a protest in which I *hadn't* seen Johnson leading, speaking, acting as marshal. Now I remembered his recent epithet: pigs. Pigs, indeed! "Sam, you're dating yourself. No one calls us pigs anymore."

"What the hell are you doing here?"

"You first, Sam." Put back together, this house would sell for close to four hundred thousand dollars. A rich man's house to the likes of Sam Johnson. Had he just decided to "liberate" some of the owner's possessions? To share the wealth? Under-write the counterculture weapons budget? Or was there some-thing specific in there he was after? Until now there had been a light touch to Johnson's forays against us. "Sam, I've known you for years now. You've made a religion of trespassing on public property. You've broken the law for your causes countless times. But you've never broken into someone's house! What are you doing here?"

"This is my house."

"What?" Howard got that statement of amazement out be-fore I did.

"I own the goddamn place, cops!"

Johnson could be lying, but he'd had too much practice to concoct a story like that. Had his slogan changed from "Power to the People!" to "Joy to the Gentry!"? I couldn't keep myself from choking back a laugh. Murakawa had to take over and talk Johnson out into the open and make sure his "gun" was no more than a threat.

I pat-searched Johnson. "If you own this house, why are you lurking in the basement?"

"Not in the basement. Upstairs. Hatch door."

"Why were you *dropping* into the basement, then?"

"To catch 'er."

"Catch who?"

"She's got a hole in the fence the size of Nebraska."

"Slow down. Who are you accusing?"

"Her," he spat out, jabbing his finger eastward. "The damned diver."

"Bryn Wiley! Why would Bryn Wiley cut your fence and beam?"

"Poachers. She lures 'em in. Lets 'em know what's to steal. I've had crap all over the place, tools broken, tools boosted. Place stinks of piss."

I didn't doubt Johnson had done his share of drugs. But noth-ing prior to this suggested he'd snapped loose his synapses, or that they had reconnected to create this kind of idiosyncratic path of thought. Or maybe both he and Bryn Wiley had spent too much time in their health clubs pedaling to nowhere.

I took a breath and said slowly, "Why, Sam? Why would a respected woman, famous even, with her own house, bother to sabotage yours? Yours, which is already half falling down the hill."

He glared toward Bryn Wiley's house. "They all think I'm ruining their neighborhood. They're always bitching: I'm not working fast enough. I've got too many workmen; I'm clogging the street. I've got too few workers; I'm leaving the house an eyesore. If they had their way, I'd spend all my time getting permits. But her"—he let out a snort of disgust—"she just can't let things alone."

Strategy and blame, they were two things Sam was good at. It didn't surprise me he was barging ahead on his remodel, permits —and neighbors—be damned. Or that he castigated them for objecting at all. What *did* interest me was his not mentioning the health club war. "Are you ruining the neighborhood?"

"Sure, that's what you'd think. You cops want the whole city to be single-family mansions."

"This isn't exactly a tenement, Sam." Before he could comment, I said, "Show me proof of ownership."

That order would have left most law-abiding homeowners grumbling about papers in the bank vault. But Sam Johnson's reaction was that of one who had spent years looking for flaws and loopholes in police procedures. It delighted him to show us up. "It's upstairs. Come on."

We followed him to a ladder that led to a staircase. Through a hall and up another flight of stairs, and we found ourselves in a back-facing living room level with the street. All things considered, I was surprised Johnson was still allowed inside the building. But of course, nothing as inconsequential as an official notice would keep him out.

The room we were in now clearly was his center of operations. It held one of those huge, heavy, scarred wooden desks assembled in the forties and likely to last another half century.

There were a bunch of chairs of similar vintage, and a gut-popped sofa that would do well to make it through the night. And most amazing of all was the bookcase holding weighty tomes on military campaigns, strategy, and heroes from the Caesars to H. Norman Schwarzkopf—all right over his bed! Was the man such an anarchist he ignored even the laws of nature?

From the desk, Sam pulled bank papers and held them out as if he were challenging me to a duel.

Which, of course, he was.

Responding in kind, I read them more carefully than was necessary. "Four hundred six thousand dollars?" I said, amazed.

"It's damaged," said Howard, who longed for the day when he could afford the brown shingle he lived in.

"Sam, *you* paid over four hundred thousand dollars for a house?"

He shrugged, clearly uncomfortable for the first instant since we'd found him. Another time I would have laughed. "Must be quite a surprise to your friends in the movement. How did you come up with that kind of money?"

He shrugged. "Wife."

"You have a wife! With money?" There's a lid for every pot, they say. But who would have thought Johnson's pot would be filled with gold? Still, a wife might be a stabilizing factor.

"My wife inherited money."

Not just a wife, but an heiress. "She inherited enough to buy a four-hundred-thousand-dollar house?"

Johnson shifted his body so he faced the dark windows instead of me. "It's a long-term loan and I'm doing the work here myself. Me and my friends."

Which meant the lot would be torn up for years to come. With the prospect of years of hammering and sanding, Dumpsters and deliveries, it was no wonder the neighbors were furious. And Johnson's friends, who were neither likely to respect property rights nor show up for work on time, whose goals were to overthrow or undermine the system, weren't going to endear themselves to anyone on the block. At the rate Johnson was working, maybe he and his wife *could* keep the operation afloat if they hadn't used their entire windfall for the down payment. "But the down payment, Sam. Twenty percent is over eighty thousand dollars. Your wife could spare that kind of money?"

"Not all of it."

"Where'd the rest come from?"

"I got support."

"Support? You mean for your work? Your work in the movement?" Behind Johnson, Howard and Murakawa were struggling to keep straight faces, but this kind of bridge burning made me edgier yet about Johnson. "Sam, someone gave tens of thousands of dollars to you as an anarchist and you used it so you and your wife can live in the hills?"

"I'm not going to be the only one living here," he insisted, lamely, but not nearly so lamely as I'd expected. "The city's always squawking about lack of rentals. I'm giving them more."

"You're turning this building into low-cost housing? A shelter for the homeless?" I asked, sure that couldn't be true. Berkeley is a compassionate city, whose citizens agonize over the plight of the homeless. People are concerned. But if Sam had even considered opening a shelter for the homeless up here in the hills, the neighbors would have had a lawyer here to outflank him before he could get H. Norman off the shelf.

"Yeah. So? You got a problem with that?" Now he was in his element.

I turned to Murakawa, and nodded at him to go and pass the word to Levine and Sapolu. This was hardly a five-officer operation anymore.

"Sam, how long have you been here tonight?"

"An hour."

"Did anyone run through here?"

"You got a description?"

"Naked."

Johnson laughed, a sound not of humor but of victory. "You lost a bare ass? I wouldn't turn him in to you on principle, if I had him, which I don't. I got enough problems with crazies sleeping here, without this becoming a nudist's dressing room. But look, why don't you ask *her*?"

The hated *her*. "Bryn Wiley?"

"Yeah, maybe she's recruiting the sartorially challenged to camp out here, too."

"Sam, are you saying that Bryn Wiley is harassing you?"

"Is English your second language?"

"And what are you doing about it?"

"I'm telling you."

I let a beat pass and looked him straight in the eye. "Since when is your method of handling confrontation calling the police?"

He didn't answer. He picked up the bank papers and busied himself folding them and returning them to the desk.

"Do you own a gun?"

"Why? Was Wiley shot?"

"Answer the question."

"Yeah, and I've got a permit. But before you start celebrating, I haven't been carrying it around in my pocket. It's a rifle. For hunting, you know. The American Way."

"A rifle," I said, tensing. "Where is it?"

"Where? In the Great American Place!" He jerked his head toward the dining room. I walked through the doorway and looked toward the mantel.

There it was, needing nothing more than a moose head to complete the picture.

"Take it with you," Johnson insisted. "Have your lab guy go over it. I haven't fired it in a year, but listen, don't take my word for it. Spend the taxpayers' money finding out." His trim little beard quivered.

"You've got plenty of bricks," Howard said before Johnson could gloat too long.

"What's that supposed to mean?"

"Where were you last Friday night?" I demanded.

"A week ago? Who the hell knows?"

"Think."

"Why?"

"Because that is when someone bashed in the logo of The Girls' Team van."

Johnson put down the papers and looked up. For the first time the man was smiling, albeit not pleasantly. "So that's what's got a bee up her ass. Someone's after her van, huh? Hitting her right in the logo."

"She said you're deceiving your customers. Yanking them in by their bleeding hearts."

I expected a roar of protest. But Sam Johnson looked me in the eye and said, "I haven't shot at her; I haven't come at her with bricks. But let me tell you, the woman's a fucking pain in the ass. You can believe I'm not the only one she's ticked off. And if she doesn't stop sabotaging my fence here, I won't say I'll take matters into my own hands—the law frowns on that—but if someone wants to know where she is, wants to sit in my house and take a look around the neighborhood, I'm not going to stop him."

CHAPTER 5

FEELING LIKE A PLAYGROUND monitor, I headed back to Bryn Wiley's to get her explanation of the hole in Sam Johnson's fence. The Girls' Team van was gone, and so, apparently, were Bryn and her cousin. "They must really have the inside scoop on the city," I said to Howard as we walked back to our cars. "I'd give a lot to find a place to get a doughnut and a cup of Peet's at this hour."

"Hang on," he said, giving my stomach a pat. "There's pepperoni pizza in the fridge at home."

"*If* the tenants haven't scarfed it down."

"I'll pick up a carton of ice cream before you get there."

I squeezed his hand, still perched on my stomach. "The way to my heart."

People think of Berkeley as a town that doesn't close, with jazz slithering under the doors of off-hours clubs, Cal students partying, Avenue crazies honing their routines till the sun comes up. And California Cuisine for the asking anytime night or day.

Au contraire. Finding a place that will cook you a hamburger after 10 P.M. qualifies you for Detective Detail. From the trunk, I grabbed my garbage bag and jacket and headed inside to write up the reports on the nudist, Bryn Wiley, and Sam Johnson.

To those citizens who hate spending tax dollars on their police department, this building should be a comfort. Everything is shabby. In the basement there's a lunchroom you'd have to be starving to consider. The most visually appealing space in the entire station is the jail—if you like salmon pink.

The squad room is essentially a large foyer surrounded by offices. Through one window I could see both sergeants in their cubicles. I glanced down the squad room table past the box of forms that sat on it like a centerpiece. Occasionally there is a class in the meeting room and Community Service provides bagels or cookies. Less occasionally a few crumbs survive till 1:30 A.M. Not tonight. I pulled out a plastic chair and began on the reports.

I'd finished the first two when Connie Pereira came by. Pereira had been on patrol as long as I'd known her, but she had worked with me on a number of homicides. Now that I'd been deposited in her domain, she could barely contain herself from mentoring.

"Smith," she said, propping her butt on the table beside me. "I ran into Howard in the lot. He said he left a box of papers in your old office. Can you bring it home tonight?"

"Sure." I looked at her more carefully. "Connie, I do believe you've got a few of those blond hairs out of place." For Pereira that was virtually dishevelled. "Hard night?"

"A ten thirty-three audible up on College. The alarm that was waking half the neighborhood came from an open door on the roof. I had to climb a hedge to get to the fire ladder. And once I found the damned thing, it still took half an hour to raise the owner to come and reset. After that I had a four-fifteen with the husband and wife screaming louder than the alarm. He's threatening to bloody her right in front of us. And her, she'll be back with him in a week. Why do we bother?"

"You called mental health?"

"Yeah, they came. They've been before." She shrugged. "You ready to go?"

"As soon as I finish this." I pushed up and went to the end of the table to find a second sheet for the Johnson report. "What's this? J. Smith? I didn't leave anything here." I pulled the carton toward me and pawed through the pencils, notepads, clear nail polish, empty Tylenol bottle, three different strengths of sunscreen. It was the stuff I hadn't been able to get in the first boxes I'd taken out of my office when Brucker moved in. These odds and ends had been in the bottom drawer. "Look what was sitting on top, Connie," I said, holding up a Tampax box.

"Right. Very sensitive of Brucker."

"Whole thing's real sensitive. Would it have killed him to leave me a note that he needed the drawer?"

"Well, come rescue Howard's papers before he finds them cast out in an box with his boxer shorts on top."

I added the last two sentences to the report, deposited it in the team tray for the sergeant to approve and headed downstairs to the tiny office that Howard and I had shared only last week. Then I had kidded him about his upcoming position as patrol sergeant. While he'd race around to check on 415s and car stops ▴ in the night, I would take over his old desk and cover it with reports, forms, graphs, and notes and have every item of every homicide case at hand. It would be Homicide in Heaven, I'd told him. If heaven were an eight by twelve institutional green room with one window that never admitted sun. The office was barely big enough for one person. Presumably it would suit Brucker. He'd probably already hung the framed news photo of himself shaking Ronald Reagan's hand. The accompanying article proclaimed that private citizen Reagan had stopped in Sacramento to encourage the troops. The picture, the talk of the station, would make a change from the notices and memos Howard and I were so familiar with.

We had had our desks facing opposite walls; when he'd rolled his desk chair out, I'd had to slide mine in. And when we'd both turned around to talk, we'd shifted in choreographed moves perfected after a number of minor crashes. If he'd stretched out his long, long legs—the man is six foot six after all—he'd had to angle them toward the far corner of my desk. It had taken months to get the routine down. We'd both grumbled about the tiny space. But after a week on patrol with not even a desk of my own, I really missed it. I pushed open the door.

It stuck halfway. I braced my palm against it and shoved.

The light came on.

"Surprise!" Connie called out.

"Welcome to the Wacky World of Patrol," Paul Murakawa said, grinning. Leonard was there, and Acosta. And of course, Howard, all squeezed into the tiny room.

"We were going to get you a box of doughnuts and a thermos of coffee, but, well, you know, stuff's not too fresh this hour of night. So . . ." Pereira passed me a can of Calistoga water, orange flavored.

"So how's it going, Smith?" Leonard, the old man of patrol, who had been on the Telegraph Avenue beat longer than I'd been with the department, had commandeered my old desk chair. I boosted myself onto my old desk—Brucker's now—next to Paul Murakawa. Connie Pereira had taken "her" seat on the end of Howard's desk, kicked open the bottom drawer, and propped her feet there. She patted the spot next to her for Acosta, and, I noted, he wasted no time taking it.

A smile settled on my face as I looked at my friends. Hanging around the station after a ten-hour shift was a sizable gift on their parts. And, I thought looking at them, in this case a gift from the best-looking guys in patrol. Tall, sleek, Mercurio Acosta looked like he should be holding a French cigarette between his fingers. Paul Murakawa, at thirty-two, still abashedly brushed a swatch of thick black hair off his forehead before he spoke and would probably always look like the all-American kid. Howard had his head of red curls, his lantern chin, and his "something's up" grin, and Leonard . . . well, Leonard wasn't going to be doing beefcake calendars, but he was still in with the best in my book.

"I suppose Howard"—I nodded at him as he pulled out his chair and stretched his legs at the required angle—"told you about Sam Johnson, the nouveau entrepreneur."

Leonard shook his shaggy head. The man looked like the oldest bear in the circus. The joke around the station was the department should get him a funny hat and transfer him to bike patrol. "I wondered what happened to Sam. Haven't seen him on the Avenue in months. He even skipped the last People's Park confront. To tell the truth, I almost miss the guy."

"Loses the pizzazz without him?" Acosta asked, wiping off the top of his can before he drank.

Leonard nodded, but before he could go on, Howard leaned back in his chair and said, "Do you remember the Persian Gulf protest on San Pablo?"

Leonard nodded—no department-related maneuver escaped him. But Acosta frowned questioningly. That was enough for Howard.

"The Persian Gulf protest was vintage Sam Johnson. I've got to hand it to him, pain in the ass that it was. He gets fifty of his disciples to sit down in the intersection of San Pablo and University. Twenty after five on a Friday afternoon. Traffic's pouring off the freeway, all four lanes of both streets are full. Calls are flooding the station like every driver in town's got a cellular phone—and this was back when every driver *didn't*. I go flying out of here, get in the car code three."

Pereira thrust one hand on top of her head for the light and the other in front of her mouth, more of a bull horn than a siren, but no one quibbled.

"I get to University and it's stopped dead. Up here, a mile from the site. It hasn't been five minutes since the first call! I drive on the grass divider as far as I can then I just give up, leave the car, and run the rest of the way. "Course when I get to San Pablo, Johnson's crew is long gone. Traffic jam lasted another two hours."

"But you knew it was Johnson," Murakawa put in.

"Oh, yeah. It had his touch. But what could I do? Blocking an intersection is a traffic infraction. Believe me, citizens who've just spent hours sitting in their cars aren't anxious to sign a

citizen's arrest form so they can repeat the experience in municipal court."

"When the press guys asked Sam why he'd felt free to inconvenience half of Berkeley," Leonard said, "he did the tried-and-
true thing—he blamed George Bush!"

We had all heard the story before, but we laughed anyway.

Pereira and Acosta smiled and drank as if their Calistoga cans
were operated by one switch. But Leonard held his thoughtfully.
"Yeah, Sam Johnson really believes he's . . . well, not *making* a
better world as much as hacking away at the bad one. But the
thing is"—now he was talking to me—"what you see is not what
you get with him. Maybe it's a midlife crisis."

"What are you telling me, Leonard?"

"To be careful, Smith. Sam could have gone over to the good
life, but maybe not. Maybe he's got one last, desperate move in
mind. And if he does, it'll be a beaut. Don't get lulled by Howard's prank tales. Or Johnson's Puckish charm. The man's like
an IRA terrorist. One minute he's buying you a pint and filling
your ears with blarney about freedom for the masses. But after
he's charmed you—just like that—he'll step outside and blow up
your car." He let that sink in, then added, "Johnson's got dangerous connections. No proof, but we *know* he's been involved
in sabotage, a fire bombing that left one woman with scars all
over her leg. He started in the last of the Vietnam era working
the follow-up protest to the Golden State Savings holdup, the
one where one of the customers died after falling off the curb."

I nodded. "But he wasn't involved."

"Nah. The two robbers—Wilson 'Red Fist' Wright and Tim-
othy Anderson—got caught outside. The driver—Mary Lou,
Mary Jane, Mary Something Nash—had the smarts to pull into
traffic and disappear. But Johnson didn't have anything to do
with it, because if he had, the operation wouldn't have been such
an amateur deal. It would have gone off with style. The point is,
Smith, Johnson's been around this stuff and, well . . ." He
trailed off, suddenly realizing he'd made the point twice before.
"The guy's like Howard, but he's *not* Howard."

Pereira came to his rescue. "You guys see the box of Smith's stuff plunked in the middle of the squad room table? How could you miss it, huh? Brucker's to thank for that. Couldn't wait another moment to fill *all* the drawers here. He's like a two-timed wife tossing the lech's clothes on the porch."

Acosta shook his head.

"What the hell was—"

I cut Howard off. "It's no big deal. Still, I can't let that kind of disrespect ride." Acosta, Pereira, and Howard nodded. "I'll call him on it." After a moment the trio nodded again.

But Leonard just sat.

"Leonard?"

"I don't want to tell you to let things slide, Smith. But Brucker . . ." He looked toward the door and then shrugged as if he'd just remembered it was nearly three in the morning and there wasn't likely to be anyone in this end of the building but us. "Be careful with Brucker. He's a good cop, does his job, pulls his weight, but the thing is you always get the feeling he's holding something back. He's an okay guy and you end up talking to him, not watching what you say, and then six months later what you said comes up against you. By then it could have come by four different routes. Maybe Brucker had nothing to do with it. But you wonder."

Acosta nodded. "The guy's got a way of getting what he wants. That post in Sacramento, that was a plum, part of the esteemed research team doing a standard study on serial killers."

"Brucker'd worked Homicide but he didn't know more than Eggs or Jackson," Howard said. "But Eggs and Jackson didn't apply."

"I heard them bitching about it afterwards," I said. "By the time they heard about the job, Brucker was in Sacramento. Not that either of them seriously wanted it."

"But they wouldn't have gotten it." Murakawa said it softly, and with such uncharacteristic bitterness that it took a moment for the words to register. I realized then that he hadn't spoken at all before. Now he leaned forward, brushing at the hair on his forehead twice even though it hadn't had time to fall back down between swipes. "I never mentioned this to you, Smith, but when Brucker applied for the Homicide slot, I put my name in, too. This was before the slot you got came up. Before the leave I took. But then I really wanted the Homicide job. I figured I had a good chance, until the interview with Inspector Doyle. The first thing Doyle asked me was how interested I was in chiropractic school."

I nodded.

"No, Smith. Then, I wasn't talking about chiropractics. Then I hadn't mentioned it to anyone but Brucker, and that was just because he found a folder in my car. I wasn't even seriously considering it then. And maybe my plans weren't the deciding factor."

"Brucker told him?"

"Brucker denied it. Maybe he didn't." But everything about Murakawa's posture said Brucker did. "And of course, after that I did think seriously about chiropractic school, and I did go on leave and take enough science labs to find out I *didn't* want to be a doctor. So I can't make much of a case, right?"

"Still . . ." I said.

Murakawa shrugged and brushed at his hair. "I'm not asking for sympathy. Things happen. It's just, well, I wanted you to know."

"Right," I said, leaning back against Brucker's wall. "I guess I'd better stop worrying about getting myself back into Homicide, and get used to Patrol." But I could feel my throat tightening. Howard rested his hand on my thigh and gave it a rub.

"Next time the sergeant's test comes up . . ." Murakawa's voice trailed off.

I didn't comment on how many years that would be. "Look, forget I said anything. I made my decision, and I'm okay with it."

"You've got a three-day weekend," Pereira said. "That's the joy of Patrol. Why don't you guys go to Tahoe?"

Howard shifted uncomfortably. "Can't."

"Why not?" Connie insisted. Connie had been in this office so often, perched on Howard's desk, scarfing down half my doughnut, finishing the coffee I'd intended to finish myself, that she'd assumed squatters rights in both our lives.

"The downstairs tenant moved out. I've got to spackle his walls and repaint before I can rent his room."

"Howard," Connie continued, "it's not your house. You're just a tenant there. You slave over that place like it was the family mansion."

Connie's words could have been mine, *had* been mine more times than I was comfortably remembering. But it was harder for Howard to deal with them from her. I rested my head against the wall.

"Someday the house will be mine and—"

"Yeah, sure, if the landlord is dumb enough to sell when he's got a tenant handling the shit work and spending all his free time increasing his investment."

"Connie, I just—"

"Howard, you are obsessed. You're so obsessed you can't even take a break to enjoy your free weekend."

As one Leonard, Acosta, and Murakawa shrank back; things were getting too domestic for them. I was beginning to feel protective of Howard myself, but I could hardly jump in on his side when everything Pereira was saying she'd heard from me.

"Anyway," Howard said, "I can't go to Tahoe because I'm going on loan to Fresno next week."

But Pereira was not to be deterred. "And how are you planning to spend your last days here with your live-in lover?"

I expected Howard to tell her that wasn't for her virgin ears. But clearly he'd had enough. "Connie, whatever you think, the room needs to be painted, and done before I go."

"And if it isn't?"

"Then—"

"Howard, you *are* obsessed."

Howard looked at me.

There are moments in life when Truth flashes clear and

bright. This was one of them. "Howard," I said, "do you remember that fifty-one fifty call you got when you were first on patrol years ago, the guy who had kept every newspaper he'd ever gotten stacked in his house so he'd never lose a fact of his life?"

Howard tapped his finger on my thigh. He was considering the argument more seriously than I had expected. I was impressed. I was just about to tell him so when I spotted the hint of a smile. He turned to me as if we were alone in the office. "Jill, I realize you don't understand. It makes you uncomfortable to have your name on the house lease. You'd rather cut off your foot than actually own a home. You can't even bring yourself to think what it's like to feel as I do about this place." There was no resentment in his words; they were just statements of fact. But statements that were clearly leading somewhere. "You once made a point of showing me how difficult it is for someone to really understand a situation he never wants to face."

I nodded. Leonard, Murakawa, Acosta, and even Pereira didn't know what he was referring to, but none of them interrupted. I knew exactly what he meant. I'd wanted Howard to realize what it was like to be a woman confined by society's proscriptions—don't walk alone after dark; don't wear seductive clothes; never stop in a bar alone; always, always be careful—because if you break these rules and lure some man to attack you, it will be your fault. I'd engineered a sting of my own so that he, the six-foot-six cop, used to walking where he wanted with gun and baton could really feel bound by the walls inside which women have lived. I'd shown him, but the manipulation of that sting had left him with a debt unpaid. Now he was calling it in. I had no choice but to say, "Okay."

"You want to know what it's like to give up something I care about as much as this house?" he said.

I *didn't*, of course. Murakawa and the rest of them *really* didn't want to know. I could see Connie Pereira behind Howard and her expression said she would have given up almost anything just to get out of the room. "Okay."

Howard lifted his hand off my leg. "I'll stop working on the house for the rest of the month, Jill, if you will make a similar commitment."

I'd have been better off dealing with Sam Johnson. Not for nothing was Howard known as the king of sting. On the spur of the moment he could come up with great gotchas. Given a week's preparation time, he created cons worthy of Hollywood. He had had over a year to lick his wounds from my sting, to recall how easily he'd fallen in with it, to grasp vainly for the signs he should have seen, the things he should have done, to take to heart how the sting had changed things between us. To plot his revenge. With a year's prep time Howard could make the Trojan horse look like a lawn flamingo. I squeaked out, "Just what kind of commitment do you want me to make?"

"Give up junk food."

"Junk food?" Relief washed over me. Howard was letting me off easy. It would be no big deal to adjust my food intake for the rest of the month. Food was not a big item in my life. I ate what I could grab. So I'd grab something different.

"Starting now."

"Okay." Ridiculously easy, but I wasn't about to argue. I leaned down and gave Howard a kiss. "Okay, leave your work clothes in the closet. Tahoe, here we come. Hey, we could even drive partway tonight. I'm getting a second wind, how about you? I can make us a thermos of coffee. And there's still some pizza in the fridge, right? We can eat that—"

Howard grinned. "I don't think so."

CHAPTER 6

AFTER FORTY, THEY SAY, dimmed light is a boon. In the case of Howard's house, that was an understatement. The neighbors to the south had already complained about the sagging porch off the corner bedroom that looked like the top of an antique canopy bed. At least they didn't have to worry about a noisy neighbor sitting out there at night listening to the A's game. (The last tenant who had used that balcony was a large man who did, in fact, sunbathe with the A's. He went through the floor one bright afternoon, sort of a pop fly unto himself.)

We had had a call from the neighbor to the north about the decrepit garage, and one from the guy across the street about the condition of the wood shake roof. But we already knew the shingles were thin, old, cracked, and separated. We had discovered that during the previous rainy season.

The six-bedroom house had many flaws. But at night, in the softening glow of the moon, it stood dark and appealing under the graceful umbrella of the jacaranda tree in front, crowned by the evergreen in the back.

At 3:30 A.M. the tenants—an increasingly motley array Howard had been forced to accept for need of rent—were most likely asleep, or at least in their rooms. Howard and I had decided to leave for Tahoe in the morning. Now all I could think of was food. I headed inside.

So I wouldn't have pizza. Like as not, the remains of last night's pepperoni and black olive had been devoured hours ago when the night was young and the tenants prowling. But just yesterday I'd bought a gallon of chocolate marzipan ice cream, the kind with swaths of dark chocolate cutting the sweetness of the almond paste. I'd hidden it behind the ice trays. Some of that was bound to be left.

I started toward the kitchen—I could taste the marzipan, feel the ground almonds between my teeth, smell the— I stopped. No. I couldn't have ice cream, either. Howard classified that not as the staff of life, which it is in my life, but as junk food.

Damn, I needed to eat *something*. There was a box of chocolate chip cookies Howard's mother had sent in the . . .

No.

There were some Snickers in the bedroom.

He'd probably consider them junk food, too.

Suddenly I was starved. What *could* I eat? It was way too early for Noah's Bagels to open. The scones at Peet's Coffee wouldn't be available for four more hours. What else was there? I was ravenous and there wasn't one thing available.

I was going to shrivel and die. And the only keening at my wake would be Howard's laughter.

In the meantime I'd spend the rest of the night lying awake thinking how hungry—and stupid—I was.

In the end I—and Howard—decided to test the theory that sating one appetite dulls the others.

It was close to 11 A.M. when I woke up. Starved. I went through the whole food litany again—pizza, ice cream, cookies, the emergency Snickers in the night stand. The Snickers was out anyway. Howard, the crumb, had devoured it after concluding that the Law of Cross-sating is erroneous. He'd taken it into the bathroom as a courtesy to me, but I could still hear the wrapper crackling and catch a whiff of that chocolate and caramel. It had been the last smell in my mind before I fell asleep. It must have stayed there all night—I remembered a dream in which I was buried, happily, in a mudslide—and now the whole bedroom smelled like suburban Hershey. Miserably, hungrily, I sank back under the covers. What did Prozac taste like? But even if it came in chocolate, the tablets had to be too small to matter.

In a wicker chair across the room, Howard sat, elbows on thighs, chin in hands, eyes glazed. "Walls are filthy," he grumbled. "Need a coat of paint."

The walls—deep green—could have gone half a century without showing dirt. In fact, Howard had painted them a year ago. I smiled. "A little lost for things to do?" Caught in my own anguish, I'd almost forgotten Howard's half of the bargain.

"Nah. I'm going to the Y. Or maybe I'll just come back to bed."

"Maybe you should just do that."

He was dressed, but undressing was another of his skills. He dropped his jeans to the floor, exposing his long lightly furred legs, stretched, and wriggled out of the yellow turtleneck I'd gotten him from Eddie Bauer, displaying his lightly muscled chest and those sinewy shoulders that told of hours of crawl and butterfly. And when his Jockeys hit the floor, I noted once again what a fine tight set of buns the man had. I clasped one of them as he slid under the sheets and kicked off the blankets. My nipples hardened against his chest; I ran my lips across his collarbone, and when he pulled me closer, I arched my neck so I could continue to breathe. I loved the man; he had a great body, but practically speaking, in bed there was too much of it. And there had been times when he'd clutched me to him and pressed my mouth and both nostrils hard into his chest. Sex is like swimming, though, and over the years I'd learned where the air pockets were. And now I luxuriated in the smooth warm feel of his skin, the communion of his kisses that required no words.

But an hour later, after we'd traipsed sweatily to the shower, I was hungry.

"Let's get on the road," Howard said.

"Okay, if we can go by Peet's first." At least I could have a latte. No one in Berkeley would label Peet's as junk food.

A scone occupied me till we crossed the Carquinez Straits, the latte all the way past Vallejo, but after that the road rolled on undifferentiated like a giant cruller. Howard and I were on the far side of Sacramento when we figured out exactly how long it had been since we'd been out of the Bay Area together. Between tiling, shingling, spackling, and painting commitments and my overtime in Homicide (a little obsession of my own I decided not to bring up), we had become the stable homebodies of our neighborhood.

It wasn't until we started up into the Sierra that I realized we never had gotten around to discussing either of the cases. With all the conflict and accusations between Bryn Wiley and Sam Johnson, I'd almost forgotten the Bare Buns Brigade. "Any word on the naked runner?"

"No."

"We have an ID?"

"No."

"Didn't his friends ID him?"

"No."

"Howard, why not? It's not like the Bare Buns Brigade lures passing men off the street to a life of lewdity. They had to know the guy."

"Right, but they knew him as Dingo. I suppose I could contact the Australian Feral Dog Society and see if any of their charges have hightailed it east."

"The guy knew the terrain better than I did," I insisted, a mite churlishly. Sugar deprivation does that.

"Could be a transient who cased the area."

"A transient casing beat two? Naked? It's not like he was planning to burgle, at least not and hide the loot."

Howard shook his head and concentrated on the road, and the bittersweet pleasure of driving his new truck. He would not be taking it to Fresno; if it had been made of marzipan, I would have been pleased about that. The road was clear, but snow sugared the trees and bushes. I turned the heater up. If I had stayed home, I would have sat out in the yard, lapping up the warmth of that big caramel sun and reading the latest Oliver Sacks article in *The New Yorker*. In the Bay Area you sunbathe in March and drive to see snow. Even ghetto schools close for Ski Week.

Howard downshifted as the traffic slowed. "I questioned the two guys, them bitching the whole time about being cold, like the salmon-pink Hilton should have offered them terry-cloth robes instead of jail clothes. What I got out of them was that Dingo'd been in town a couple of weeks."

"And he'd masterminded their routine?" I speculated.

"No, they'd done the dance before."

"But the location, Howard, Dingo chose that, didn't he?"

"They swore they didn't."

"You believed them?"

Howard hesitated. "Yeah. They'd given their performances before, on the Avenue, on Shattuck, outside the Ashby BART station, places where there are students and the like. But Rose Walk, for them it made no sense."

I nodded. "It's not like they're an outreach program taking their art to nudity-deprived neighborhoods. But they did choose Rose Walk, or Dingo chose it." I sighed. "I just can't believe it has no connection to Sam Johnson or Bryn Wiley."

Howard laughed. "Jill, you *want* to believe that."

"Well . . ."

"Okay, here's the question: If you could choose to discover Dingo was Sam Johnson's spy, or that the hotel in Tahoe served broccoli that tasted like chocolate, which would you pick?"

"Low blow, Howard. And this from a man who's missing the antique baseboard sale at Recycled Home."

The vacation would have made Connie Pereira proud. We cross-country skied enough to develop aches in places I didn't know I had muscles (and I guess I didn't have them *before).* We took in shows. Howard won a hundred thirty-six dollars at blackjack, and our only argument was whether maple syrup pushed pancakes into the junk food category. (I won twenty of Howard's dollars when ten out of ten people agreed with me. Then to rub it in, I ordered the manhandler's special, forgetting that I don't like either pancakes or maple syrup.)

On Wednesday our 10 A.M. to 8 P.M. day I left for work, knowing Howard would be gone when I got home.

The first thing waiting for me at the station was a message from Herman Ott, Telegraph Avenue detective. A message from Ott is never a plus. I tossed it. The second was a note from Brucker: "Need to go over your cases. I'll be here until noon." There were no open homicides and I had left him notes on all the felony assaults that required explanation. Still, his wasn't an unreasonable request. I would answer his questions, after we were eye to eye about sticking my belongings on the squad room table. And after I'd dealt with Bryn Wiley.

I didn't know how serious Bryn Wiley had been about her threat to force Johnson's hand at her press conference Saturday. She'd expect me to be on Johnson's tail, not "wasting time" reminding her how unpredictable the man was and objecting to her plans. She wasn't going to be pleased to see me at her own door.

Which is why, when I got there, I was surprised to be greeted with a look of panic followed by a smile. And more surprised that the woman at Bryn Wiley's door was not Bryn Wiley but Ellen Waller. "Come on in," she said. In the daylight she looked less like Bryn's deflated ghost. I could see now that the resemblance was more general than it had seemed last Saturday—two thin, tallish women with short, full, chestnut brown hair. But Ellen Waller's face was softer than Bryn's. Her eyes were brown, not blue. And she was older than Bryn. Forty-five or so to Bryn's thirty-three.

"Can I get you some coffee? It's decaf," she said, in that wary tone we police officers hear so often we begin to think of it as normal.

I pulled out a line that always puts female witnesses at ease. "I wish I could take you up on that coffee. But not in the middle of a ten-hour shift driving around."

She smiled. "The dangers of police work they don't tell you about, huh? Well, sit then. Oh, I guess that's not really possible with all that stuff hanging off your belt? How about a stool? I'll get the one from the kitchen. It's not real comfortable, but—"

"Thanks." I was impressed at how quickly she'd sized up the situation. Bryn hadn't noticed it at all. Still I followed Ellen to the kitchen door and held it open as she carried the stool in. I didn't think she'd make a break for it, but I wasn't about to take the chance.

She put the stool in the middle of the living room, moved toward one of the sofas, and then, reconsidering, she moved the lusting Shiva to an end table and sat in its place on the end of the confessional bench. She curled her feet under her and rested her right arm familiarly on the penitent's shelf, next to the priest's seat. It was a remarkably uncomfortable-looking pose; one, I thought, that merited whatever forgiveness she might request. A clever hostess puts her guest in her debt by offering her the best of the food, the most comfortable chair. It's not easy with a police officer, but Ellen Waller was managing better than average.

"Where is Bryn?"

"At a planning meeting. She should be back anytime."

"Planning for the press conference?"

"No. For the fall's lecture schedule at The Team."

I nodded. I considered asking Ellen about her sudden departure last week, but the level of potential cooperation was four hundred times what I had expected and I wasn't about to undermine it—yet. "What can you tell me about the attacks?"

She was wearing a gray sweatshirt and those loose sweat shorts. Now she rearranged her bare legs on the bench, using the time to prepare her answer. I wondered if Bryn had cautioned her about me, or if Ellen herself knew something she hadn't decided whether to say. Or if she just had more sense than her cousin about pushing Sam Johnson too far. "First off," she said slowly, "Bryn's really undone by them. She's unnerved, but more than that she's shaken to find out that she is unnerved. She thinks she should be able to handle this, like she did the handstand on the ten-meter platform."

A meter is 39.37 inches. Upside down, 33 feet above the water? My stomach lurched. I'm better about heights than I used to be, much better. Hardly anyone knows I had a problem. But standing at the edge of a cement block 33 feet above the water . . . I'd cut off my foot before . . . "In a handstand?" I must have sounded more horrified than I'd intended.

She reached out automatically and almost patted my arm before she caught herself. "Yeah, and they don't cancel competition just because it's windy. Of course, Bryn wasn't afraid. Fear isn't something she deals in. For her it's all challenges to be mastered. Like life's a finite number of trophies waiting to be moved into her room. There's no question whether she'll get one, it's only a matter of when. If she makes a mistake, she learns her lesson and moves on. Athletes are trained to block out the thoughts of their mistakes, and concentrate, over and over, on the way the thing should be done." Ellen paused, noting my reaction. "I'm hoping some of that rubs off on me."

She was observing me as carefully as I was her, as if assessing whether I was adequate to protect Bryn. Or maybe take her on. I'd heard the "past behind you" theory of athletic trainers: that thinking about the road to the mistake wears that sequence of thoughts into the brain and into the body and then, under performance stress, the athlete is likely to veer onto Mistake Road. So block out the errors, mentally rehearse how the performance should be, and create the freeway to Success. Useful in sports, and in life? If all-for-my-goal were a sign of character, Brucker would be up for Role Model of the Year! "How about social things? Relations? Does Bryn handle those as well?"

"If she did, she'd be too perfect to tolerate. Surely you know that." Ellen's wide mouth pulled into an ironic smile—it looked like that was the kind of smile for which it had been created. "She's tolerable, socially, but it's not her medal sport. Really she's had to focus too much on her performance to . . . or maybe it's just that she's never *had* to fit in." She jerked toward me. "I don't mean that as a criticism. You can't be everything; what she does is important. For instance, she *handles* problems when someone else, a *lesser* person, would fall apart."

"Such as?"

"Well, right before she had to dive at the very last Nationals meet, she heard that one of the other Cal divers had been seriously injured in a dive. It unnerved everyone, but she had to block it out and climb up on the same kind of diving platform and dive. Then at the Olympic Trials every time a reporter asked about her dives, her making the Olympic Team, overcoming her scoliosis and that year off, it was always coupled with questions about Tiff. You know the type: 'Your problems are gone and your friend is in the hospital, how does that make you feel?' Bryn couldn't let it get to her." She shook her head. "It would only have taken one look at a newspaper to make me a basket case; but of course, Bryn didn't—couldn't—let herself read those papers, let Tiff's error taint her." Ellen must have read my expression; she added quickly, "She's not callous. Look at how hard she worked, and all the people she's helped since then. There's no benefit to wallowing. What's done is done; she knows that."

"But do you—does Bryn—think the attacker could be someone from her diving days?"

"She thinks it's Sam Johnson."

I leaned toward her, matching her movement, trying to slip into her mental motion. "May be, but it may not be. Either way, I've got to have some leads. You've been thinking about this, Ellen, and I can see you're concerned about Bryn. Who do you think might possibly, in the widest range of consideration, be angry enough, hurt enough, crazy enough . . ."

Ellen shook her head.

I didn't break the silence.

In Ellen, there was none of Bryn's smooth, controlled movement so characteristic of the athletic. Her nods and headshakes, the abrupt reach of a hand gave her the semblance of Bryn with the top layer scraped off. Like she'd thought so much about Bryn, observed and pondered her, tried on her skin, that her own effect was evident only in reaction to her brave, demanding cousin. She drew back again, quivering softly in the gray sweats in the beige room. "I haven't been here that long. And, well, we weren't close before. So even though we're family, she's got friends who know lots more than I do."

"Who? The friends?"

That threw her back farther. "I don't know. I guess I mean she should have friends like that."

"What about a lover, present or past?"

"No one now; no one she's mentioned. She's so busy and her schedule's so peculiar. She's so focused on her work . . ."

"How long have you been here?"

"Why do you ask?"

I laughed. "Because I'm a police officer, Ellen."

"Lest I forget, huh?" She smiled but the movement looked forced. "It's been about two months since I started here. Before that Bryn wouldn't even admit she needed a secretary. Everyone else knew it. It took me three weeks just to deal with her unanswered correspondence!" Ellen laughed.

The blue Volvo wagon pulled into the dirt space in front.

The laugh was gone. She glanced from the window to me and back, and said in a quick near-whisper. "The thing I want you to know is that no one's as perfect as Bryn seems. She's got devils she can't face. So when she snaps at you, it's not because of you, it's her. She can't deal with being undone by this. You do understand?"

It was Ellen I didn't understand. Or what she really thought of Bryn, or of me. "Ellen, I appreciate your concern." I did. Most subsidiary interviewees paid as much attention to my feelings as I do to those of the clerk who sells me my Snickers. I waited till she flashed a nervous smile. "Why did you go out the door when you saw me last night?"

"Last night?" she repeated, looking beyond me at the car outside. "Bryn wouldn't . . ."

The car door slammed.

"Bryn wouldn't what?"

Bryn got out and took the steps to the door in two bounds. Ellen jumped up and pulled open the door, ready for Bryn.

"Ellen," I said, "the question still stands."

Bryn strode in, chestnut hair gleaming, bright blue eyes glowing, shoulder muscles peeking out of a sleeveless Girls' Team T-shirt that just matched her eyes. But when she spotted me her face hardened. It might as well have been a marquee flashing: I let you see me emotionally naked. Now I'm going to wrap myself in so much anger, blanket you with so many demands and accusations, I'll entirely cover over that shameful incident. She flopped on the couch and glared up at me. "Have you interrogated Johnson?"

"We question. They only interrogate in the movies. And yes, I've questioned some of your neighbors, including him." I didn't allude to the humiliated anger; she'd take that as poking her wound. "Has the guard started yet?"

"No."

"When—"

"He doesn't. I'm not spending hundreds of dollars on a rent-a-cop because you real cops can't do your jobs."

"Your choice. For yourself, your employees, and your customers." I paused just long enough to air the implication of irresponsibility. "Then let's talk to other suspects. I know you're convinced Johnson is our guy, but believe me, an assailant can be someone so unimportant to you you don't remember a name. But lets start out easy. Ex-lovers."

"No."

"Think. Who have you dated in the past year? Make me a list. You can drop it by the station for me."

Bryn's face tightened, but before she could retort, Ellen said, "I'll get the calendar and your address book for you later."

Bryn nodded dismissively.

"Girls' Team customers—"

"*Members.*"

"Or employees? Is there anyone who feels he or she has been pushed aside?"

"I don't push people aside!"

"Should she add them to the list?" Ellen asked. I glanced at her just in time to see the smallest of grins fade from her lips.

"Ellen!" Bryn snapped. "Get me some tea."

Ellen blanched, jumped up, and pushed the kitchen door to swing closed behind her.

Glancing after her, Bryn sighed. I had the sense that she wanted to say something ameliorating but had no idea just what was appropriate. And she wasn't about to wimp out in front of me, not again. My *guess* was that she was as unnerved by Ellen's jab and dance as Ellen was frightened of her knockout punches.

Bryn had said she was so strapped for money she couldn't afford to hire anyone but a relative. That explained her half of the bargain. But Ellen? Surely she could do better than be at the beck and call of a tetchy, self-absorbed cousin . . .

"Bryn, just what does Ellen know about this?"

She started to protest, but I held out a palm. "No. Ellen knows something. The two of you are bouncing it back and forth out of my reach. It's key to this investigation, right? What is it?" I gave her a moment to respond, then demanded, "What about diving competitors?"

"You can't cheat in diving, for Chrissakes! Can't hide anything. You're up there on the platform like a pimple on the end of a tongue. Only thing you can do is kiss up to the judges. And *I* damned well didn't do that!"

It was a big defensive burst for a series of incidents that she'd been living off ever since. If she had done anything amiss in the Olympics, the media would have jumped on it. "If it's not that, what is it?"

"Either arrest Johnson, or stop pretending you're doing anything but wasting my time."

With anyone else I would have walked out of there, and written a report loaded with "refused cooperation." "I won't tell people how to exercise if you won't run the police department."

"I don't need—"

Taking a deep breath, I translated *grow up:* "Ellen told me one of your strengths was putting problems behind you and focusing on the issue at hand. I'd appreciate your doing that now."

She hesitated, then shouted, "Ellen, the tea! It doesn't have to be dead black."

Ellen hurried in, cup in one hand, pot in the other. She moved to the far side of Bryn, put the cup on the end table next to the Shiva, and bent over to pour. The bitter smell of green tea cut the air. Her movements had the same deadpan quality of her earlier comments. She didn't look at Bryn at all. It was to me she gave the smallest of smiles before she settled on the penitent's seat.

Later, I told myself, *get Ellen later. You can't let them bounce you back and forth too.* "How about nudists, Bryn?" I asked, recalling my speculations with Howard. "This is an out-of-the-way place for them."

"Don't bug me with your other cases. You want to know about Johnson?"

I gave up. "Okay, let's talk about Sam Johnson. He opens a health club a couple blocks from yours, he buys the house next door to you. Why?"

"I have no idea. It's like locusts eating your crop and then your children. Flood washing away—"

"I get the point! But the man had to have had some reason, even if it's a crazy one. Which came first, the house or the health club?"

"The house. It's been going on forever."

"Forever?"

"Over a year. The rip-off gym's only been open three months." Now she was sitting up, leaning forward toward me, her eyes sparkling the way I remembered them from the Olympic interviews.

I shifted my weight on the stool, jiggling the baton and flashlight as I moved. "I know, Bryn, that you spent years preparing The Girls' Team, but it wouldn't necessarily take Sam that long." I held my hand out to forestall her sarcastic comment. "Could it have taken him nine months or less?"

"The place is a storeroom of machines. In a week he could order them and take delivery."

I nodded. "So, okay, even allowing for coming up with the idea, finding out how to convert movement into heat, getting the necessary permits, even in Berkeley that could be done in less than six months. Chances are he bought the house, then came up with the idea for the gym. So Bryn, what happened between the two of you when he moved in next door that would make him intent on hitting you where it hurt most?"

A malicious smile flickered on her lips. "I threatened him with the Blight Ordinance. The place is an eyesore. He's doing the work himself, and is prepared to spend the rest of his life poking along at it. So I got on him. And then there were trucks all over the street, radios blaring, hammering and sawing till after midnight. So I had to get him again. He's turning the damn place into an apartment. 'You can't do that,' I said. 'There are zoning ordinances.' Does he care? Not hardly. Permits? Are you kidding? Well, maybe he gets one or two. In Berkeley, you don't put up a trellis without going through six commissions and paying for enough permits to cover the thing in paper, and you can believe he didn't bother with that. And why doesn't anyone care?"

I waited for the inevitable. Citizens elsewhere may play with municipal spats but Berkeleyans have honed them to Golden Gloves caliber. Better we should have citizens slinging ordinances and suckerpunching with subpoenas, than duking it out with deer rifles . . . though, in this case we could be dealing with both. "Why doesn't anyone care?"

"Because the goddamned city's afraid to hassle with Johnson, that's why! Everyone in City Hall knows him. If they push, he'll sue the city and every commissioner in it. They say you can't do that, but Johnson's been hip high in lawsuits for a quarter of a century; he'd find a way. Guy's made tactics his life. Our neighborhood organization files a complaint with a commission; they subpoena him, his lawyer postpones, and he doesn't do it till the afternoon of the hearing, and half of us don't find out till we're there."

That sounded like the Sam Johnson of the Persian Gulf street blockage. "He can only do that so often."

"Yeah, but while he does, he keeps sawing and hammering, and pouring cement. So by the time the complaint is heard, it's a moot point."

"But some complaints are heard."

"Right. Gets two or three postponements. When he *does* come, he manages to shift our complaint to last on the agenda. Do you know what that means? Those meetings start at eight and run *routinely* till two in the morning. The Lupicas and Croys have to go to work. The Johansens are in their eighties. By two A.M. we're lucky if a pair of us are still in the room." She gave one of those disgust-abbreviated shakes of the head, as if she couldn't keep from reacting to behavior so egregious, but was in too great a rush to pause. "Tactics; guy's a master."

That was an understatement. And something she should have considered before she took him on in his own arena. "And so you decided on some tactics of your own, right?"

Ellen got the point before Bryn. Neither of them spoke.

"Bryn," I said, "not only is it illegal to destroy property—you know that. But one small shake and that house of Johnson's will be a pile of plaster. If someone wanders in there through the hole in the fence that you cut, they could be killed. And Bryn, their heirs will sue you for every cent you ever thought of having."

"I didn't do anything to his fence," she said lamely.

"Maybe it was the eighty-year-old Johansens?" I asked, not bothering to control my sarcasm.

Bryn stared at me and matching my tone said, "And maybe it was Karl Pironnen, Johnson's other neighbor. I took his side when the Johansens complained about his dogs barking. Ellen's taken him to the vet and the bank. For us he'd be glad to get out the old metal shears. Of course, he'd have to have done it after dark because he's afraid of everyone. Or maybe his dogs chewed through it. Or—"

I'd had enough. I stood up. "I'm here to end the attacks on your vehicles. But you and Sam Johnson are enjoying your little war too much to stop."

"Hey, don't lump me with him!"

I let a beat pass and used the time to force a calm I certainly didn't feel. "Okay, then you be the adult. Handle the issues through the channels your taxes pay for." I took another breath and said, "And don't provoke Johnson with a press conference."

"Oh no." She jumped up to face me. "He's done his tactics game, now I'm doing mine."

"Bryn, you are dealing with a desperate man, who knows explosives, who thinks you are trying to take away the only property he's ever owned, and who's surrounded by adoring, young loose cannons who view death as a tactic."

"Tough."

"Bryn, you denounce him in public and you could get shot. Or they could miss you and hit a bystander."

She crossed her arms over her chest and leaned back. All she needed was a cigarette with ashes ready to flick. "That's why we pay for police, to protect the bystanders."

I steeled my face and aimed for the athlete's jugular. "Or Bryn, more likely, a kid would be jumpy, not a good shot. He'd miss your heart. But the spine is long and there are lots of possibilities for paralysis. Why don't you call your friend Tiff and ask her what it's like?"

The color drained from her face. If I'd had any question about this being a low blow, that was gone. She looked terrified.

A draft sliced in the armholes of my vest that might or might not stop a bullet. The green tea smelled like long dead bracken.

The color began to return to Bryn's face. She turned at Ellen. Slowly, powerfully, she breathed in, arching forward like a wave about to break. I didn't need a glance in Ellen's direction to tell me she was in danger of drowning.

"Don't look at me like that," Ellen forced out. "I don't know what you two are talking about. You never told me about anyone called Tiff."

But Bryn was already crashing toward her. "How could you . . ." She stopped, swallowed, and said, "Oh . . . I guess I didn't."

Purposely, I didn't look at Ellen. Instead, I tucked away that desperate deception for later use. "Bryn," I said, "think about this. One instant can change your life forever."

Bryn stepped toward me and the wave crashed. "I don't scare; I don't back down. The press conference stays. You want to see if I live—and if Sam Johnson lives—be there. Saturday. Four o'clock. People's Park."

An anti-Johnson speech in People's Park; she might as well have gotten a flight to Mecca to bad-mouth Mohammed.

CHAPTER 7

Bᴙ ᴛʜᴇ ᴛɪᴍᴇ ɪ got back to the station, I was exhausted even though it was only midafternoon, and my head was throbbing. I verified that Bryn Wiley had a permit for People's Park Saturday afternoon. The event was a looming disaster, the kind of stupid conflict born of ego that we see from Bosnia to Somalia to wherever else. And there was nothing I could do to forestall it. I took two aspirins and had dropped my quarters in the candy machine before I remembered my bet. Aspirin can do only so much; it was chocolate I needed. And sleep. And, well, chocolate!

On the way out of the lunch room I ran into Leonard escorting a drug-thin woman who couldn't have been anywhere near as old as she looked. On her wrists the cuffs were small as they get and still looked like she could slip her hands through at will, *if* she'd had the will.

"Four eighty-four." He sighed.

I nodded. If I hadn't seen it so often, I wouldn't have believed she'd had the energy to shoplift. But from the looks of her limp, stained T-shirt and chinos, she was boosting from need.

Waiting for me upstairs were three phone contacts to return —all to 484B victims who would be hoping I had better news than I did about their stolen bikes—and one message from Herman Ott I ignored. Brucker was transporting a prisoner to Santa Rita. At the best of times the station is a depressing reminder of government neglect, but this afternoon sooty windows looked black, the copy machine roared, and when I went up to our jail, the sole prisoner was a screaming drunk who managed to transpose one noun into verb, adjective, adverb, and dangling participle, and employ it for fully fifty percent of his vocabulary. He had, I felt, summed up the day.

Thursday, the team shifted back onto Swing Shift, 4 P.M. to 2 A.M. Brucker, a nine-to-fiver, was already gone when I got free of the team meeting. But the framed photo of Ronald Reagan and himself hung like a castleward keeping watch over Brucker's fiefdom. Bryn Wiley's list of contacts hadn't materialized. I called her number and left a reminder message. At nine thirty a drunk ran into a utility pole near the Oakland line. He ended up in Highland Hospital, ten blocks in the southeast quadrant of the city ended up without power, and I spent the rest of the shift dealing with the 10-33 audibles set off by the power outage.

I vacillated on warning Sam Johnson to be cool on Saturday. He would be no more responsive than Bryn, but I couldn't do nothing. I compromised with myself: drive by and if he was outside I'd stop. I was almost there when the dispatcher called.

"Six Adam nineteen?"

"Adam nineteen," I said to the dispatcher.

"We've got a fifty-one fifty on the one thousand block of Shattuck, complaining she's getting harassing calls from the former President."

"Former president of what?"

"The country."

"Which one? President, not country."

It was a moment before the dispatcher answered. In that moment I suspected he, too, had pondered whether our caller was hallucinating Ronald Reagan nudging himself awake to give her a buzz or Richard Nixon bugging her from the Great Beyond. "RP is Candace Upton."

When the dispatcher gets a 911 call, the caller's number shows on the screen. "Her phone number?"

The dispatcher laughed. "When I told her you'd call, she said she'd already hung up on the President twice, and she wasn't touching her phone again tonight."

"Okay, I'll swing by."

But when I came by the Upton apartment, the lights were off. I knocked but Upton didn't answer. Did she mistake me for one of the pushy ex-Presidents? Or had she moved on to other cosmic offenses? Chances were I'd get another chance to find out later in the week.

I drove on, occasionally aiming a side spotlight at a moving shadow, mostly just keeping the police presence on the beat.

Friday, I didn't wake up till noon and was still tired. I went through the whole litany of breakfast hopes—doughnuts, pastries, ice cream, Snickers, before the awful truth struck me once again. If it hadn't been for the prospect of Peet's, I would have pulled the covers back up and stuffed them in my mouth. They'd have tasted good as anything else I could eat.

I went to the Y, did half an hour on the StairMaster, twenty minutes on the stationary bicycle, hit the pool for another half hour, and fell asleep in the sauna. Then I ate a chicken sandwich the size of Des Moines.

I got to the station early, and headed for my old office. As soon as I opened the door, I could feel bile rising in my throat. Beneath his news photo of himself and Ronald Reagan, Brucker was half sitting, half sprawled in my chair, with one of my old case files in his lap, and piles of his papers lined up on Howard's desk where I had dreamed of laying out mine. Brucker looked up, a small smile on his tidy lips. You couldn't say it was smug, but you wouldn't swear it wasn't, either. On the corner of his desk was a Hershey's with almonds, half-eaten.

I looked down at Brucker's square face, his boxy features. If he'd been a gingerbread man, he would have been cut entirely in right angles. The only curved thing about him was the oval of his bald pate, and that was so white it looked undercooked.

"Brucker, if you were desperate for the bottom drawer, you could have called me."

"You knew I'd moved in."

"I assumed two desks would suffice. I don't like my belongings left on the squad room table; I don't want my personal items on top." There was doubtless a more diplomatic way to handle this. I didn't bother looking for it.

"So sorry to break the etiquette."

"Not etiquette, common courtesy." A guy, he'd say was setting things straight; me, he'd label bitchy. The look on his face said he was tempted to do just that but caught himself.

Instead he said, "I'm going up to Sacramento tomorrow for the rest of my papers. Reports from some interesting studies."

Ignoring his implicit request for questions about his prestigious posting in Sacramento, I settled on the corner of Howard's desk. "You've got questions about m—*the* assault cases?"

"Oh yeah, there are a lot of loose ends."

"Right. That's why they're not closed, Brucker."

He pulled open Howard's bottom drawer, fortunately the one that was not behind my feet, and presented me with a five-inch stack. It took half an hour to go through it and neither one of us was in a better mood at the end of that time. As is so often the case, the only thing that knowing I was behaving like an ass gave me was one more thing to be annoyed about. It was ten to four when I put down the last case and headed to the door. I was going to have to throw on my uniform and I'd still be lacing my shoes at team meeting.

"Oh, and Smith," Brucker said when I was half out the door, "I hope you won't get your back up: I told the dispatch sergeant to remind his crew you are in patrol now."

I could have protested that I'd been on patrol two weeks now, getting calls from those same dispatchers. Instead I waited, forcing his hand.

"I caught them after the first misdirected call."

I crossed my arms.

"For you."

"From?"

"Ott. That's the slimeball PI on the Avenue, right? What's he up to, Smith, trying to squeeze you like those scumbags do the city council?"

"Got me, Brucker." I walked out feeling like I'd been frisked. My pockets were empty. The man had my job and my office. There was nothing more for him to find. But I was glad I'd kept my mouth shut. It sort of made up for not answering Ott's calls, not that Ott would ever know, much less appreciate.

Two weeks ago I'd been making a difference. Now I was putting up with crap so I could . . . what? Keep Bryn Wiley and Sam Johnson from acting like two-year-olds?

When I got to the squad room, shoes unlaced, still snapping the keepers that hold the equipment belt to my pants belt, a box of macaroons was making the rounds. I took one and, while Pereira watched, squeezed it until it broke in two mangled parts.

The clouds Saturday afternoon should have been big and black and centered over People's Park. In fact, the sky had a thin dusting of gray. Good shooting weather, Leonard said as we headed toward People's Park, eyeing jackets slung over forearms, baggy shirts, loose jeans for signs of concealed weapons.

It was also good crowd weather. Half the people around were drinking coffee or Italian sodas from paper cups or eating cookies, pastries, or slices of pizza. I stared longingly as a slice of pepperoni made its way into park and mouth.

"Looks bad for a cop to pull a four eighty-four, Smith," Pereira murmured as she headed to the far end of the park. By now, of course, half the force knew about Howard's and my bet. After four steps Pereira stopped and turned, just in time to catch me checking my cheat sheet for the 484—petty theft. She grinned. After all the hours Connie Pereira had spent perched on the corner of Howard's desk, ogling my coffee or doughnut till I gave in and relinquished what was left, this bet was going to be hard on her, too. Not that that would keep her from enjoying my frustration. But what are friends for?

When I come to People's Park, I am always struck by how

much I care about the sixties symbolism of the place, and how little I actually like being here. And if I weren't in uniform, I wouldn't want to walk through it at all. As it was, I spotted one of the coke dealers I'd surveilled when I was on this beat just as he raised his hand to his mouth ostensibly to cough. If we'd had a camera on him, maybe we'd get a shot of the rock going from his mouth into the buyer's hand.

Set behind a row of stops on Telegraph Avenue, People's Park occupies the rest of the block. The far end, about a third of the park, is trees and underbrush and transients in sleeping bags with grocery carts packed full. In the middle, the University (owner of the land) built volleyball and basketball courts and a public bathroom—not without years of protest. On those courts, Cal students wearing bright blue and white now run and shoot hoops. A university-hired guard stands by. And the homeless, in dusty brown clothes, hang around the edges, tacitly announcing it's their park still. In true Berkeley fashion, years of controversy, demonstrations, scores of arrests, complaints, review hearings, and a spattering of lawsuits have resulted in nothing changing.

I took up a post at the northwest corner of the park, near the free box. A roofed container about five foot square, it's sort of a pound for clothes. Clothing owners who've become bored with or outgrown their garments drop them off there to be adopted by new owners. By four-thirty the afternoon wind was picking up, flapping the collar of my wool uniform shirt, carrying the smell of life on the street.

I surveyed the crowd. Peaceful enough now, though there were clumps of young male adults who'd killed more than one six-pack this day, and half a dozen older guys nodding off under the trees. Bryn Wiley's talk was likely to be only slightly more popular than I was here. I scanned the crowd for Sam Johnson, but he wasn't visible. But I counted six, no, eight, of his protégés sprinkled around the park, and that made me wary.

The crowd had thickened to a hundred fifty, about half the increase in media: reporters from both San Francisco dailies,

The Bay Guardian, the *Oakland Tribune, The Daily Californian,*
and the *East Bay Express,* plus crews from three television stations. A full house. Press conferences are a dime a dozen; the
press is leery of being used by talking heads seeking legitimacy,
and delivering tedium. But Bryn's call was a sure story for them:
local star, yuppie controversy in historically yuppie-phobic
Berkeley. The background of People's Park was the perfect "vi-
sual" to illustrate the yuppie-Berkeley dichotomy. It was a shoo-
in for the broadcast's cute windup story, and a coup that meant
the last words before sign-off would be the reporter's name. And
it could turn into a lot more than that. No wonder every station
had crews already taking background shots.

"If Wiley takes a dive," Leonard muttered with a straight
face, "we'll have it from every angle."

"She called this thing for four o'clock. It's already twenty-five
after," Pereira said. "Maybe she got a better offer."

"Gives her a wide, wide range," I said.

Leonard ambled back through the crowd. This was his territory. Even in uniform he moved easily through the sleepy sub-
cultures of the park. The regulars trusted him, as much as they
did anyone, and they counted on him to protect them from the
dealers and the crackheads, as much as they could anyone.

"Getting antsy," Leonard said as he circled back. "You don't
leave guys hanging this late on a Saturday. Too much loose time.
Before Saturday night, they're too ready-to-go."

Reporters checked watches. Camera operators fiddled with
their equipment. Two of Johnson's allies chatted them up. They
were right in front of the stage.

"How long are we giving it?" a rookie asked his team sergeant.

"Till they disperse. We're not here for Wiley; we're here for
them." He nodded at the crowd. "It's not getting smaller. It's
growing on itself. If Wiley doesn't show, we'll end up dealing
with a blowup here from the frustration alone."

On Haste and Dwight streets cars slowed nearly to stops.
Radios blared a cacophony of strings, horns, and rappers. The

smack of hands batting the volleyball was as regular as clock-work.

It was four-forty when Bryn Wiley mounted the platform, eighteen inches above ground level. News crews jostled anew, shoving closer, trying to figure where Bryn would be on the podiumless dais. Reporters extended their microphones, cameramen shifted their minicams. In the crowd the tenor of voices lowered as people shifted toward the action. I checked for faces, looking for those who lived to confront and those who felt "their" park was being invaded. And for the young bullies who preyed on the homeless. Three guys standing together I recognized from every demonstration I'd been to here—Johnson's crew. I moved between them and the stage. Murmurs bubbled up here and there, but mostly the crowd was quiet, waiting, ready for . . . for something.

I checked again for Sam Johnson. He had to know about the event. Nothing happened on Telegraph without Johnson's knowledge. So why wasn't he here? Was he "not dignifying" the event with his presence? Or maybe he had no answer to the charges Bryn would hurl. Either way, avoiding confrontation was not like Johnson. Particularly when the battle was in his own kingdom. Or maybe Johnson, the great tactician, had set himself an alibi elsewhere for whatever came down.

Bryn stepped to the microphone just as the sun broke through the clouds for that final startling gleam it gives on overcast days. The beam may not be stronger than it is all afternoon long on a sunny day, but on a gray day it's like the piercing light that precedes a divine proclamation. Dressed in walking shorts and tank top with The Girls' Team emblazoned in gold, Bryn smiled as the beam hit her and still cameras flashed. Her angular face was tan, her curly chestnut hair shining in the sunlight, the muscles of her lightly oiled arms and shoulders visible. All she needed was a red, white, and blue ribbon with an empty circle hanging from it for the Olympic medal she hadn't gotten. I couldn't help wondering if she had kept us waiting for forty minutes so she could catch the heavenly glow.

There was no podium to protect her. She strode to center stage and stood, slowly surveying the crowd as if to put each clutch of men—and the audience was almost entirely male—on notice that her words were meant for them. "Berkeley," she said, in a deceptively lazy voice, "is living in the past." She paused, staring into the crowd, daring them to object.

When no one did, she went on in that pulling-theories-from-the-back-of-the-mind voice. "What is 'Berkeley'? Not this patch of land we're standing on, not the National Guard troops that pointed rifles to keep you out of it, not the peace marches that brought you to it."

Low murmurs ran through the crowd. Bryn took a half step closer to the microphones. "All that was twenty-five years ago! A quarter of a century ago! You"—she pointed to a boy with long blond hair and baggy clothes—"weren't even born then."

"Hey, what do you know? You weren't here! We were talking about freedom!" yelled a dark-haired guy fifteen feet from the stage. I couldn't make him. I glanced at Leonard. He shook his head—unknown to him, too.

"Right you are, man," Bryn said. "Freedom, it was Berkeley against the state, Berkeley under siege from armed militia. Berkeley committed to freedom. Those were glorious days, important days, days when we stood for something—when we stood up for the truth, when we faced the government eye to eye, and said: We . . . will . . . not . . . be . . . deceived." She paused, eyeing the heckler. "And what is the legacy of those days? What have we got now?"

"Ain't honest government, that's for sure!" That was one of the park regulars.

"Right on, man!"—another guy I couldn't make—"They lie in Washington, they lie in Sacramento, they lie in City Hall."

Bryn broke into the calls. "Right, and they lie right here on Telegraph Avenue."

"Yeah! Damn cops, they tell you—"

"Back in Those Days, the cops stood with *us*, against *them*! Now they stand for nothing!" She waited, but kind words about police, even a quarter century ago, didn't reverberate with this crowd. Before the hoots could start, she shifted focus. "We will not be deceived!"

I tensed, hand poised over baton.

"We will not be deceived by our government!" she called. "And we will not be deceived by those who tell us they are helping us, and then rob us."

A murmur of confusion ran through the crowd. Bryn's was a sentiment that could hardly be disagreed with, but no one could tell where she was headed. They eyed her suspiciously.

"What am I talking about?" She flashed a smile. Cameras flashed in return. She let the anticipation stretch. "Sam Johnson, that's what! That's who! Where is Sam Johnson? Not here! But you all know Sam. And you—"

"Hey, who the hell are you?" a voice called from the back. One of Sam's crew. The crowd stiffened, shifted in toward the stage.

I stepped in closer and eyeballed the two Johnson friends in front of Bryn—no visible weaponry.

"And you," Bryn repeated more firmly, "know what he promised with The Heat Exchange. He promised people like you, people who have to choose between food and heat, he promised you help. And are you getting that help? No! Have you seen one cent from Sam Johnson? No! And why not? Because the Emperor has no clothes on!"

"Like the Olympic phone call!" Sam's friend from the back yelled.

Bryn stopped.

"Hey, lady, you're—"

"Don't be fooled." Bryn stepped forward till her mouth was an inch from the cluster of microphones. Her voice blared. "It's Sam Johnson who's cheating you. Sam—"

Like a wave the crowd's attention swept to the right. Like the Red Sea, a path opened. And like in the Garden of Eden, a bald, naked man ran out, holding a banner: THE HEAT EXCHANGE.

Camera operators made 180-degree turns and, seeing the

crowd five deep in front, backed up onto the stage, nearly knocking over Bryn Wiley.

But the nudist was quicker. He skirted around them, onto the stage, and reached out.

"Hold it!" I yelled.

She flung an arm at him.

He grinned. In one swift movement he rubbed his hand down her bare arm, then spun, jumped from the stage, and ran through the crowd.

"Move aside!" I shouted, shoving between two brown-jacketed men. They gave way, but the crowd in front was rush-hour thick. Everyone was cheering on the nude Mercury. Murakawa and Pereira pushed toward him.

Bryn was alone on the stage! I turned and shoved back between the jackets and pushed onto the stage.

She was gone.

Frantically I scanned right and left to Dwight and Haste streets. I spotted her on the sidewalk by Dwight Way, next to her Volvo wagon, holding a reporter by the sleeve and pressing a paper into his hands.

The crowd cheered louder. By now the runner had dropped his banner and was loping by the free box. No uniformed officer was near him. He turned to the crowd, pointed to a truck at the curb, and disappeared behind it. Doors on the side of the truck sprang open, and two men passed cardboard cartons of cans and lunchbags to the guys nearest them.

The nudist was forgotten. Bryn Wiley wasn't even a memory.

Murakawa and Pereira moved toward the truck. The sergeant pulled the radio free and called for backup.

Murakawa reached the truck. Two guys pushed in front of him. "Hey, cop, this food's ours!"

He glanced at the cans. "Enjoy," he said, "we're just watching."

But he was wrong about that. Within minutes we were breaking up fights. The sergeant was calling for more backup. By six o'clock the food was gone, the park was a mess, and we had two men in custody and one in the emergency room.

At six-thirteen I cut the engine in front of Sam Johnson's construction site. No lights were visible from the house. Big surprise there. I made my way over the rubble and banged on the door. There was a hole where the bell used to be. In half a minute I banged again. Footsteps? Or was that just the wind? Behind the house eucalyptus trees waved their spindly leaves like finger bones from a dangling skeleton.

"Po-lice! Open up, Sam."

He didn't.

I could picture him holed up across town in some buddy's room overlooking People's Park, hefting a beer in a return salute and laughing. Still, I made my way down the cement steps of Tamalpais Walk. A rusted pipe railing ran shakily beside them. In the dusky light, moist leaves blended into the stained cement. Earthquakes and ground settling had thrown the flights of stairs forward, threatening to slide the unwary foot off each step. It was not a descent for the nervous. To my right Johnson's house loomed large, dark, ragged. I shone my light underneath it. "Sam, you in there?"

"Who wants to know?" he demanded.

"Police. Come here."

Another time he would have told me what I could do with my order. Now he trotted out from under the house and stood opposite me inside the hurricane fence, looking for all the world like a brown-haired, buttoned-down kind of guy with no concern but working on his house. His yellow oxford cloth shirt was rolled to the elbow, his forearms streaked with dirt, a smudgy line across his forehead. Sam Johnson was as befouled as I'd ever seen him.

"Okay, Sam, let's talk about this afternoon."

"This afternoon? You want to hear about the two by eights I'm cutting? Or the cement guy I contacted to come Monday noon? Or—"

"Skip it. Who's your nudist?"

"Officer," he said, less smugly, more angrily than I would have expected, "I wasn't at the diving woman's press conference. But I heard about it. She got off easy."

"Is that a threat, Johnson?"

"Nah, nothing's ever a threat, is it? But if she takes it as a warning, she's wise. Tell her—you'll be reporting to her . . ."

I wouldn't, but I didn't feel obligated to explain that to Johnson.

"*I* wasn't at the park today. What happened today, *I* didn't do it." He paused, that puckish grin of his teasing me from behind the empty metal diamonds of the fence. "You don't create an itch then expect a guy not to scratch it—tell her that."

"Spoken like a teenager in heat." I sighed. "Sam, I really expected better of you."

"Tell her," he snapped in a voice that turned his grin hollow. He turned and strolled out of sight.

I climbed back up the slimy steps, avoiding the rusty pipe railing, thinking of what Sam Johnson could have done to Bryn had he chosen to. And pondering his uncharacteristic message. Boorish wasn't his style. Sam Johnson was *not* Howard, but they were both star performers. On the protests he created, he'd given himself near perfect style points. And his threatening comment had wiped out all today's style. Why would he . . .

I was getting into the car, repeating: "You don't create an itch then expect a guy not to scratch it," when I remembered my last encounter with a nudist. *The* nudist. I couldn't swear he was the same one, but how many bald nudists could there be in Berkeley? The last time, my nudist had run up Rose Street, then down through the underbrush, through the *poison oak*!

I smiled. Howard wouldn't give it a ten, but it'd be close. Bryn Wiley wouldn't be smiling. She'd be scratching her arm.

In the car I called dispatch, got Pereira, Murakawa, and Leonard on channel 2 and—the first positive event of the day—we could all go code seven. "My place. Ten-four."

* * *

"It was a master work," I said twenty minutes later as my three colleagues opened the white containers on Howard's dining room table. The one thing I'd been dead sure of after Bryn Wiley's rally was that Murakawa, Pereira, and Leonard would need a banquet. I owed them. I handled banquet preparations Berkeley style, or at least my style. I called *To Go Getters* to deliver a feast gathered from four local restaurants that would accommodate Leonard's ulcer, Paul Murakawa's vegetarianism, and Pereira's insistence on meat, spices, and a wide variety of tastes—all in finger food form so she could filch from carton after carton. And of course, my own Howard-enforced proscription against junk food.

If Howard had been home, he would have built a fire worthy of Celtic kings in the living room's huge hearth. It would have crackled and snapped and sent smoke across the room. As it was, the air was clear and the normal eau de mold hidden under garlic, onion, chili, and curry. Sixteen white cardboard and plastic containers (Styrofoam is outlawed in Berkeley) sat on the big, well-scratched mahogany dining room table that had probably come new to this house in the thirties. The chairs around it had obviously dribbled in singly like the tenants and were about as compatible. In uniform, her blond hair permed but still shiny, a touch of eye shadow and mascara visible to the discerning eye, Connie Pereira looked entirely too professional to be sitting on a half-runged ladderback chair—too professional to be reaching greasy pincer fingers. Leonard, on the other hand, looked like he usually wasn't allowed in the house.

"Bryn Wiley," he grumbled, yanking a captain's chair in closer to the table, "what the hell did she do a fool thing like that for?"

Pereira snared a plump lamb samosa, surveyed the other boxes, and shifted her shoulders preparatory to a cross-table lunge at the pot stickers. Inconsiderate criminals could end a code seven meal anytime; our most important dining skill was speed. "You got anything on the nudist?"

"Nothing," I said in disgust. "But I'll keep on it. Leonard's putting out the word on the Avenue."

Leonard, midway through a slice of polenta with sour cream, nodded. No fool, he carried a cloth napkin to tuck under his chin. Patrol officers pay for their own dry cleaning.

Murakawa was gnawing on a gray thing I took to be a vegetarian drumstick. It even had a faux bone in the middle and ersatz "skin" that made the whole concoction resemble something left in the morgue for a decade. Everything in his boxes looked like the last stop before compost.

"What about the nudist, Smith? He your Bare Buns?" Pereira asked.

"If there are two bald nudists covered with poison oak, I may have a question. If not, it's Bryn Wiley who's got the problem—he rubbed his hand down her arm."

"The gift that keeps giving, huh?" Pereira laughed.

"No," Murakawa said.

"No, what?"

"Poison oak isn't spread from person to person. You have to get it directly from the plant or, if the plant burns, from the smoke."

"Surely, Sam Johnson would know—"

"Yeah, Smith, sure as you did." Pereira laughed.

"Dogs," Leonard barked. "Two weeks I was scratching, all because I rubbed a dog in Tilden Park."

"Well there, of course," Murakawa admitted, "the sap was still wet on the dog's fur."

"So if the nudist had a handful of sap?"

"Then, Jill," Leonard said, "Sam Johnson's got himself one helluva committed nudist. Or a guy who's got no more sense than he has clothes. He's already covered with itch and he's going back for more."

We looked at Murakawa for the nudist's prognosis, but he was busy forking in nut and bean salad. Pereira had predicted that his calorie intake from any of these meals would be minus and eventually his teeth would be worn down to the gum. Then, she'd added, he could move to a diet of bean paste and tofu. When he finished chewing, Murakawa looked up and asked, "What about the food truck in the park?"

"Gone before we could get the crowd under control," Leonard said.

"Didn't you even get the license?"

"No. Don't matter. We could bust our butts running it down, but I'll tell you what we'll find: rented with phony papers. You been around the Avenue as long as I have—since the trolleys ran to Oakland and they still had the telegraph lines, in case you're asking, Murakawa . . ."

Murakawa, the last person to ask an intrusive question of a colleague, smiled uncomfortably, and helped himself to more fried gluten balls. Pereira shook her head.

"We all know who's behind it," Leonard said.

I nodded. Sam Johnson had done a great job of manipulation all the way around. When the late night news came, it would have discreet shots of the rash-red running nudist carrying his banner. As for Bryn Wiley, she would be just a comical footnote. I put down my fishburger with fried onions and mushrooms. "So, Leonard, where do you see this going from here?"

"Where could it?" Pereira demanded. "Johnson's won."

"Yeah, but Wiley was handing the press something afterward," Murakawa said.

"Press release. By that time it was already outdated." Pereira had already eyed my burger, and recognizing it as a lost cause, she shifted her eyes quickly over the gluten balls to Leonard's remaining meat loaf.

Leonard pulled his plate in closer, looking every bit the shaggy carnivore. "If you'd asked me a couple years ago, I'da said Johnson's one of the 'think first' rads. Not in it to spite his parents, if you know what I mean. He really cared about justice, or justice as he saw it, and a fair share for at least the people he was focusing on."

"But?" I prompted.

"But since he got married, he's changed. Maybe he's just

worn down with losing, maybe he's sick of mediating the squabbles of the kids who *are* in the movement to spite their parents, maybe he's sick of seeing them waste their energy to make a point no one cares about."

"Like his own traffic clog at San Pablo and Uni?"

"Yeah. Great tactic, but the movement came out of it looking like spoiled brats, and you can believe no one caught in that traffic jam was rushing to contribute the next time Johnson needed cash or lawyers. Yeah, maybe that's exactly what Johnson's had enough of. You know, Smith, old rads either plug on against injustice until they drop, just doing it to do it, or they become old Republicans, or some—and I figured Johnson would be one—become statesmen. And some snap from the frustration."

Pereira's plate was empty. She surveyed the empty containers. "Dessert?"

"Next month," I said.

"Some hostess you are. There's nothing worse than dinner with no dessert."

I was just about to agree wholeheartedly.

But of course, there was something worse. The radio crackled. "Six Adam nineteen and six Adam one."

"Nineteen. We're both here."

"You've got a nine-one-one call on Tamalpais. Possible one eighty-seven."

"Do you have a street number for that?" I asked, holding my breath.

"I'll check."

It was Bryn Wiley's address.

One eighty-seven is homicide.

CHAPTER 8

I RAN FOR THE car, hit the lights and siren, and got the dispatcher back before I was out of the driveway. "The one eighty-seven, who's the victim?"

"Caller didn't say. Call came via CHP."

Cellular phone 911 calls go to the Highway Patrol. "Any other victims?"

"No."

"Suspect?"

"Guy who called said: 'A woman's been shot,' gave the address, and hung up."

But CHP would have recorded the phone number. "Who's the phone listed to?"

"A Bryn Wiley."

"Bryn Wiley! He called on her own phone? And then hung up? How'd he sound: angry, scared?"

"He called CHP."

"Get 'em back and find out for me. Thanks. And this scene, on Tamalpais, it's a hillside with a lot of underbrush. I'm going to need every backup unit available." I wove the car through the two-lane traffic on College Avenue until I could cut up to Piedmont Avenue—Fraternity Row. Two lanes there, too, but grassy islands between them. Lights and sirens should clear a street. They don't. Drivers freeze in indecision; pedestrians stop mid-crosswalk to gawk, as if the patrol car's in a movie and they're the audience. I yanked the wheel right, around a Suzuki Samurai, left to skirt a clutch of students, right, onto the grass and past three double-parked vans.

Like strikes of lightning Bryn Wiley pierced my mind: Bryn holding a press conference on Sam Johnson's turf. So stupid. But so in-your-face gutsy. And she'd come within a hair of winning the crowd. No wonder she was revered by scores of Berkeleyans—our own secular Joan of Arc.

But when she'd gotten home from the People's Park debacle, humiliated, and had imagined Sam Johnson chortling with his friends as I had, did she crumble? Did she stand quivering as she had by the Volvo, or did she snap back with a fury ten times greater than she'd aimed at me? I had no idea what was beneath those reactions. And my guess was that she didn't either. Maybe she was too scared to look. Maybe her campaigns were more necessary to her than she was to them. Maybe she *couldn't* give them up.

I got lucky on the road behind campus, and cut below the Ngingma Institute, Berkeley's bit of Tibet.

If Bryn had been shot in the park, I wouldn't have been surprised. But in her own driveway . . .

Maybe the victim wasn't Bryn. My stomach clutched. It could be Ellen. God, I didn't want it to be Ellen.

I picked up the mike. "Adam nineteen. Control, put me priority for the ID tech."

"Done, nineteen. Ambulance rolled from Kensington. It's already at the scene."

Ambulances usually wait till they're sure of cover. Why hadn't this one? "Any word on suspects?" Could they be behind the redwoods or on the hillside behind Bryn's, ready to pick off the medics, or us? "Who's supervising the scene?"

"Let me see. Grayson's out at the Telegraph scene. Lieutenant's . . . you are Smith, until Grayson gets there. On suspects, nothing."

"Give me a radio channel and get everyone on it."

"Channel four."

"Thanks."

"Ten-four."

I pulled up on Tamalpais Road just before Acosta. The street was dark, those tree-muted streetlights merely blurs two stories up. Cars hugged the curb, parked two wheels on the sidewalk. I gazed ahead at that sharp elbow curve. Bryn's driveway was just past the midpoint. But the redwoods across the street blocked it out.

"This is Adam nineteen. On Tamalpais half block below the curve," I said into the mike as I pulled to the curb. "We don't know what we've got here. The responsible could be anywhere. There could be more than one. Acosta and I'll do the scope from this end." Acosta pulled up behind me. On the radio, officers were checking in. Murakawa and Kendall would come down from the top of Tamalpais.

I moved in at a run, keeping close to the trees. I was nearly into the curve when I spotted the ambulance, its spinning roof light turning the sheet on the gurney red, the dark blue Volvo wagon in the driveway black, the ground around it a bloodier brown.

Behind me, brakes screeched, one after another. Ahead, a couple in bathrobes stood in a yard. Acosta sprinted to them; he'd ask about suspects. I checked the redwood stand, flashing my light into the shades of black. Pereira was coming up behind me now, checking yards, behind cars. In a dark, wooded area like this only a fool would be spotted. Any suspect with a dime of sense would be long gone. I ran on toward the ambulance.

Holding the IV, one medic was climbing into the back of the ambulance after the gurney. My chest went stiff as the protective vest. I was expecting to find Bryn dead. She wasn't . . . yet. I peered up into the ambulance and saw enough of the blood-covered face to know I didn't want to see more. Her honey-colored hair was so clean, so shiny. Every time I looked at death, it was always the same; the edge never wore off. I grabbed the second medic.

"ID?"

"Full pocketbook. Driver's license, credit cards, the lot. Name's Bryn Wiley."

Bryn, not Ellen. A wave of relief washed over me, then a second wave—guilt. "She alive?" I forced out through my clenched throat. I didn't want to hear the answer.

"Barely."

I followed him around to the cab. "She conscious?"

"Hardly."

"Any sign of suspects?"

"No."

"The victim, where did you find her?"

"In the driver's seat, the Volvo." He climbed in, hit the lights and siren.

An officer had to accompany her in the ambulance, for that one-in-a-million chance she would regain consciousness and make a dying declaration about her killer. Even then, for it to be accepted as evidence in court she had to have known that she was dying. I was real glad to be in charge of the scene; I didn't want to ride across town looking at what was left of her face. Acosta was three feet away. "You ride with the victim. Sorry."

"Sure."

"Her purse is in there," I said, shutting the door after him as the ambulance pulled away. I didn't tell him to go through the purse, he'd do that. The medics had been first at the scene, first to see the body. "Get the medics' statements at the hospital." He'd call me as soon as he knew anything. Chances were, the first thing he'd have to report would be the time of death.

I watched the red lights waver and die behind the curtain of redwoods. Now, in the emptiness, my stomach lurched. But I didn't throw up. I don't.

Pushing away the picture of her bloody face, I called the dispatcher for time and case number. Taking out my notebook, I concentrated on noting the medics' names and observations, the time the ambulance left, and Acosta's presence in it. I could feel myself go numb making the shift into "all business." I surveyed the Volvo. The driver's window was two-thirds gone, but what was left held a bullet hole. Irrationally, I thought how furious Bryn would be that she'd wasted the time to get the window replaced—when she couldn't even have delegated the job to Ellen because Ellen didn't drive.

Inside, shards of glass lay everywhere except on the driver's seat. The backseat was covered with one of the comforters from the house, the black and white one.

Headlights glowed white from both ends of the street. There was a squeal of brakes. Patrol officers from other beats. I had Leonard freeze the scene. "Run the cordon fifteen to twenty feet around the car. Wide as you can. Into the street. Include the house."

He nodded, got the yellow crime-scene tape out of his trunk, and began stringing it between two trees at the end of the driveway, around to the railing by the house steps, and on to three more trees before it made a circle of sorts. The sureness of each move reminded me how deceptive was his shambling appearance. "Scene frozen by 24—his badge number—17:24," I added to the record.

On the radio, patrol officers vied for the dispatcher's attention. House lights came on in upstairs windows across the street. Doors banged shut. I handed out assignments: Sapolu, containment; Murakawa and Pereira, crowd interviews (technically everyone there was suspect; they'd all have to be interviewed, later taken to the station for statements); two officers to go door-to-door uphill, another pair downhill. And Bryn's house, we needed to get in there. The situation that ended with Bryn in the driver's seat, shot, could have started in the house. The suspect could have run back inside. Ellen could be there, dead or dying —or she could be the suspect.

"Heling," I called as she loped up. "Take MacElroy and Zonis. Go through the house. Could be one or more responsibles inside, could be another victim." The trio would clear one room after another, keeping together, protecting each other.

"Officer, what's going on?" demanded a woman in a raincoat. She was leaning over the cordon, almost falling forward.

"There's been an injury. Step back away from the scene, please."

"Injury to who?"

"Step back, please."

"I *live* here, I've got a right to know."

"Step back, *please*. I'll be with you as soon as I can." Grudgingly, she stood upright and moved onto the street, muttering. Her only audible word was "rude."

I wrote down the last of the assignments and times. Sapolu, on contain, was moving like a terrier, barking at one incursion after another. Barking politely. The biggest problem with a homicide scene is keeping the extraneous sworn officers from tromping all over it. "Any of our friends want a look," I said, "tell them you're documenting everyone who comes on the scene, and we'll take elimination prints from them. And, of course, they'll be subpoenaed when the case hits court."

Inside Bryn Wiley's house, lights went on in the living room. Good sign. I waited till the bedroom light shone, and called to Leonard. "Spray your light on the ground on the driver's side of the car. See if there's a casing there."

"Right."

Tanner, from beat 18, ran toward the scene just ahead of a student with a notebook, a reporter for *The Daily Californian*. In another ten minutes everyone with a police scanner and an inadequate social life would be at the scene. Before the Cal guy could speak, I said, "Much too soon. You're looking at a couple hours before we have anything worth your time. Go to dinner and come back; you won't miss anything."

I noted down Tanner's arrival and the time, and that of the Cal reporter just for good measure. "Tanner, sketch the scene."

"Smith!" It was Leonard.

"Got something?"

"You bet. Number one." He flashed the light three feet inside the cordon. It shone on a bullet casing. "Number two." He moved the light six inches to the right. "Number three." The beam shifted two feet forward. "Number four. A thirty oh six, don't you think? Take down game bigger than you, Smith."

I glanced at Tanner to make sure he was noting the casings, then asked Leonard, "Nothing beyond there?"

"Nope. By the time he got the fourth shot off, she must have gone down."

"Maybe," I said, cautioning myself against creating scenarios in my mind. Once in place it's hard not to adjust every new fact to fit in. "I'd say this makes you the finder of record."

Leonard groaned. Now anyone who found any evidence at all would bring it to Leonard and he would sign it in. It was no boon for Leonard, but it meant the whole team wouldn't be tied up in court.

I took my own flashlight off my belt and aimed it at the nearest casing. Could be from a 30.06 rifle cartridge; Raksen, the lab tech, would know. And damp as the ground was in this ever-shaded spot, there should be usable prints. I suggested that to Leonard.

"Could have been a suspects' picnic here, Smith. You'll be lucky to get a decent toe or heel with all the foot traffic that's been through here."

"Maybe near the last two casings." He would have landed harder there.

"Cement. Look, Smith." He aimed his flashlight at first one then another cement disk. "Only two goddamned garden steps in the place, and he lands on them."

"Chooses them, surely. It's hard to imagine such a stroke of luck. It makes me think of the nudist leaping off the railing at the end of the path from Rose Street—like someone who knows this spot."

We were standing in front of a redwood, small in the annals of redwoods, but huge compared to normal trees. The trunk was a good three feet in diameter. "Perfect spot to wait for her to pull up. Then all he had to do was step out and shoot." I looked across the street. "And disappear into that grove of trees before anyone saw him. Rope that off and check it out, and I'll send Raksen over after he's done here."

"Right."

"Officer! What the hell's going on here!" A man in sweats pushed in between us.

My radio crackled. "Adam nineteen?" I glanced at Leonard and moved away. Leonard's beat was Telegraph Avenue; he was used to handling crowd problems.

I flicked the mike on. "Nineteen."

"I got the CHP dispatcher who took the nine one one call. The cellular phone."

Bryn's cellular phone. What kind of person would lean over Bryn Wiley's bleeding body and use her phone to call us? Why bother? You don't fire four shots at a woman and then when she's hit, call the police. "What exactly did the nine one one caller say? What kind of voice?"

"Male. No accent. Sounded young. Shocked. Said a woman had been killed and gave the address."

"That's all?"

"Dialogue, yes. But the thing was, Smith, well, CHP's embarrassed about it. And it was just a split-second mistake. But at first CHP thought it was a call from the field."

"From one of their own? Why?"

"She said it sounded professional. Momentarily. She was just about to chew him out . . . Because it's a busy night. She thought he was taking up air time on the emergency channel to call in plates. She caught the mistake in a second, but . . ."

Plates. License plates. Nora, Ocean, Pablo. "His voice sounded young?"

"Yeah. His voice, Smith, it broke."

"Thanks, Control, you've been a big help. Ten-four."

"Ten-four."

I turned toward the dark house on the other side of the construction site. Karl Pironnen's windows were dark. But I was willing to bet he was sitting inside them, trying to peer out through the coating of slobber left by Nora, Ocean, and Pablo. Pironnen was sixty years old. Did voices that age still break? As terrified as he seemed of people, when he opened the door to me in my uniform, I'd be likely to find out.

If he was still there by the time I could cut loose of the scene.

All the lights were on in Bryn Wiley's house now. I wanted to get in there, into Bryn's nightstand, her letters, her medicine closet, to see the trinkets she kept to remind her who she was. And I needed to go over the car.

The fronds of the redwoods rustled and the wind blew off the freezing night waters of the Pacific. I heard shoes slapping the street behind me, heavy, moving fast. I turned, hoping it was Raksen.

It wasn't. Looking down at me was Grayson. His arms were folded across over his chest, his mustache almost covering lips pressed together in annoyance. He was the scene supervisor; it was his scene now. "What've you got, Smith?"

I gave him a rundown on the scene and watched him listening for omissions, noting things to change. His finger was rubbing against his cuff, itching to point, to assign, to wag. I half-smiled. Guys come on the scene, they want to mark their territory.

While that finger was still rubbing, I held out my notes to it. Pages of names and times and assignments.

Heling came up behind me. "Smith, the house is clear. The small bedroom's really clear. Clothes, but nothing else. No papers, no photos, no books. Like the occupant just came for the weekend. And the weekend's over."

Behind the crowd, another marked car pulled up. The red pulsar lights took twenty years off the driver's graying red hair. But when Inspector Doyle hoisted himself out, those two decades crawled back on, weighing down his every move. He'd had surgery a few years ago, never would admit the cause. Never quite bounced back. His dark Windbreaker fluttered loosely in the wind, as if it had been made for a larger man—him, before he went under the knife.

As he hurried across the street, futilely trying not to favor his
left leg, I realized how much it mattered to me to be in charge of
a case, to be the one who got all the reports, the conclusions; the
one who could see into the soul of the case. Investigation is a
team effort. All jobs are vital. Maybe, I thought looking at Grayson, I just wanted to make my mark.

But no, it was more than that in this case. It wasn't just that
my knowledge of Bryn Wiley and her life would be watered
down in the retelling. It wasn't that I even liked her; I hadn't.
But I cared enough about her to close her file for her. And to get
the person who had stood waiting behind the redwood to blow
her face off.

Doyle would be doing assignments now. Bryn Wiley's house.
The Volvo. Karl Pironnen. He'd give me only one. The physical
evidence is vital; it was tempting. It wasn't going to change.
Heling could list the contents of a room. But interviewing suspects is the heart of the investigation. Few things are as important as those first statements, hearing them in person, seeing the
suspects' reactions, getting the small facts, the asides, the nuances you'll use to trip up suspects later. When you merely read
a transcript, you miss those little things. Without the initial interview you've got nothing to judge against. I'd seen Karl Pironnen before; I had a baseline for him.

I briefed the inspector, told him about the space under Sam
Johnson's house—a beaver dam of hiding places for a suspect, or
for Sam Johnson himself. He assigned Heling's team back to the
house, and took on the car himself.

I turned and strode down the street, rerunning my talk with
Pironnen, seeing him when he wasn't a suspect, setting in mind
the standard of innocence against which to judge his words,
gestures, silences. Despite the probable hygienic deficiencies, I
would interview him inside his house, and see what the dwelling
told about him, and I would see his face in the light.

Where to start, with the 911 call, or hold that in abeyance?
Or ask about a gun? I'd run him through files the other night.
We had no gun permit listed.

Despite the uniform and the tight protective vest, I felt like I could breathe. I realized, as I pressed the doorbell, that I felt different than I had the whole time I'd been on patrol. Now I felt like me.

CHAPTER 9

I RANG KARL PIRONNEN'S buzzer again. It pierced the interior silence then died like a cigarette stubbed out in a planter. The door was set with the smallest and highest leaded glass window I'd ever come across—a peep hole for the tall. Raising myself on tiptoe, I peered into the dark at one small light in the distance. Had it flickered, I'd have taken it for a candle. It was that kind of house.

I turned the volume on my radio down to a murmur, pushed Pironnen's buzzer again, and held it in. I'd have laid cash that Pironnen was inside, too stubborn or too frightened to answer, except that it was dead quiet in there. No barking, no scraping of toenails. Occasionally there's a dog that doesn't go racing to the door; one dog, maybe; definitely not three together. The buzzer groaned on inside. No footsteps approached. I lifted my finger. Still no sound.

But I'd be damned if I was going to walk away. I tapped the buzzer like Sergeant Joe Friday, in a series of staccato beats. Behind me, the onlookers, numbering over fifty by now, created a mosaic of sound, asking each other for facts, tossing in speculations, edging forward to hear as the radio on Murakawa's shoulder sputtered a call.

Raksen had arrived and was setting up lights around Bryn's car. As soon as he started photographing, he'd provide a show worth waiting for.

I rang the buzzer one last time. Pironnen didn't have to come to the door. Legally, he could stare through the leaded glass at me and still choose not to open up. But damn it, a woman was dying, her face a mush of blood and flesh from the gunshots. Hours ago she'd been on the stage, catching the last ray of sun. For a woman determined to stay in the center of things, who seemed alive and focused only when she was in the spotlight, it was a cruel irony to meet death with no face. Soon—maybe already—she would be just another corpse, a lump of matter in a closed box. There would be no last viewing for her friends, fans, supporters, to fix her face in their memories and give her that small bit of immortality.

Footsteps—stockinged-foot soft—approached. Pironnen would peer through his leaded peep hole at the glass-distorted night. He would spot me and pad away. And if I called out "Police!" he'd just pad more quietly.

I bent my knees and stayed close to the door. The footsteps stopped. I could hear his wheezing breath. He was looking. Seeing no one. If he left I'd have to—

The door opened a few inches.

I stood. "Mr. Pironnen, you remember me, Officer Smith. We talked the other night when you were out with Nora, Ocean, and Pablo. Where are they? I didn't hear them. It's freezing out here, do you mind if I come in?"

His eyes widened and his wheezing breaths were barely more than puffs—I'd overloaded his circuits. While he was letting them unscramble, I walked in.

I took a couple steps through the entry hall and into the living room. The whole room was brown and black and gray, the colors of the dogs, and coated with hair malamute thick. The sofa, tables, mantel, lampshades, radio, pictures were so completely covered they might have been merely raised sections of the wall.

I am not a good housekeeper—well, not a housekeeper at all

—so I understand the progression by which a socially acceptable room deteriorates into an embarrassment. I know that, like true rabbits, dust bunnies multiply. If you let them go for a month—not intentionally, of course—they will clump together. But if you fail to collect them at that key moment and permit another few weeks to pass, they will disintegrate again.

But this room was so far beyond my experience I couldn't begin to guess how long it had been in the making. Or how long since there'd been a guest in here. Not in this decade surely. Probably not in the last two.

Pironnen himself was liberally covered with dog hair. It was no wonder the man was wheezing. And also no wonder I hadn't heard footsteps. I glanced at his feet. Through the muck of dog hair I could make out the brown leather around the pointy toes of his wing tips.

Pironnen edged back till he was five feet away. His narrow mouth pursed. Deep-set gray eyes cowered in their sockets. And short gray hair hung over his forehead protectively. His navy V-necked sweater seemed inadequate for the cold of the house, and his black chinos bagged at the knees. He didn't ask me to sit —thank God. I was hoping the smell—that musty-sweet odor of dog, here layered with dust and dirt, a sort of compost lasagna—would diminish as I stood here. But no such luck—it was the aroma of the house. Hairs floated in the light like snow. With each inhalation I was sure I felt a strand entering my nostril. I snorted and tried to inhale more gently, so the air didn't move. *Give it up, Smith!* Perhaps I'd forgotten the point of breathing!

I looked back at Pironnen. He hadn't moved or changed expression. Now that I was inside the house, I needed to guide those circuits of his into usable paths. "Aren't the dogs here?"

"Out."

"For their walk?"

"Out."

"Do you usually take them out at night?"

He nodded.

"But there are too many people around tonight, huh?"

Again he nodded, the stiff lines of his fearful face tightening. Instinctively, I wanted to put a comforting hand on his shoulder, but that would have been the worst move. And of course, I didn't want to touch him. I kept my gaze on him, letting its effect seep in. Already, he was nervous enough for his voice to crack—if he spoke more than one word at a time. I wished now I'd heard the 911 tape. Distorted by multiple circuits, the voice might not have revealed much, but the syntax, that could hang him. I decided to go for broke. "What kind of gun do you have?"

"None." His voice didn't break; he looked no more frightened than before. That was the problem with the far different drummer set—with them an extreme reaction didn't stand out.

"Have you been outside at all tonight?"

He hesitated.

"When?"

"Earlier."

"Before or after it was dark?"

"Oh, after," he said definitely.

"Don't you go out in the daytime?"

"No . . . unless . . . sometimes, I have to."

"For doctors and dentists?" I was leading him, but there was no choice. I wondered what percentage of his conversation was spent with people leading him. Or not waiting for him to force out the words at all. How long had the man lived alone, where words were tools best used singly to suit the canine mind?

"Doctor, dentist. Yes."

"And business?"

"Through the mail."

I nodded, letting that thought settle before I moved on. "But you went out tonight after dark?"

He nodded.

"Do you recall the time?"

"Eight twenty."

Amazing. "How come you remember so specifically?"

"My chess match with Milwaukee is at nine. I've got to get back."

"Do you play with a friend there?"

He stared, perplexed. It was a moment before he said, "I'm on ChesNut."

"A computer bulletin board that arranges chess games? How many games are you playing now?"

His eyes shifted up and to the side as if the answer were hanging off his right brow. "Twelve."

"You have twelve chessboards set up here?" How could he tell the red squares from the black under all this hair? And the king and queen and the horses, wouldn't they be buried in the underbrush?

"No, no boards."

"No boards?"

"In my head."

I didn't know whether to believe him or not. Was the man a genius, or was he hallucinating? For the moment I opted for the former. "Mr. Pironnen, I'm really impressed. You must be a very penetrating thinker. And you must remember everything, right?"

"No." It was a single word, uttered without intonation, but it screamed: *Don't patronize me.*

Cops don't embarrass easily, but I could feel my face coloring now. "Tonight," I said, "did you see the flashing lights outside?"

"From in here. Ambulance."

"Did you call it?" I slipped the question in.

"No," he said, but this "no" had none of the nuances of the previous one. Just a straightforward no.

I pressed my lips together against a sigh. Had a confession been too much to hope for? Or even evidence that he was the culprit? I didn't picture Pironnen shooting Bryn and reaching across her dying body for the phone. I couldn't imagine him choosing to come that close to anyone.

Still, the 911 tape had radio codes in the background. "When you were out tonight, did you see the Volvo station wagon?"

"I didn't notice it."

I asked about the period before the ambulance arrived, but he denied, with that blank expression, hearing shots, seeing anyone unusual on the street, then or earlier. "At night, I don't have to talk to people. Even if they see me, they don't rush over, push in on me."

"Have you found that with the neighbors, pushing in on you, calling it help?"

He didn't smile, but he nodded more easily. I guessed that that was as close to a smile as he came. For him, was every human contact a potential smothering? Did he have the same cringing reaction outside that I had in this room?

"Bryn Wiley," I said, "did you know her?"

Again he nodded, and I noted that the quality hadn't changed. He was relaxed as he recalled her. "Ellen's cousin. I saw her over there."

"Did you speak to her?"

"No. She was always on her way."

"But you know Ellen?"

The creases around his eyes and mouth deepened.

"Did she try to help?"

He nodded.

"Nora jumped on glass. Split her paw open. I couldn't stop the bleeding. Outside. Ellen saw it. She came running. We took Nora to Dr. Abbey, the vet."

That sounded like Ellen. It made me smile. "Did you go inside the vet's?" I wanted to know whether Ellen was just doing a favor or using the opportunity to push him into social contact. I wasn't surprised when he nodded. That sounded like Ellen, too. She'd have been the right person to support him.

"Have you and Ellen gone back since?"

"Yes, Dr. Abbey's."

"Anywhere else?"

The lines deepened and he physically pulled back though he was a good five feet away from me already. It was too big a question. "The last time was when?"

"Yesterday."

"Where did you go then?"

"Vet."

"And?"

"Bank."

"And?"

"Herb store."

I smiled. A good, if very Berkeley, choice. In an herb store Pironnen wouldn't stand out; he'd be a run-of-the-mill customer there. Ellen must have given this operation serious thought. Pity she hadn't socialized him enough to be out paying attention to his surroundings, and his neighbors.

"Mr. Pironnen, Bryn Wiley has been assaulted, seriously," I said, watching his reaction. His face showed a flicker—of surprise, curiosity, fear, I couldn't say what. "Someone called nine one one to report her injury. About nine o'clock tonight. We have reason to believe you and your dogs were nearby. Did you see anyone near her car then? Think!"

"*I* was home at nine. Milwaukee is at nine."

"Well, as you were coming home, then."

"I *remember* coming down the street. I told you, no one was there."

"Her car was damaged two days ago. It might have been done by the same person. Have you seen anyone around their driveway in the last week who looked . . . odd?"

"You mean like me?"

The perception so shocked me it took me a moment to smile. After his last quixotic hint of reaction, I wouldn't have thought he could make that leap to see himself through someone else's eyes. I explained what I meant, but that didn't prompt an answer.

The interchange, or perhaps his snatching control of it, seemed to focus him. He walked toward the front door with the firm steps of dismissal. Another witness I would have detained long enough to set straight, so he didn't nurture the seed of noncooperation before our next interview. But with Karl Pironnen I wasn't sure which rules to play by, or if there would be any game to win. I turned to follow him, from habit scanning the dining room, peering in the kitchen, and noting the only hair-free square inches in view—a tarnished silver frame holding an old photo. Two young men stood arms draped around each other's shoulders. There was no question they were brothers. I bent closer, squinting to make out their long, thin, happy faces through the smudged glass. In Pironnen's I could see the fearful seed of what he had become; the other man looked like what he might have been—fuller faced, confident, smiling at Pironnen. Fingerprints mottled the soot and I realized the dog hair had not been *cleaned* off the frame but merely shaken off each time it had been picked up.

I put the photo back and sighed, sending a tornado of hairs in my face. Time is vital after a murder, and by and large I had just wasted a quarter of an hour of it. "Mr. Pironnen, Ellen is missing. I'm worried about her. Can you think where she might be?"

"Oh yes," he said quite easily. "Off with Sam's wife."

CHAPTER 10

"Ellen is with sam Johnson's wife?"

Pironnen nodded, seemingly oblivious of my shock. "Has been. Didn't say she was right now."

"Did Bryn know about that?"

His brow wrinkled in puzzlement as if he couldn't comprehend why I would think he would know such an esoteric bit of information.

"Have you seen Ellen with her before? How often?"

He shrugged.

When nothing changes, time doesn't exist. Pironnen didn't have a job, or appointments on the sixth or eighth, or friends coming by on the fourteenth. What did time mean to him? But no, wait, he did have some commitments, his chess games. "Do you remember the last time you saw Ellen with Sam's wife? What chess game were you working on then?"

"Oklahoma City. Very tight game."

"What day of the week is that?"

"Tuesdays. Three twenty."

"Always Tuesdays?"

"Of course."

"Can you remember the move you made the previous week with Oklahoma City?"

"Of course. Knight to queen's bishop five."

"While you were thinking about that move, did you see Ellen? Was she with Sam's wife then? Take a moment. Think."

"You mean did they do something together every week? No."

"But why do you"—I chose my term carefully, unwilling to condescend again—"speculate Ellen is with her now?"

He didn't answer.

"Have you seen them together elsewhere?"

"No." And then as if he was tired of stringing me along, he added, "She came another Tuesday, waited in her car, then left alone. Blue Volkswagen hatchback, three BKP three seven oh."

I laughed. "You're amazing, Mr. Pironnen. If all our citizens were like you, we wouldn't need a police department. We'd have all our perpetrators in jail."

"What's the point of putting them in jail if they don't understand what they've done?"

I was just formulating a question when he added, "They throw the pebble into the water; they're not splashed by the ripples."

"The police only apprehend, Mr. Pironnen; the courts deal with justice. Do you—"

The door scraped open. Dogs panted and yipped, toenails scraped on the wood floors. The dogs raced at us, churning up a tornado of hair. I shut my mouth and squinted till I was looking out through the protective shield of my lashes.

Two of the dogs were huge, one merely medium to large—shepherd mixed with springer perhaps. But that one, Ocean, I discovered—had enough long gray and brown hair to thatch a room of his own. Nora was all black, maybe Great Dane and setter. And Pablo, black and brown, looked like a large pi dog, the kind you see in newsreels from the third world. All three scrambled and jumped on Pironnen, licked his face, hands, neck, any accessible patch of skin. And Pironnen himself looked like someone whose switch had been flicked to On. He jostled them as they leapt on him, rubbed his forehead against each of theirs, cooed, and panted in cheerful mockery of their own delight. He could have been his outgoing brother in the photograph.

So taken was I with his transformation that it was a minute before I noticed the door shutting behind me.

"Who walked the dogs?" I asked over the ruckus.

"Down, you dogs! Down!" he said, clearly not expecting any change. "The boy . . . Jed."

"Jed?"

"Jed Estler. Downstairs."

It took me another minute to find out the route to downstairs —outside and around the house. I handed Pironnen my card— no easy task, but leaving it on any surface in the room would have been akin to burying it—and asked him to call me if he remembered anything I should know, and when he saw her to tell Ellen to call me.

Once outside, I checked in with Grayson, and waited while he freed up Murakawa for my backup when I bearded the *boy*. Activity at the scene had narrowed to Raksen combing the area around the Volvo with an extension rake. That meant he had finished photographing but hadn't gotten to anything that required walking on the frozen area, like looking in the car. The crowd, having been presented this lesson on just how tedious forensic work is, had dwindled to half its earlier number and those still here showed the edginess of short timers. The reporters for the San Francisco papers were glancing at their watches. Only the student from the *Daily Cal* looked to be in it for the duration. His grade probably depended on it.

There had been no word from Acosta at the hospital. Bryn Wiley hadn't been DOA. I couldn't decide whether that was good or bad. And still no sign of Ellen Waller.

"I hate to think it's an assault/kidnap," I said.

"Or maybe Waller shot Wiley."

"And escaped on foot? Waller doesn't drive. Car's still here." I didn't believe Ellen was the perp. It made no sense that the woman who had deflected Bryn's bark with a scurry and a grin yesterday would lurk behind a tree and shoot her today. Or maybe the truth was that I didn't *want* to believe that.

"Two women, living together," Grayson mused. "One with all the money and fame, the other the drudge. Could be the drudge got pushed once too often. Or could be there was more to their living together."

"All things are possible. But not all love relationships lead to death. And I didn't get that sense of ownership you do when people are a couple." Before Grayson could regroup, I went on, "If Ellen did decide to kill Bryn, I doubt she'd do it shooting across the driveway. She lived with her; she could have killed her a hundred easier ways inside the house." Still, in a homicide investigation everyone is suspect.

I turned and headed back down Tamalpais, walking with the sure step of a Homicide Detail Detective, blocking out that it was a fleeting masquerade. Trailed by Murakawa, I passed Pironnen's front door and came upon a bit of yard covered in ivy. But once I moved beyond a fence and started down the side path, I wondered why I would have assumed Pironnen would keep the ground outside his house better than the inside. He didn't. In a city—even Berkeley—you don't often get to find out just how high weeds will grow. Here, doubtless amply fertilized, they reached above my waist. The cement path was like a part in a long crew cut, but it did lead to what might have been a basement door. Inside I could hear the shower going.

I could have knocked immediately, but if Estler was reacting to the sight of a blue uniform upstairs by busily destroying evidence, contraband, or flowerless plants, he would go on doing so under cover of the shower. Murakawa was already flashing his light around the backyard. There the grass was mowed, a lounge chair sat on a level spot, and beyond it was a sliding gate in the fence to the staircase between Pironnen's and the construction site. I caught Murakawa's eye and grinned. All the yard needed was a bright flowered border to scream: *Not responsible for the rest of the lot.* Murakawa would appreciate the need to make that distinction.

The shower stopped. I knocked. And in a minute the door snapped open. A head leaned toward me and said, "You the one upstairs with Karl?"

I almost laughed. Garbed in a thick white terry-cloth robe with a white towel around his head, Jed Estler looked like the ugliest girl in the dorm.

I must have shown some reaction. He shrugged. "You're eyeing the towel, huh? Feels dumb to me, too. But it's better'n icicles on my scalp. Karl's not into heat. Come on in.

"I'm from back East," he went on as I walked into the ten by fourteen room, what in the euphemism of realty lingo would be called a "plus room" or, considering the Lilliputian kitchen and bath at the far end, an "in-law unit." "Back there you forget about heat, you die. Here, you don't die, you just wish."

"You could get a space heater."

He shrugged off the idea. Ah, the greater warmth of complaint.

Estler shut the door after Murakawa, hurried across the room, turned the desk chair around, nodded at us, straightened the dark blue plaid blanket on the bed, plopped down, and started to spread his legs and stopped abruptly, obviously remembering his attire. He was like one of those battery-run toys. I'd have thought the friction alone would keep him warm.

I perched on the edge of the chair, flashlight hanging down one side, gun and baton on the other. Murakawa leaned against the door frame, as out of Jed Estler's sight as was possible in this tiny room. I took a moment to study Estler: Early twenties; not much taller than me, maybe five-nine; thin, little pointy features that made him look like a child, a child you wouldn't leave unsupervised. *It's too quiet in there* must have been words he heard like a mantra when he was growing up. He seemed like the last person you'd pick to be caretaker for Karl Pironnen. And considering Karl's description of shrinking from the push of human contact, I'd have thought one dose of Estler would drive him under the covers for a month.

Estler crossed his legs—pale, almost hairless legs. I eyed them for signs of a rash. The inner right shin was flaky and looked like he'd been scratching it. "Officer, what's going on out there? I saw all the lights and police cars."

"A woman's been injured."

"How?"

"We'll talk about that later. But now, tell me how you got this job for Mr. Pironnen."

"Chess."

I waited, knowing it wouldn't be for long. This was one guy who would fill in the blanks to overflowing.

"Karl's a senior master, did he tell you?"

"What's a senior master?"

"You know anything about the chess scene?"

"Zip."

"You've heard of grand masters, right?"

"Well, yes."

"That's the top ranking. To get it you've got to play at tournaments, a lot of them in Europe. Karl could be a grand master, but he won't do the tournament scene. Compared to the academic scene, grand master is a Ph.D. and senior master's like a terminal masters."

"Right. And you?"

"I'm the master of the minute clock. In the sixty-second game I can lay you out."

"Might money change hands on such a game?"

He uncrossed his legs, rubbing the right shin over the left as he moved. "It's a unique skill, half chess smarts, half intuition. I'm not ranked—can't be bothered—but I'll take on any ranked player in the minute game. Beat him nine times of ten. More than that." He recrossed his legs. "See, with guys like Karl, he's never met any of his opponents, but he's played their games in his head until he knows how they think, how they plan their strategies, how they'll react to what he does. He talks about tossing a pebble in the water and watching where the ripples splash. He says if you throw the pebble, you should feel the splash. When he tosses the pebble, he knows where these guys will get wet. When they toss back, he knows they know he's wet." He uncrossed, reaching toward his shin and then apparently catching himself before he let himself scratch. If he had the urge to check my reaction, he caught himself in time. Then, as if nothing had happened, he looked up and grinned. "In minute chess you don't deal with the small stuff. Moves too fast. Guy sits down across from you. You eyeball 'im, and mow 'im down! One after another."

I took that with a tablespoon of salt. Estler might be as good as he said, he could be hustling games daily, but clearly he was not making enough to support himself in more than a Sheetrock cubicle in a hermit's basement. What was he doing here? A live wire like him wouldn't be satisfied stored in a basement. Was it the proximity to Sam Johnson he wanted? There was something of the younger Johnson I recognized in Estler—always on the outlook for an angle, charming you while he sized you up and edged you out. I sat silent a few moments to throw him off his rhythm, then said, "You and Karl don't seem compatible."

"Think I'm too lively for ol' Karl, huh? Brightens him up," he said, choosing the most favorable interpretation of my comment. "No, really. He perks up when I come in. I was surprised too. Not everyone can keep up with me. And the slow ones, they say I suck out their energy—like I'd need that little mouthful, huh?"

"But Karl Pironnen doesn't feel that way?"

"I remind him of his brother. Life of the party. Made Karl go out, see people. Pulled him out of his shell. He's the one who got Karl to go to tournaments. Only reason why he's ranked at all."

"And this similarity, who noticed that? Karl Pironnen or, Mr. Estler, was it you who brought it up? Did you point it out and then convince him to give you this room?"

If I thought I was going to jolt Jed Estler that easily, I was wrong. He grinned. Just like a younger Sam Johnson would have grinned. "Yeah, right. I'm on top of things. Guy up the street told me Karl's story, and I thought: 'Hey! There's something for both of us here!' And right I was. Best—"

"Guy up the street? Who?"

He paused, startled. "Just some guy. I don't remember his name."

"Try Sam Johnson."

His reaction was instantaneous—the slightest widening of the eyes, mouth opening just a little—then he was back under control. "Wasn't Sam. I've only talked to Sam a couple of times—about the noise."

"Nothing else?" I said, eyeing the towel on his head.

He didn't shake his head—too dangerous. "No, nothing. But getting back to Karl, the best thing that's happened to him is me! I make it possible for Karl to live alone. I make his appointments with Dr. Kendall, the dentist, Dr. Orris, the internist, Dr. Abbey, the regular vet. I make sure he gets places so he's not missing medical appointments, or pissing off the emergency vet because he's afraid to show up—and getting charged a bundle for a no-show." He was back in his stride now. The younger Sam Johnson couldn't have done better.

"And the dogs," I asked, "when do you take them out?"

"When Karl doesn't."

"Today?"

"Just tonight."

"How long were you out with them?"

"About half an hour."

"Was Bryn's car in the driveway when you left?"

"Don't know. I went the other way, down Tamalpais."

Good save. "Do you take the dogs to the vet?"

"Yeah. I've been to Dr. Abbey so often I could be a dog."

"So why was Ellen doing that? Was she afraid Karl would miss another appointment?"

"Maybe. Look, it was an emergency. I'm an assistant, not a slave. I get my room free, nothing else. For that I'm not here twenty-four hours a day. Ellen wants to help out, fine with me."

I let a beat pass. "You don't like Ellen then."

"No, Ellen's fine. Actually she's real nice. Willing to help."

"Compared to Bryn Wiley, you mean?"

"Yeah, well, that one, she's got her nose too far up her ass to care about anyone but herself." An observation from familiar ground. "She the one who was 'injured'?"

"Yes."

He was on edge; doubtless, he was always on edge. I'd have to press harder. I put down my note pad and stared first at his bathrobe. I wished I had had a chance to observe him from the back. But with the bathrobe covering his memorable features, it wouldn't have helped much. Police can request many things, but we can't ask a citizen to disrobe in his own apartment. I asked one of the things I could. "Where were you Wednesday night?"

"Here."

"All night?"

"Yeah."

"Did you hear anything unusual, when you were in here, all evening and all night?"

"Wednesday? Why do you want to know that?"

"Just answer the question."

"Am I under arrest?"

"No."

"Then I don't need to answer any damned questions."

"Take the towel off your head."

"What?"

"You heard me."

"I don't have to—"

"There some reason you don't want to expose your scalp?"

"I told you, it's cold in here."

"Fine. Put some clothes on, we're going to the station."

"Hey, I don't have to—"

And that was when his voice cracked.

CHAPTER 11

Jed Estler's voice had cracked just like an adolescent's. His little peach of a mouth was shut so tight that his lips were barely visible. He was as stunned as I was.

"Take off the towel," I repeated.

He looked at me wide-eyed, shrugged, and pulled an end. The terry cloth fell to the floor.

I stared, almost as wide-eyed as he.

Damp brown curly hair covered his head. Estler wasn't bald. He didn't even have a receding hairline.

A smug little grin appeared, but he said nothing.

So Estler wasn't the bulldog-masked nudist. He hadn't been the naked man running down past Johnson's house or through Bryn Wiley's rally. He could be exactly what he seemed: a perky little neighbor involved in nothing more than tending Karl Pironnen.

I didn't believe that for a moment. "You found Bryn Wiley's body."

"That was her?" His grin vanished. His sharp little-kid face scrunched; he looked like he was going to cry. There was no way not to like him; but I knew better than to trust him. He was picturing the bloody pulp of her face. I could have led him away from that vision, and the memory of reaching for her phone. I didn't. When twenty seconds had passed, I said softly, "Tell me about it."

He swallowed. His skin was the sweaty near-green of someone who has already thrown up.

"Jed, the phone you used? Where is it now?"

"In the car," he said in a throaty whisper. His words were slow but each one seemed on the verge of exploding with fear.

"Her car?"

"No . . . Karl's."

"Karl's car? The Subaru wagon in the driveway?"

"Yes."

"Why did you put it there?"

"That's where it was."

"Jed, it's Bryn Wiley's car phone from her *car*. You used it to call the police."

His face went gray-green. "Oh my God, you don't think that I did that to her? What kind of man do you think— How can you—"

"Tell me what happened," I said in a monotone.

"The phone . . . was already there . . . in Karl's car. Ellen left it there, this morning, after she and Karl went to the bank. I saw it later. I was taking the dogs out after lunch. I checked the car for Nora's collar. Nora wasn't wearing it. It wasn't on her leash. Karl had taken her when he went with Ellen this morning. But it wasn't there."

"The collar."

"Yeah. But the phone was. Bryn's phone. I was going to call Ellen to pick it up when I got back with the dogs."

"Why didn't you call her then? You had a phone right there."

"I didn't want to leave the dogs wandering around loose in the middle of Saturday afternoon. Neighbors get real uptight about the dogs. Nora's collar was gone. I couldn't even put her on a leash. I just wanted to give them a run and get them back in the house before anyone came down on me."

"Why didn't you drop the phone by Bryn's on your walk?"

He scraped his fingers across his thigh in three quick motions, finally coming up with the end of the terry-cloth bathrobe tie. Once in hand, he began kneading it. "I couldn't. That was the point."

"Why?"

"Because Bryn might be there."

"And?"

"Then Bryn would know that Ellen had been out with Karl this morning."

"Would Bryn have cared?"

"Ellen sure thought so. That's why she took the phone with her, so if Bryn called, Ellen could say she was at home, working. Ellen said—you know Ellen?"

I nodded.

"Ellen said Bryn wouldn't object to her going with Karl if he needed support, that Bryn would really be pleased to help out—vicariously."

That I believed. I could picture Ellen's grin as she added the zinger.

"Bryn *would* be pleased, Ellen said, if she weren't so preoccupied with the press conference. But because dealing well with people *was*, um . . ."

"Not her medal sport?"

He grinned. "Yeah, that's how Ellen might put it. Big euphemism, huh? But Ellen just said she didn't want to put Bryn in the position of saying something she would regret later."

I hoped Ellen hadn't postponed sex or chocolate waiting for *later*.

We Berkeleyans frown on those who condescend to their in-home employees. Fortunately for Bryn and Karl Pironnen there is no such censure of domestic weirdness. I'd seen married couples who had worked for years to develop that level of pathology.

The color was returning to Estler's face in hesitant blotches. His hand was still working the terry-cloth tie, but not so frantically. I'd wanted him on edge, too wary to watch what he said.

But now I needed more concentration from him. I let him sit a moment until he felt safer, then said, "Let's go back to the scene outside Bryn's house. Before you called."

"Well, the phone—"

"No. Start at the beginning."

"You don't think that I—"

"Start at the beginning."

He looked like he'd taken a misstep and fallen to the bottom of the well. Slowly he said, "I heard the shots."

"Where were you?"

"Here. Right here. I mean I didn't know they were shots till I saw her—omigod—face."

"Take your time." I would let him give me his whole story before I started pulling the errant threads out of it.

"I thought it was Sam next door, hammering or something." His hand worked the tie harder, scraping his fingers against the rough nap. "Okay, I know that sounds dumb. Gunshots don't sound like hammer hits. I wasn't sure what I thought Sam was doing. It was after nine o'clock Saturday night. He has no business doing any kind of building or tearing apart at all. But whatever he's doing he can't be doing it that late Saturday night. It drives Karl crazy."

"Does Karl go to bed early?" Surely not. Jed's answer would be one test of how far out his story was.

"Who knows when Karl sleeps? He's a first-class insomniac; he sleeps when he's too exhausted to move. The only time he's near normal is when he's out backpacking with the dogs. That's when he feels most at home. Here, in town, it's like sleep has to creep up behind him and take him by surprise."

"But Saturday night?"

"Saturday's match is his hardest one. If I'd heard Sam banging away *before* nine, I would have called him, except that Karl was already on the line."

"The modem's on the only phone line?"

"Sure. It's not like Karl's got friends who call. He doesn't do friends. He does chess. Chess is his life. Tonight Milwaukee

made his move. Karl was looking forward to that all week. As
soon as it came in, he started considering his counter." He
glanced up at me. "Not just the next move, but its implications
for the rest of the game. All in his head. And if that game plan
doesn't work, then he tries another and another. But he's got to
keep in mind the attacks and defenses that don't work here. He
can't be interrupted."

Murakawa shook his head in amazement.

It *was* amazing. Also diverting. "So, Jed, you say you were
here alone, and you heard the shots which you took to be an
unidentified noise from next door . . ."

"Yeah, I flew out of here before that asshole Johnson could
ruin Karl for the whole night," he said, as if he'd missed the
skepticism in my voice. But he didn't look at me, or Murakawa,
and he was shooting out words like he was desperate to smother
me with the whole explanation before I could attack. "I got out
the gate and there was no light under his house. So I ran up the
steps—"

"On Codornices Path?"

"Yeah. I figured the noise must be coming from inside his
house. I expected to see a light from the front. But when I got to
the street, the house was dark. Then"—he shut his eyes and his
whole body went still—"then I heard a noise. I thought it was
one of the dogs giving out with a moan, but it couldn't have
been. It must have been her."

"Her?"

He swallowed. "Bryn. I . . . I, uh, started over there. I
started to run, I think. I don't remember really. I think I ran. I
got to the car and I reached for the door. And then I saw her,
that bloody . . ." Sweat coated his face; his hands stopped dead
on the terry-cloth tie.

I waited for him to go on, and when he didn't, I said, "And
then you leaned across her body and reached for the phone."

He clasped his mouth and ran for the bathroom.

This was no act. I could hear him throwing up. But that
proved only that he was unnerved, not that he was a terrified

murderer. I moved next to the bathroom door where I could keep an eye on him. I wasn't ready to read him his rights; he was still free to tell us to get out, but chances were he wouldn't.

When he finally pushed himself, wan and shaking, up from the sink, he said, "I need to get dressed. And take a shower."

"In a minute. When we're done. You saw Bryn in the car, then what did you do?"

He turned away, clutching the sink. "I can't . . ."

"Of course you can. Pull yourself together. You're not the one lying in the hospital, bleeding."

"She isn't dead?"

"She wasn't when the ambulance roared out of here." I repeated my initial demand to him.

For a moment I thought he was going to launch into the familiar *What kind of woman are you?* routine, but he was too drained for that. His hands clasped white against the sink. I was sure he was seeing her bloody face anew. I could see it too as the medics had loaded the gurney into the ambulance, her hair stuck in the blood. I blanked out the memory, walled off any feeling, any thought, everything but questioning Estler.

"I was sure"—his voice cracked—"she was dead. I never thought . . . I didn't think at all; I guess I panicked. I turned and ran for the house, Karl's house, I mean. But when I got to the sidewalk, Nora let out a howl. She doesn't usually do that. I started to go to the front door to check that everything was all right. Then—it was like a sudden realization—I realized everything *wasn't* all right, and I had better call 911. I didn't want to tell Karl what had happened and upset him. And I remembered Bryn's phone in his car. So I used that."

"Is it still there?"

"What? Where? In the car? Yeah. I mean, I left it there."

"And then? Did you go back up to the scene? To Bryn."

"I couldn't. I was just too undone. I stood outside Karl's door for a few minutes until I thought I could carry on normally. Then I went in to make sure he and the dogs were okay. Karl hadn't noticed anything. If he'd heard the shots at all, they'd passed out of his mind somewhere between the pawn and the queen. He was in the computer room—"

"Where is that?"

"On the far side of the house from Bryn's. He didn't even look up when I glanced in."

"Is that normal?"

"For him, yeah, it is normal. And then—I know you're going to ask—I took the dogs back out and walked—ran—half way to El Cerrito. Now can I get dressed?"

"When you've given me an answer to this: You found the body; you called it in. I have only your word the phone was in Karl's car . . ."

"Ask Karl; he'll—"

"You just admitted you saw Karl after the shooting. You had time to cook up a story then."

"Are you crazy? Why would I shoot Bryn? She's never done anything to me. And if I did, I'm not crazy enough to hang my alibi on someone as weird as Karl." He pushed himself free of the sink, his body steadier than it had been half an hour ago. "If I shot her I wouldn't have called an ambulance. The reason you shoot someone is so they die."

"People change their minds. They make mistakes. They fire in anger."

"Well, I didn't. I just tried to do the right thing. And God, am I sorry I did. Now I'm going to get dressed, if that's okay with you."

"Go ahead," I said considerably more offhandedly than I felt. I sat in the icy room—he'd been right about the temperature here—and tried to get a feel for what he'd said. He could be just what he seemed: the chirpy little guy flitting here and there. He could have transformed Karl Pironnen's life. But if he'd caused improvement, it wasn't in Pironnen's living room, or in his social functioning.

Jed Estler made me want to smile. I hoped he was innocent. But even if he hadn't killed Bryn Wiley, he still had left her to spend her last minutes on earth alone.

I glanced at Murakawa. He shrugged. He was right. In Prairie Village, Kansas, Karl Pironnen and Jed Estler might be considered downright strange, but here in Berkeley, they were a variation on one of a number of familiar themes. People who had eschewed goals for getting by, for hanging out, for smelling the roses. People who were fulfilled by the challenge of chess games. People who lived in single rooms because that was enough.

There was a time when I had looked at people like this, who could dispense with the extraneous, and felt admiration.

Now I thought of Pironnen's house and flashed on Howard's. I looked at Jed Estler's room and saw my own. I pictured Pironnen playing one *game* after another, pretending they did more than fill his time. And me? I answered one call after another.

"Smith?"

I glanced at Murakawa. He didn't speak again, and I wondered how much of my horror had shown on my face.

In the bathroom something dropped, water turned on and off and back on again. I could imagine Estler dervishing around in there as he grabbed clothes. Jed Estler might have no great purpose in his life, but he was the last guy to find taking care of Karl Pironnen enough. There was more going on with him than he'd admitted. Or than he was likely to admit until I knew the right questions.

I walked with Estler outside, through the level, mowed backyard to the wooden gate and onto the Codornices Staircase.

We topped the stairs and started up Tamalpais. It was one of those crystal-clear, almost still Berkeley nights when the cold of the heavens floats unimpeded down on us. Those nights take me in every time. The mornings after, I wake up expecting thick yellow sunbeams to be striping my comforter—not the quilt of fog that has stolen in after I've gone to bed. When I moved west it never occurred to me that "sunny California" would be not a reality but a hope.

The scene—Bryn's driveway—was quiet. The patrol cars on the street were dark; Raksen had finished photographing and was now hands-and-knees-ing it toward Bryn's car. Not much of a show. The crowd was gone entirely, and the only sworn officers in sight were Grayson and Leonard, the finder of record, waiting to claim whatever Raksen came up with.

When Murakawa had driven off with Estler, I walked the five feet to Grayson and lowered my voice. "Anything of value from the neighbors?"

"Two of them saw the Volvo here about five thirty. Could have been here earlier, that's just when they got home."

I nodded. "And from Acosta at the hospital?"

"DOA."

I felt as if my elevator car had dropped ten stories. I'd seen her face; I knew the odds. I hadn't even really liked the woman. And yet I felt stunned and bereft, deserted by life and meaning. I wanted to close my eyes, or walk over to the little redwood grove and stand in the dark middle surrounded by those trees that would be here centuries after we, and maybe Berkeley itself, were forgotten.

Even Grayson had a little of that look—eyes wide, skin almost sagged in a sort of pervading disillusionment. Not grief for the victim, per se, but distress because one who had become ours had died. I put a hand on his arm momentarily and he didn't pull away.

Behind me footsteps slapped the night silence. Heling, I hoped, ready to report she had looked through all of Bryn Wiley's windows and found nothing amiss inside. I turned and looked at the woman loping toward me. It wasn't Heling. It was Bryn Wiley.

CHAPTER 12

Bryn WILEY! I WAS so stunned I couldn't move. She was glaring at me, and Leonard, and Grayson, but I didn't care. She was alive!

I finally smiled as she demanded, "What the hell's going on here?" And as she turned her indignation on Grayson. "Now what's happened to my car? Oh, shit, it's the window again. *Again.* Can't you cops do anything to protect property in this city? I can't even park in my own driveway!" I was still feeling the warmth of her prodigal return as she raged on: "I'm not asking much. The goddamn culprit lives right next door. How easy do you people need it to be? I'm not dealing with beat cops anymore. I demand a detective."

It was only then that I registered that Grayson wasn't taking charge in the face of her tirade, that he looked every bit as bewildered as she—because he had no idea who she was and therefore why she was carrying on. "Bryn Wiley," I said to him. And to her: "Bryn, there's been a shooting."

"What? Who?"

Who was shot? The answer broadsided me. I found myself staring at Bryn's living room window, wordlessly pleading with it to show me Ellen standing inside. My eyes clouded and I blinked futilely trying to clear them. And when Bryn's chestnut hair came into my muddied vision, for an instant I thought my plea had been answered. Then the horror hit harder, striking the already bruised spot. There was something so unutterably sad about Ellen being dead; something so unfinished. My voice sounded far away and wooden as I forced out, "Not on the street. Inside. Can we go inside?"

"Tell me what the hell—"

"Bryn, a woman was shot. She was sitting in your car."

"In *my* car?" She was shouting. "I can't believe—"

"*Inside!*" My voice caught. I had to swallow, and when I spoke again, the words sounded like they were coming from a different person. "Come on. Come inside."

She hesitated, then shrugged and started for her stoop. I glanced by Grayson, ignoring his silent *What the hell is going on here?* His mustache twitched—he was on the verge of telling me I couldn't just trod over him—but something stopped him. I don't know quite why he backed off—it wasn't like Grayson—but I nodded a thanks and said, "Let me have Pereira or Leonard to take notes as soon as one of them is free."

Bryn had already turned on the interior lights when I walked into the living room. She stood looking from one white sofa to the other and ended up staring at the confessional bench and the lusting Shiva. I would have expected her to settle on the couch as she had the other times, but she picked up the Shiva by his head and moved the statue to the central section of the bench. Then she sat on the right and pulled her legs up under her.

Just like Ellen had.

"Ellen?" she asked in a voice so small I almost missed it.

The stool Ellen had brought in for me when I was here before was next to the smaller sofa. I carried it across from Bryn and sat close to her. "We can't be sure. We know that a woman was shot in the driver's seat of your car. The only identification she had was your purse, your driver's license. She was about your size and had hair like yours. But Ellen didn't drive, she told me that, and you told me. And this woman was in the driver's seat."

The color washed from her face. "Omigod, Ellen! Why Ellen? Who would want . . . ? Ellen? God, she didn't even know anyone, she'd barely moved in. How could anyone have . . . ? Why Ellen?"

I shook my head, shaking off that last feeble hope. Of course it was Ellen. Of course she *could* drive, even if she didn't often choose to. Almost anyone *can* drive. "Why did you tell me Ellen didn't drive?"

"She had no license. She never drove, not until tonight. She didn't want to. But I couldn't leave my car there at People's Park, could I? She had to take it home." Bryn's voice was squeaky, her scrunched forehead and eyes pleading. "I gave her my license in case she got stopped, so she'd be safe," she added desperately.

"Yeah, it saved me from thinking it was she who'd been shot. And if she needed blood, Bryn, maybe they gave her your blood type. Your gift could have killed her."

Bryn just stared.

I should have felt guilt. But I felt nothing but the cold of the room. The smell of that bitter tea hung in the air like long dead leaves in the rain. My eyes clouded. It could have been Ellen sitting there. If only . . . I pushed the thought away. Ellen would have been pale, too, but at least she would have been sobbing out her horror and her sorrow. I would have reached out to comfort her, told her we'd pull out all stops to find the person who had done this to her cousin.

Bryn's arms pressed hard against her side but she sat dead still. She looked like she had been abandoned in the most desolate place on earth. She sat that way for a full minute, her feet under her, bare ankles pressed against the hard wood penitent's seat. When she spoke, her voice was barely controlled. "It's not a question of who would kill Ellen, is it? My car, the car only I drive. Ellen didn't drive; that's what we told people. That's what he'd have believed." She paused, eyeing me for agreement. "He shot her because he thought she was me! He's trying to kill me!"

"Who?"

"That bastard Johnson!" Color was creeping back onto her face, and the quaver in her voice was from anger. "I expected him to sabotage my press conference. But this . . . I never thought he'd do anything like this." Her fists tightened into balls. "But damn it, I won't let him get away with it. You've got evidence now, don't you? I saw that cop crawling around by the car. You've got bullet casings and footprints. You must have footprints; the ground's soggy as a pond. You don't need to worry about me pressing charges; I'll sign whatever you need. Damn it, I will not allow this."

"The lab tech will find any evidence on the ground. What can you tell me that definitely ties Johnson to this scene, here, tonight? Give me facts."

"Facts? Search his house, find his gun!"

"If he killed someone, he wouldn't leave the murder weapon over the mantel"—I'd have Leonard or Murakawa check on that —"and there's no way we can track down all the places he could stash a gun. We can't even search his house without probable cause. So, tell me about tonight."

"How should I know what went on here?"

"Okay, so you weren't here. Where have you been all evening?"

Her face tightened and eased warily. "Trying to salvage that shambles of a press conference. I spent half the night running down reporters and giving them the text of my talk and the corroborating information. For all the good it'll do. They don't care about facts like Sam Johnson ripping off his clients and ripping off the poor. All they want is pictures of naked butts. If you'd seen the eleven o'clock news you'd know that." She leaned closer to me, blue eyes narrowed, head forward like a hawk's. "It's set me back . . . I don't know. I'll never get another press conference. At least not without them leading in with tales of the bare-assed runner. The whole thing's been turned into a yuppie joke. That bastard Johnson—"

"How did you round up the reporters without your car?" I

was amazed at how focused she was in her anger, how righteous she seemed. Had she already forgotten Ellen?

It took her a moment to shift gears. "Oh that. I had a colleague drive me."

"A colleague who was at the rally?"

"No."

"Her name?"

"Why do you want to— Oh shit. Herman Ott."

"Herman Ott?" The words were out of my mouth before I could catch them. Herman Ott, seedy Avenue private eye, living relic of the sixties, was a spiritual brother of Sam Johnson. Herman Ott would disdain The Girls' Team as a socially irresponsible yuppie indulgence. In Bryn Wiley's book, I would have guessed, the best that might be said of the sallow, paunchy, carelessly dressed Ott was that he was not asking for spare change. "What on earth could make Herman Ott drive you around to distribute flyers for a fitness center?"

"He concurs on my point," Bryn said matter-of-factly, as if there was no irony to be considered. "He knows Johnson is deceiving his club members and abusing the poor."

It was then that I thought of the old building where Ott worked. Above the shops on the ground floor, offices from the postwar era (post–World War One) had been converted into housing. The conversion had been informal—and illegal—for years. But now that it had the blessing of the city, the tenants who remained were too poor to afford better than two tiny rooms with plumbing down the hall. The Heat Exchange perched on top of that building.

Conviction makes strange bedfellows.

So that's what those messages from Herman Ott were about. Those messages I'd tossed. They might have told me something that would have kept me from standing here now.

And Ellen Waller might not be lying dead.

I swallowed hard and shut my eyes against the picture of her being carried into the ambulance. It just wasn't *right* that she had been erased so easily. It was like her life meant nothing.

I turned back to Bryn. "This is going to be a big, complex investigation. Let's start at the beginning and get everything clear." I pulled out my pad.

Bryn's response was instantaneous. "Oh no! I'm not dealing with a beat cop on this. I told you: You get a Homicide investigator in here."

"You got one. I've worked Homicide for four years. Maybe later, your case will be transferred to one of the men in Homicide. But for the moment it's you and me on this."

"I don't—"

I held out the flat of my hand. "Bryn, even you don't pick your investigator. But let me tell you, I am going to find Ellen's killer, not because you're kicking up a fuss, but because it's my job. If this person aimed to kill you, then I'll find your assailant, but not for you. For Ellen."

I stood up, took a breath, and said, "You can help or you can get out of my way. Your choice."

It was a moment before she said, "Okay, okay. But don't think I don't know you're manipulating me."

If she'd been Ellen, she would have said it with a grin.

I caught her eye and nodded. "Where was Ellen going when she left you this afternoon?"

"Joy riding, that's what she said. She thought it was funny." Her mouth quivered.

"So you don't know where she went?"

"I'm sure she drove straight home. She didn't want to drive. I had to insist . . ." Bryn swallowed, then hurried on. "She wouldn't have driven a block more than she had to. Look, common sense—"

"Common sense says you don't get shot."

It was a moment before she admitted, "Okay, I don't know."

I nodded. "That was four thirty or so. Witnesses remember the car here at five thirty. Another witness heard shots about eight thirty. Why would she be in the car then?"

"I don't know. Look, there was a reason Ellen didn't drive. No, don't look so vulturous; I don't know what it was. Maybe it was just that she was such a wretched driver. God knows, I wouldn't be behind the wheel if I was as jumpy as she was."

"And yet at eight thirty, four hours after she left you, she was sitting in the car, presumably coming back from somewhere or headed out."

She stared at me, only for a moment, but long enough for me to see the flicker of desperation in her eyes. It was the same look Ellen had had, the one that had made their physical similarity so pronounced. Seeing it in Bryn shocked me—I almost wondered if I'd imagined it. When I checked her face again, there was nothing but anger. "What difference does it make whether Ellen was coming or going or just sitting in the driveway? The point is she never drove. *I* drove the car. Johnson saw it in the driveway, and of course, he assumed it was me driving. He shot to kill *me*. That's what you need to concentrate on."

The door rattled; Pereira walked in. I explained the procedure to Bryn and went over her statement, asking again for other suspects, she, insisting again that no one in the Bay Area but Sam Johnson had reason to kill her.

"You won't be in any shape to do this tonight, but as soon as you are, I want you to think about everyone you've met in the last ten years. No, don't protest. People go away and resurface; you forget about them but they're still obsessing about you or some supposed wrong you did. Start from the present and think back. Think," I said, "like your life depends on it."

"Okay, okay."

"I'll need to have someone identify the body; you can do that tomorrow. And Ellen's next of kin? Who should we contact?"

Something in her face changed, so fast I almost missed it. Then she shook her head. "I don't know; I have to think. But if it's just the courtesy of informing someone, you've informed me. No one else is going to care."

She paused but I didn't say anything. I wanted to scream at Ellen: How can you be dead? You hadn't even found what you wanted to do in life; you were still marking time taking care of

Bryn. How can you be dead before you've even found out why you're living? And there isn't even anyone to care.

I'd asked this question before, at other murder scenes, and I'd always reminded myself that the city doesn't pay me to conduct existential investigations. But tonight, with Ellen Waller, that didn't work.

"I'll pay for burying her," Bryn went on. "That's what the county needs to know, isn't it, so they won't get stuck with the bill for a potter's field. And what about me? He's still wandering around out there, gunning for me." Her arms pressed hard against her sides and her hands bunched into fists. "You better have guards here, day and night. I mean it. If my police force can't be bothered protecting me, I'll scream bloody murder. And you will be hearing from a lot of other people, too."

I didn't doubt it. Getting an okay for around-the-clock protection was another matter. We weren't set up to give that kind of service, even to the mayor. "But first answer me this: When did you finish dealing with the media?"

"About seven. Why?"

"And then what did you do?"

"Ott got a pizza and we ate it in the car," she said with an unreadable expression.

Another time I would have laughed. I knew Ott. In a dark car, sitting next to him with no direct view of his mouth was the least repellent way to dine with Ott. "He got the pizza?"

"Yeah. He's got a special place that does double everything." She cringed. "The cheese was oozing over the edge."

"So no one saw you after seven o'clock."

"I guess not. Look, why are you—"

"Because, Bryn, the press left here thinking you are dead. The killer thinks you're dead. Let's see what the consequences of that 'death' are."

"I can tell you what they'll be."

"No! Let the killer do that." I waited until she gave a small sign of agreement. "In the meantime, you can't stay here."

"But if I were dead, Ellen would still . . . Oh, okay, I'm not Ellen. Okay, so . . . what then? Where can I go?"

"How well do you know Herman Ott?"

Her eyes widened.

Her look of horror told me she knew him well enough. Ott would be appalled, too. But Bryn Wiley had hesitated too long before answering some of my questions. There were things she'd mentally scurried to hide. And Herman Ott, for all his faults, would not overlook dissembling. He would be insulted by it. And by morning, I hoped, he would expose the truth.

CHAPTER 13

Perhaps Berkeley does not have an abnormal number of domestic deficients, but if there were a *Poor Housekeeping* magazine, it could feature a different resident for every cover story. Much of our local slovenliness is the result of youthful rebellion solidified into habit, and a reluctance to admit we've become middle-class enough to "exploit the poor" to muck out our tubs. There are, of course, plenty of devotees anxious to underwrite their meditative spiritual and physical practices by mucking at twelve bucks an hour. But it would take a truly enlightened being to cross Herman Ott's portal, pail in hand. The room he lives in is not much more inviting than Karl Pironnen's.

Herman Ott reminds me of a tatty old parrot, one of those birds you buy on a whim, and delight in teaching embarrassing phrases, before you realize just how many decades it will be around to annoy you. His particular perch overlooks Telegraph Avenue. Most of his clients are regulars there, but simple longevity has widened his nest of knowledge. By now no one dies in Berkeley without his knowing.

Ott has his code. He never discusses his clients, particularly with us.

Still, in the last two days he had called me twice. And now, with minimal fuss, he had agreed to come to the station to pick up Bryn Wiley.

Across the reception area I eyed Ott's short, slouched frame. He was glaring at the five plastic stacking chairs lined up across from the unmanned reception window on the second-story walkway. From either side, staircases descended to what might have been a gracious entryway. Instead, a bare cement room reminded entrants that the police department was not a destination of choice. At two in the morning it was ill-lit and so empty that voices echoed. Ott surveyed the area. "No wonder everyone hates the cops, if this is the way you treat citizens who obey your laws."

"I'll take it up with the municipal decorator." I cut to the chase. "Where is Sam Johnson?"

"Not in the Fraud Exchange, that's for sure. He's never set foot in that scam parlor since it opened." Now Ott perched on a yellow plastic chair, wearing a gold beaked cap. His little round belly was covered by a mustard-tone polyester shirt and a cream and tan argyle vest.

"Is The Heat Exchange doing much business?"

"Not enough to heat my office. Yeah, yeah, I know I wouldn't qualify. But the people who do aren't getting anything off their bills either. They're barely making it, Smith. They've abandoned everything, escaped from wars and famines, and used every cent to get to this country so they have a chance. And then what happens? Johnson promises them help with their utilities. They spend what little they have on other luxuries—like food and clothes—and now they're huddled together trying to keep warm. We've had the fire department out three times in the last month!"

"Why doesn't the city—"

"Because Johnson keeps telling them it's just a matter of time. And Smith, the city *wants* to believe. It'd be such an environmental feather in its cap." He glared at me. "And the city'll be such a laughingstock if this harebrained scheme fails."

So Berkeley has become wary of environmental folly. The

same city that spent half a million dollars to create a "slow street" with two to three speed bumps per block, three to four foliage islands jutting irregularly in some, and a white line that snakes between them like it was painted by a drunk.

"So what's with Johnson, Ott? You've known him for years. For two decades Sam Johnson is the king of the anarchists. Now suddenly he's a homeowner and entrepreneur. What happened? Does he think he's going to make a killing on his exercycles? Use the money to speed up work on his house in the hills? Or does he really believe he's harnessing the bourgeoisie for the benefit of the oppressed?"

Ott looked away, embarrassed. For a moment I thought his shame was for the fall of a former colleague. Then I realized it was because he couldn't answer my question. And Ott prides himself on knowing everything about life on the Avenue. "One thing I'll say, Smith. Sam knew that gym was never going to heat apartments."

"So it was a scam from the beginning?"

"Yeah."

"But why, Ott? Has Johnson sold out since he came into money?"

"Yeah, but not the way you think. Sam's no fool. He knows he'll be lucky to break even on that gym of his. He's too dependent on Cal students and faculty. Their devotion to the poor won't last beyond this semester. When they come back in the fall, they'll trot right on back to the free university gyms."

"So if he's not doing it for the poor, or to make money, and he's not a fool, then why?"

"Because," he said, jerking the beak of his cap down, "he got married."

"Ott, give me a break!"

"Okay, forget it." He started for the stairs.

"Wait." I had to get to the bottom of this. "What's marriage got to do with this?"

Ott turned slowly, but he had no smile of victory. "Here's the thing, Smith. Fannie is ten or fifteen years younger than Sam.

She's attractive, arty in that European way. Like a young Jackie Kennedy. And Johnson's crazy about her." Ott shook his head in bewilderment. "He wants her and he wants his principles. She wants him, but she doesn't want to live in a movement safe house."

"She's not enamored of fugitives arriving in the middle of the night, guys camped out in the kitchen drinking beer and grumbling about the system. Big surprise."

"Look, Smith, you want to mouth off or you want to listen?"

I smiled. I'd forgotten how hard it was for Ott to *give* me something, with not a thing in return. "I'm all ears."

"Sam wants the house in the hills to be apartments for him and Fannie, and for the poor. Fannie's got the money. She'll give it to him, on the condition that he keep his gym open."

It had all made sense until now. But this was crazier than any of the other speculative reasons I had heard for Johnson running the gym. "Why does she care?"

Ott mumbled.

"What?"

His answer wasn't much louder. It took me a moment to realize it was: "I don't know."

"What do you think?"

"I don't know." To not even have a speculation, for Ott that was astounding.

"You tried—"

"Yeah."

"Ott," I said, "Sam Johnson said she inherited the money."

He brightened. "Not a chance. She was on full scholarship at Cal."

"So where did she get her cash?" The words were barely out of my mouth when I recalled where Fannie Johnson worked. "The public guardian's office, where she is charged with watching out for the funds of the incompetent."

A smile flickered at the corners of Ott's pale, narrow mouth.

* * *

The Johnson house was just what I would have expected for the long-term leader of the movement—a small, stucco bungalow in a neighborhood we on the force knew too well. The shrubbery in front of the streaked picture window was virtually mummified, and the cracked and dirty white paint attested to more important commitments than home maintenance. It was not a dwelling that a young Jacqueline Kennedy would have chosen. Especially not with the old Rambler and Nova parked on the lawn.

Every light in the house was on. The front door was open, and music and men's voices flowed out. At this hour, in beat two up on Tamalpais, neighbors on both sides would have called in complaints. The screen door opened before I could knock.

"What do you want now?" a guy demanded. I recognized him from demonstrations on the Avenue. "You can't wait to hassle us, can you? Some rich, white woman gets offed in the hills and the first thing you cops think is: let's shake down the movement. You got a warrant?"

I wasn't surprised he'd heard about the murder. "You living here now?"

"What business is that of yours?"

"Right. You're not. Tell Fannie I'm here."

"What is this, the local doughnut shop? You cops have been here every hour all night."

"Fannie," I insisted.

"Hey, leave her alone. She's had a hard day."

"Oh, really? Why is that?"

"Every day is hard for her," he said after a moment. Behind him, the music had stopped and the voices had gone quiet. I had told the dispatcher I wouldn't need backup on this call. Had I made a mistake? Over his shoulder I could see two sets of male legs. But there could be ten guys sitting inside, having spent hours bitching about the system and its protectors.

"Tell Fannie I'm here."

"You've got no—"

"Do it! A woman can make up her own mind."

He hesitated a moment then, apparently failing to raise an objection, trudged off.

I moved back down the two steps to the path, stood beside the old Nova in the driveway, and called the dispatcher for backup. As I waited I heard her call 6 Victor 8. I'd never worked graveyard. At this hour the eighteen beats we worked in swing shift were condensed into nine. I had no idea who Victor 8 was or how far away he was likely to be.

"Whatsamatter?"

I turned, startled. Whoever had spoken was behind the Nova. "You worried we're going to take you, cop?"

I couldn't see him, but his voice was edged with hysteria like he was on something. In the light from the windows I was virtually spotlighted. "Should I be worried?" I sounded way more offhand than I felt. This could be the kind of situation Pereira and Leonard had warned me about: a crackhead or crazy coming out of nowhere, where logic is useless and there's no place to run. It was like facing down a growling dog: I couldn't back off without giving him the go-ahead to attack. I wasn't about to retreat back up the steps, not and find myself surrounded. I needed to lay the framework here, to set the rules. "I know you, don't I?" I bluffed.

"Huh?"

"From the Avenue, right? You're—"

"You don't know—"

"Sure I do. If I see you, I'll remember your name."

Silence. Inside the house I could hear muffled voices, a man's and a woman's, arguing. Not in the living room, though; farther away. My throat was dry. On my shoulder my radio crackled— the dispatcher calling 6 Victor 4 for a 911 hang-up.

"Not again," Victor 4 said. "I've been out there twice this week. They've got ten people there. No one knows anything about the call. But I'm on my way."

I strained, listening for street noises, for the sound of my backup. This kid was probably harmless; if I hadn't just seen

Ellen Waller dying for no reason, I wouldn't have thought twice about him. But God, I didn't want to get shot.

I pushed back that thought, and said, "Come on. Walk out here."

"Hey, I don't have to—"

"Yeah, you do." I flipped the flashlight up, still in its loop, and aimed it at the car. It turned night to day and the anonymous speaker into a skinny guy in his twenties with a greasy blond ponytail.

Simultaneously the backup car pulled up and the door to the house opened. I spun toward the door, hand on gun.

The woman behind the screen pulled both of her hands shoulder high.

"Just a minute," I called to her. To Victor 8, I said, "Our blond friend here thinks I should be afraid of him. Let's see what we've got on him?" Then I turned to the woman. "Open the door, please."

"Hey, I don't—"

"Please," I repeated. For the first time I realized I was shaking. I stepped up to the screen door.

The woman waiting behind it may have once resembled the First Lady who charmed General de Gaulle, but not now. She looked anything but charming or happy to see me. "Goddamn it. He wasn't here an hour ago. He's not here now."

"Sam?"

"Who else?"

"It's you I want to talk to."

"In the middle of the night? Why not talk to me tomorrow."

"Can't wait."

"Well, I can."

"You're right. It's late," I said. "How about we flip to the last page of this script. You don't want me inside, but you might as well get it over with."

Behind her a guy muttered, "Hey, you don't have to—"

"Forget it!" she snapped. She pulled a patchwork Japanese jacket tighter around her. I'd seen it in one of the stores at

Walnut Square, and coveted it, and resisted paying well over a hundred dollars for it. Her rayon slacks I recognized, too. I had tried them on in the same store, and they tempted me because of the wonderful way they hung when I stood, and wafted when I walked. But they didn't hang well on her. They bunched to one side and looked more in keeping with her long brown hair fingercombed back into a rubber band, and the irritable expression on her square face. It was a face that didn't expect people to be in the way.

Behind her I could see a sofa that had once been a montage of blousy pastel flowers. Now it looked like it had seen too many years and countless guys who scorn material possessions.

"Inside?"

"Look, I'll answer your questions. But you can do the asking here."

"How long have you and Sam been married?"

"Three years."

"Are you a partner in The Heat Exchange?"

"Yeah, so?" Behind her I could hear feet skimming carpet as if someone behind her was getting ready to spring up to her defense.

"You know the people in need in that building aren't getting any help from it."

"That's Sam's concern."

"And yours?"

"Mine is the business. If we choose to give something back to the community, that's gravy. We opened the Exchange like any other gym."

"No, it's not like any other gym, not up there on Telegraph. Without the heat gimmick, people connected with Cal would find a gym free on campus, or they'd go to The Girls' Team."

"But they don't." She couldn't, or didn't choose to, hide her satisfaction.

"Is your goal to run The Girls' Team out of business?"

"My goal is to succeed. Look, I spent forty hours a week working among the walking dead. I dreamed of having a place like the Exchange. I researched the business; I know marketing. I put everything I have into the Exchange. I had good reason for every decision I made. If I'm better than the competition, well, I should be." She caught my eye. "You know what they say: life isn't fair. If Bryn Wiley is squealing now, tough. Fairness hasn't always been such a big issue for her."

"What do you mean?"

"Maybe she kicked up some spray."

"What—"

"No! Is this what you disturbed me in the middle of the night to ask?" She moved her hand to the door. In a minute she'd slam it closed.

"Where did you get the money to open a health club, and buy a house in the hills?"

"So that's it?"

"Where?" I demanded again.

She shrugged.

"You work at the public guardian's office. We can check your cases—"

She laughed. "You figure I stole it, don't you? Sam Johnson's wife came into money; she must be a thief. Well, you're going to be disappointed. The University of California gave me that money. It took them ten years and three lawsuits before they'd finally settle. But now, twelve years after the fact, they've admitted their liability and I've got a house and a health club."

Herman Ott knew that; he had to. No wonder he was laughing at me when he left the station. "What exactly—"

"That's all." She reached for the inside door.

"What about Ellen Waller? How come you were seeing Bryn Wiley's secretary?"

She looked at me and laughed before she shut the door.

I got back to the station at 2 A.M. Inspector Doyle was on the phone. With a case like this, he could be on the phone for hours. Certainly, he'd be up all night. I tapped on his glass door, waved to let him know I was back, and headed for the squad room to write up my report supplement. It took well over two hours to record the essentials of the scene, and the three interviews. As I carried it back to the inspector's office, I reminded myself mine was just one of many reports. I should be glad I didn't have to coordinate the rest, deal with coroner, the D.A., and the press, like he did. In half an hour I would be home in bed. Tomorrow, I could hike at Pt. Reyes, visit my friend Virginia in Stinson Beach, or catch a movie. My team wasn't back on duty till Wednesday morning; I had time to drive to Fresno and surprise Howard.

But I didn't want off the case.

I stuck my head in the inspector's doorway. "I know you're short-handed in Homicide," I said, as soon as he put down the phone, "and I—"

Doyle laughed. "Smith, I could have made a bundle betting you'd want in, *if* there'd been anyone naive enough to take the other side. So skip the polemics. Your report; anything you need to add?"

"No, it's all there: coordinating the scene, and interviews with Pironnen, Estler who made the 911 call, and Fannie Johnson, Sam Johnson's wife. I also talked to Pironnen last week about the nudist. Pironnen's a recluse; he's not likely to open up to most people. He—"

"Okay, Smith, I take your point. And I do need someone to head up the interviews until Brucker gets back Monday." He eyed his watch. "Jesus, it's after four. Get yourself back here by ten."

CHAPTER 14

IT WAS 4:30 IN the morning when I got home. The house was dark and silent. That is so rare an event that I had to feel around to find the light switch. I was exhausted, wired to the point of giddiness. Forgetting that it was Spring Break, I glanced around for the tenants: two adults with part-time and poorly paying jobs, a teaching assistant, and a pair of career students committed to stopping to smell every rose. They and their friends (and enemies, and lovers) have made vocations of huddling near the fireplace grumbling about the smoky air. The TA, a Medieval Studies major, felt it gave an aura of verisimilitude when he graded papers. Sometimes they sprawled in postcoital or precoital bliss on the sofa, rug, or—on more than one occasion—the coffee table, or they lined up three-deep at the fridge. Stereo and CD players from all rooms battled for supremacy. Dogs snarled, cats hissed, coldblooded beast friends scurried or slithered as their owners grumbled territorially. Normally the place was a zoo. What Howard needed to do—what I'd told him to do—was to get rid of them all, man *and* beast. The rent would be manageable, he'd agreed, on *two* cops' salaries. That always stopped me. I wasn't about to give up my freedom and my salary so Howard could spend every spare moment keeping up this brown-shingled money shredder.

But it was, indeed, Spring Break. The tenants had headed off to places even smokier and more crowded. The house was so silent I could hear the fridge hum. For once I was sorry the tenants were gone. I could have used a normal conversation—even one about medieval farming techniques or reptilian egg fertilization—or even the grunts and moans of passion to remind me I was in the world of the living. In the absence of which, I headed to the fridge.

I had two scoops of blueberry swirl in my dish before I remembered my bet with Howard. Damn, why couldn't I have forgotten?

The whole silly bet was so trivial now. Still my stomach was churning with panic, and a Bar None, the crème de la crème of chocolate bars, would have put everything right; or an It's-It's, that ice cream confection not even known on the East Coast; or a doughnut with that red jelly which defied connection to any known fruit. If Howard missed working on this house as much as I did sweets, it was a good thing he was in Fresno.

Well, rats, I thought, if he's away from this house and *his* temptation, then the whole bet is off!

I had the spoon almost to my mouth. Then I put it down. Not because of the bet, exactly. I missed Howard. *I* certainly had no grounds for complaint. A cop swap is standard procedure. *I* was the one who loved the idea of getting behind the wheel and driving until the dawn found me on a road I'd never seen. It was I who insisted on keeping all gates open.

I stared at the ice cream. All of a sudden, hungry as I was, I just couldn't bring myself to eat. Death, divorce—nothing had ever put me off food before. The feeling was so strange it was like I was in someone else's body.

I ran the water in the tub and lay back. If Howard had been here, we would have been sitting in bed, discussing my 187. He'd be shaking his head at the mistaken identity, nodding with his Only-in-Berkeley expression at my description of Karl Pironnen's dust-carpeted house, laughing at the prospect of

Bryn Wiley camped amid the discarded papers and clothes that covered Herman Ott's floor.

Fannie Johnson, what would I tell Howard about her? It was hardly her intent to be accommodating. And yet, if I could get beneath that automatic antiestablishment shell, there would be something more inside.

I could picture Fannie Johnson glaring at me. "You think there's fairness in the world?" she'd ask sarcastically. Of course there wasn't. That's why I was a cop, so I could try to bring a little of it to Berkeley.

When I went to bed, I yearned to curl up on my side of the California King, turn my back, and press against Howard's ribs and groin, letting his arms slip around me. Instead, I rolled over to the middle and lay there until I slept.

I slept fitfully and finally gave up the attempt at 8 A.M. My arms were tense, my shoulders ached, and my fists were clenched. Clutching onto my portion of the case?

There were secrets Bryn Wiley wasn't revealing, and things Fannie Johnson had been holding back. One more try apiece and I could get to those secrets. But it would be two hours before I could even see Doyle.

Maybe Ellen had been the intended victim. She was, after all, dead. Maybe the attacks on Bryn Wiley's vehicles were aimed at Ellen, and she, who resembled Bryn, sitting in Bryn's car, which *she* never drove, with Bryn's purse . . . well, all things were possible.

And when the coroner was done, Bryn would have her body cremated and deposited somewhere. Would there even be a service? It pained me to think that Ellen's life was gone, just like that. Like the Zen dictum: Walk through life and leave no footprints. I hated to think Ellen was not even a shifting of the sand.

I tossed on good jeans and a navy turtleneck, and headed to Peet's to think.

The courtyard between Peet's and Rick and Ann's Cafe is crowded every morning, but on Sundays it's like the First

Church of Free Time with worshipers on their al fresco pews, communing in scones and caffe lattes, offering silent hallelujahs for another warm, sunny day. Dogs and toddlers make the rounds seeking tithes. There is even a poor box of sorts for the Free Clinic or the Food Project.

I sat on the bench sipping my latte (doppio alto = double everything), thankful I hadn't been forced to sacrifice that, too. Wooden benches get hard quick, and I found myself remembering Bryn sitting on hers with her feet crossed and her ankles pressing into the wood. She hadn't gone near that bench before Ellen died. Ellen had been a woman who wanted to straighten out the wrinkles in life, to make nice, or at least make up for what had not been so nice. It was Ellen's confessional bench, after all. She had gone to considerable effort and expense to refinish it. Why? Slowly, I drank the coffee and steamed milk. What had she wanted Bryn to confess, to repent? What was in that confessional?

I finished the latte and held the cup down so a particularly fine black lab could lick out the foam.

"Haircut?" a young woman with short crisp red hair asked. "We're having a grand opening special. I could lob that tail of yours right off."

If my mind hadn't been on the confessional bench, my senses concentrated on the black lab, I never would have agreed, at least not without six weeks of indecision. But now, remembering the nudist yanking that tail, the crisp-haired woman seemed like a gift from the cosmos. "Fine, but I don't have much time."

The minute I walked out of the hair salon, I was sorry. When I looked in the car mirror at my tiny brown cap of hair, so short it could have been painted on, I groaned. My face, oval an hour ago, was now round. Sixty minutes ago I had looked thoughtful; now I looked perky. I was spunky, feisty—all those adjectives that mean a flash of ineffectual energy from a person too small to take seriously. I glowered—a feisty little glower.

And when I got to the station, I was sorrier yet.

"Hey, Smith," Lieutenant Davis, the watch commander, said. "Got your hair cut, eh? You look . . . cute." Lieutenant Davis was a man of precise actions and solid taste. By "cute," he meant someone who had no place in the squad room.

"Wait up, Smith," he said, taking a call-back card from a file on his immaculate desk. "These are yours. This one was misrouted to your old office."

"Thanks." I glanced at the date and time: Friday morning. "It's been sitting down there all this time?"

"Someone just brought it by."

"I didn't mean to suggest that *you* had had it more than twenty-four hours." I smiled. Lieutenant Davis routed forms so quickly he could have rented out space in his In box.

Davis flashed a smile, a conservative little smile. "You know, Smith, I don't countenance putting off call-backs. Yet and still, in this case you're probably just saving yourself work."

Now I looked at the caller's name: Candace Upton, the Presidents' phone pal. "Shit!"

Davis normally doesn't countenance profanity, either. Now he laughed.

The second sheet was from Inspector Doyle. I realized before I read it what it meant: He wouldn't be meeting me to confer as he had in the old days when I was in Homicide. He was merely leaving me an order: "Take Bryn Wiley to the morgue and get an ID on the deceased."

Still, there was a lot to be learned about a suspect as she views the corpse. I signed out a patrol car and headed for Telegraph Avenue.

Telegraph was blocked off for Sunday street market. Racks and tables that normally lined the sidewalks on weekdays filled the streets, and shoppers who normally craned and crammed now ambled around the displays of T-shirts: GO BERZERKELY! (with the requisite tie-dye background), SUPPORT ELITE LAWNBOWLERS (the latest municipal controversy), CHINESE COLONIALISTS OUT OF TIBET! I passed the table of Sally, the tarot reader, who had always turned over a card for me when I was on this beat four years ago. She glanced up, but if she recognized me she was too polite to admit it. Next to her were open shelves of pottery and multicolored candles of the same vintage as the tie-dyed long johns next to them. The sun was warm, the air light with incense, and music from open car windows sailed like ribbons in the wind.

I crossed the street and glanced in a sunlit store window, spotting a slightly perplexed-looking woman with short hair and a vaguely Asian look to her face. Wearing my clothes. I felt a flash of fear, like I'd lost my . . . self, and then, after a bit, I relaxed. I had walked these streets in uniform, with gun and baton. I'd always thought of myself as more of a Berkeleyan than a police officer. But to the people on the Avenue I'd been the Man. Even out of uniform. No matter how long I lived in Berkeley, I was always an outsider, the person whose very presence made others flinch, reduced them to children about to be found out. It was one of the ironies I bemoaned when I woke at four in the morning: I loved the city, I protected it; but I could never truly be a part of it.

But now, in the costume of my new hair and casual clothes, I could at least pass.

I wished I had time to stop, finger crystal earrings, or cedar boxes carved in the shapes of animals. I walked lightly, like I was just another civilian strolling among the blankets, looking at displays of handcrafted leather belts and pressed flower hangings, smiling at the shouts from Hate Man, dropping a dollar into the violin case of a guy in a tux playing something too formal for the day. My stomach lurched toward the garlic-onion-tomato aroma of the pizza place beside the entrance to Herman Ott's building. Pity that I couldn't be free of my junk food bet!

The momentary pizza-lust was gone almost as soon as it had arrived. The short-haired, bejeaned Berkeleyan that was me seemed to have a stranger's stomach.

Even Ott's building looked different. The "lobby" was an eight by ten square accommodating an old cage elevator—the one that had been a decoration since '62—and a double-wide iron-railed staircase. But today it was missing its carpet of napkins, pizza plates, leaves, and dirt. Many times, when I'd trudged up the extra long flights of stairs to question Ott, I had lugged pizzas to lure information from him. I'd taken the steps two at a time, arriving panting to pound on his third-floor office door and threaten him for evidence withheld. I had been up these steps more than anyone in the history of the department. But never had I seen them so clean, or so crowded. Tanned, muscled, shorts-clad climbers raced up the steps like they were on the slopes of Everest.

I cut across the traffic at the third-floor landing and headed around the south side of the square hallway loop.

When I had first come here, the building was still home to the last of the hippies who had liberated the two-room offices and hung beads over the doors in the two bathrooms down the hall. Soon it became a crash pad for addicts who kept their doors locked for good reason. Only Herman Ott had bobbed with each wave of tenants. And when refugee families took over and children filled the halls and the aroma of coconut satay floated out from the open doorways, Ott felt like the elder statesman of the building. It was he the newcomers asked for advice. His door had never been unlocked—his clientele was too casual about possessions to encourage that kind of foolishness—but I'd seen him respond by name to soft knocks made by small fists low on his door.

The enthusiastic shouts of the Heat Exchangers heading to or from the top floor accompanied me. That was the only noise. All the doors of the offices-cum-apartments were shut. The hallway was empty of children, clear of cars and pails. Even the aromas were muted by the closed doors. The hall looked like it was under siege. No wonder Ott was so outraged about The Heat Exchange.

I knocked on Ott's opaque glass pane. Not waiting for his requisite refusal to answer on the first try, I knocked again and called out, "It's Smith, Ott."

I was just raising my hand for the traditional third round when the door opened.

Ott stepped back without my forcing him—another rare greeting. His sallow face had none of its normal curmudgeonly verve. He was wearing the same gold-billed cap, tan and cream argyle vest over mustard polyester shirt, and bronze-ish khakis he had on last night, which meant he had probably slept in his obsessively well-ordered office and given Bryn his pack rat's nest of living quarters—an arrangement that must have equalized their discomfort and inconvenience. He couldn't get to his clothes; she couldn't get out to the bathroom. This was not an arrangement destined for the duration.

I stepped into the light inside the office.

Ott didn't move. He stood staring at me.

"Don't even think *cute* or *perky*!" Before he could come up with a spunky little adjective of his own, I said, "Where's Bryn?"

"Gone."

CHAPTER 15

"Bryn is gone? gone where, Ott?"

"Gone gone."

"How could you lose her in less than twelve hours? What kind of detective are you that you can't watch a witness for half a day?"

"I didn't have her shackled to the wall. If you wanted that, you should have put her in Q for the night. You must have buddies there, Smith."

"I don't have to send a witness to San Quentin, Ott. One witness! A cocker spaniel could guard her!"

He eyed the door but he was too far into the room to reach it. He wanted to throw me out. *I* would have thrown *him* out if it hadn't been *his* office. And if I hadn't planned to squeeze a recompense for his admitted failure. "When did you realize she was gone?"

"Seven this morning."

"How'd you discover that?"

"I made that deduction when she slammed the door."

"You mean she just walked out?"

"Right."

"Where did she go?"

"She wasn't making a run to the grocery, Smith; she was *leaving*. She didn't hand me her appointment book." Ott kicked the door shut and sat hard on his clients' chair.

I was so taken aback I almost reached out to him, but I caught myself before I made that terminal faux pas.

Ott, for all his counterculture clientele and antiestablishment code, has an unspoken office etiquette that would send Miss Manners back to school. Rule No. 1 is Ott sits in the ripped mustard leather swivel behind the desk. The client, or in my case, unwanted intruder, takes the other chair, a hard wooden affair that must have been designed by a chiropractor in need of business. Often I shoved one of his tidy piles of papers into the middle of his desk and settled on the edge, just to ruffle his feathers. Very occasionally, he perched there to stare down at me in the chair. But never had I seen him elect to take that seat himself.

I wanted to ask why he was so unhinged by a departure he had no authority to prevent, and really, no reason to. But that I couldn't do either, at least not head on. "Ott," I said, "what happened before Bryn left?"

"I made breakfast."

I'd seen the electric coffeepot—a carbon dater's dream—and the box of lemon-iced doughnuts Ott gets on sale Monday morning at Half Price Foods. By Sunday morning that meal would have made Salman Rushdie take a hike. "Did you turn on the radio?"

"Nah."

"So you talked."

He nodded.

When Ott was silent, I knew I was getting warm. "Talked about?"

"Are you sure you want to know, Smith?"

"Ott, a woman was murdered. What did you talk about?"

"You."

"Me?"

"Yeah. She wasn't happy about you handling the investigation. I . . ." Ott's sallow face flushed to an unhealthy orange.

"Yes?"

He looked downright embarrassed. Ott heard people complain about the police all the time; he did it himself all the time. I couldn't imagine what in their innocuous conversation could have brought on this blush. "Ott?"

"I told her"—he forced it out—"she should count her blessings."

I laughed. "That must have impressed her." I was touched by Ott's defense, but I was not about to mention that to him. I went on. "So she was saying she wanted a Homicide officer in charge —she already told me that. What else did she ask? What I was going to do next?"

Ott nodded.

"And you told her I was headed for Fannie Johnson's?"

Again he nodded. But it wasn't a final nod. "And then what, Ott? You two were sitting, eating breakfast, and something happened and Bryn walked out. What?"

Ott swallowed. He'd rather have choked than disgorge information to a cop, especially one he'd felt forced to defend. "I told her you were going to interview Sam's wife about his whereabouts. She says: 'At *her* mansion?' I ask her why she assumes that. She says she's never seen Sam's wife at the construction site. She asks me what Sam's wife is like. I say: Hasn't Ellen told her? She looks so surprised that I say: Ellen knew her from before she came to work for you. She knew her through people at Bootlaces. Bryn's face—it was like someone flipped the card. She picks up her stuff and walks out. No response to me asking how come? Or where are you going? No thanks for taking her in. The card, Smith, it was dead white."

"Why was she so stunned, Ott?"

I couldn't quite label Ott's expression: part put out, part appalled he didn't know the answer, part something else. The incident didn't make sense to me either. "The re-entry center, Bootlaces, did Ellen volunteer there?"

"Volunteer?" Ott laughed. "Smith, she came for the food."

"Bryn Wiley's cousin needed free meals?"

Ott pushed himself up out of the clients' chair and walked around behind the desk. "No, Smith, Bryn Wiley's cousin did not need free food."

"Wha—"

"Ellen Waller wasn't Bryn's cousin."

Landfill. The case was like the filled land that turns to mush in an earthquake. By now Ott had stood up and I sat in his clients' chair—where I clearly belonged—and tried to grasp some straw of truth in this case before it all turned into mud. "If Ellen Waller was not Bryn's cousin, who was she?"

"Ellen Waller. What makes you think they were related?"

"They said so, both of them."

Ott raised the pale skin where his eyebrows would have been if he had any. "And you didn't question that?"

"Why would I, Ott? Two women, who have a familial resemblance, who are *victims* not *suspects* of a crime, say they're cousins. It's not like being married. You don't get special privileges for being cousins. Why would they lie?"

"But they did." Ott was smiling now. In a minute he'd be perching on the back of his chair, looking down.

"Why?"

"Don't know. Didn't know they were using that story."

"Well, why do you think?"

He just shrugged, not an easy move for a man with virtually no shoulders. "Live-in help?"

Admittedly, it was the kind of bourgeois arrangement many Berkeleyans would be embarrassed to make—or admit to making. "Okay, Ott, if Ellen Waller wasn't Bryn's cousin, then Bryn didn't call her cousin to come to Berkeley because she needed a secretary."

"Well, a secretary she did need. Look, Smith, the thing with Bryn is she's a great motivator, an idea person. But she has no patience with the small stuff. Like answering fan mail."

Staring at Ott, I laughed. I glanced through the connecting door at Ott's other room. It was not the sun-lit study of a social secretary's dreams. The only rays that made it in there had traveled down the air shaft and squeezed through a four-decade accumulation of window soot. Covering the one ancient, formerly overstuffed chair and most of the floor were newspapers, magazines, books, and a spectrum of yellow clothes that belied the notion that yellows don't clash. If clutter were dog hair, Karl Pironnen would have felt right at home.

"I represent all types, Smith. There are business people I'll take on. I know about networking. And Bryn had a big campaign going to publicize her gym. She went through a number of secretaries early on. Wide-eyed and adoring when she got 'em; white-fisted by the time they stormed out. She wasn't a considerate employer."

"Tell me about it!"

I'd meant it as agreement but Ott took it as a question. "She'd go full-blast at one thing. Meanwhile, people want her to speak; they're trying to confirm dates she's already agreed to; get her commitment to be on this board or that. They need answers. The letters pile up unopened. The people are calling; they're desperate; Bryn doesn't answer. Then she dumps the whole thing in the secretary's lap and expects her to come up with the kind of excuses that make her look good."

"Like saying she screwed up and Bryn feels terrible she has such an incompetent for an employee?"

"Right. But once the gym was on its feet, she didn't bother with a secretary. She hated having that efficient little person around, reminding her she was failing at things that she didn't give a damn about but that she had to do because she'd hired this secretary."

"She told you this?"

"Yeah."

"So how did Ellen come into this marvelous job?"

Ott leaned forward onto the desk, a little less majestic than before. "This I got secondhand, from a source at Bootlaces. I haven't checked it out. No reason to."

"Go on."

"Bryn was doing a motivational talk at Bootlaces. She's a supporter. It wasn't a big crowd."

"That surprises me."

"The reason was she was scheduled to do it a couple weeks earlier and she forgot. The people at Bootlaces were annoyed but they knew her well enough to insist she make good and be quick about it."

"Safe to assume they felt she'd let her last secretary go too soon."

"They may have thought so, but Bryn still didn't. Bryn wouldn't have put up with anyone wanting to straighten her office or put her on a schedule. If anyone was looking for that job, that evening was not the time to approach Bryn about it."

"But Ellen didn't have to, right?" I was almost out of my chair. "Bryn noticed Ellen because she looked so much like her? Right?"

"Yeah, right," Ott said with a definite lack of satisfying finality.

"So what's missing here. Ellen lucked into this job because she happened to resemble Bryn."

"She didn't *happen* to look like Bryn, Smith. A couple days before the event she didn't look anything like Bryn Wiley."

CHAPTER 16

I ASKED ABOUT ELLEN'S background, but Ott didn't know. "Find out, Ott!"

He didn't object.

"And Bryn Wiley, Ott. The woman walked out of here with nothing but an overnight duffel. She doesn't have a car—we've got that in impound. If she's in town, I want to know where. If she's gone, I want to know where."

"I'll call you," he said, opening the door to indicate our meeting was over.

"No, Ott, I'll call you. Tonight."

I was out in the hall before I could wonder what it was that motivated Ott's incredible docility. Ninety percent of my requests he turned down flat. There were times he'd thrown me out of his office on principle. And here he was not only agreeing to track down Bryn Wiley, but acting like a chastened schoolkid when I snapped demands. Something was making him anxious to learn about Ellen Waller and to find Bryn Wiley. And I wanted to find out what that was.

I drove slowly back to the station, thinking about Ellen Waller. Ellen had presented herself as the poor relation, long-suffering but able to preserve her sense of humor. I had bought her package without question or thought. Foolish as it was, her deceit hurt my feelings.

That I could have shrugged off. But I couldn't dismiss what it said about my judgment. I'd let my instincts block out my training. More Berkeley than cop, indeed. Maybe I *wasn't* Detective Division material anymore.

A cold swirl of panic filled my chest. Homicide was life and death; any other assignment was . . . a lot less important. After probing the psyches of men and women desperate enough to take another person's life, how could I ever be satisfied with separating 415 squabbles or searching for stolen cars? It would just be a way to fill forty hours. If I couldn't make it as a detective anymore, what would *I* do?

Only Herman Ott would understand, because, I was sure, he felt that way, too.

The station was Sunday-afternoon empty—no harried officer at reception, no one going through the card files for photo lineup shots, no one from Community Relations looking for volunteers or warning us off a plate of pizza squares intended for the civilians in their academy class. I checked my mailbox for papers, my voice mail for phone messages, and the computer for print-out backgrounds. Sam Johnson's was a mile long. He was known to the FBI. He was a major player on CORPUS (the countywide arrest information network which listed each arrest and its progress through the legal system). The man had had more dates—arraignments, court hearings—than a prom queen. But it was on Records Management System that he really shone; there every contact with the department is listed, whether the subject is the responsible or the complainant. Between his political activity, The Heat Exchange, and the home building site, Sam Johnson must have ticked off every citizen in town. About half of The Heat Exchange complaints—mostly for noise— came from Herman Ott. Was Ott, I wondered, the *finder of record* for his neighbors, or was he merely representing his own pique? On PIN (warrants) and NCIC (nationwide warrants) Johnson was clean.

Karl Pironnen was known to Records Management via residents on the routes of his nocturnal dog walks. I could imagine Pironnen so caught up in pondering his next chess move that he lost track of those three big dogs till one of them knocked over a trash can and the householder assumed there was a prowler.

Jed Estler had made his mark with Traffic. Another speeding ticket and he'd be walking.

Bryn Wiley's contribution was just as I would have guessed. Her complaints about Sam Johnson probably justified half a clerk's position here. Otherwise, she was clean. Not so much as a stop sign roll-through.

On Ellen Waller there was nothing at all. It was like she didn't exist. And maybe she didn't. Why should her name be more real than anything else about her? We had followed the state law and sent a set of Ellen's fingerprints and a forensic dental chart to the Department of Justice in Sacramento. They'd be inputted into the John and Jane Doe computer and checked it against the Missing Persons reports. They'd be sent to Criminal Identification and Investigation Division to see if the prints matched anyone known to CI&I. We'd also forwarded the prints to the FBI; but the feds would take weeks at best. In the meantime she would remain a Jane Doe, listed with all the other unknown dead lying unclaimed in morgues across the country.

I looked at the last of the records: Fannie Johnson's. For the first time I smiled. Her driver's license said Fannie Johnson. Probably the deed on their property said Fannie Johnson. But our records said aka Tiffany Glass. Tiffany Glass! Poor woman. She probably would have married anyone just for his name. I scanned up her records. There were a few minor traffic violations but no 415s (disturbance) or even 602s (trespass), the most minor arrests made in demonstrations. From the look of this, while Sam Johnson was staking out People's Park or blocking off intersections, his wife was home with a good book.

But it was the earliest entry that stopped me. It was from

Records Management. Tiffany Glass had been transported by ambulance from the Harmon Gym pool to Alta Bates hospital. The date was a month before Bryn Wiley dove off the high platform in the Olympics.

Tiffany Glass. Tiffany? Where had I heard that name? I thought hard. Wasn't Tiff the Cal diver who'd been injured when Bryn Wiley was at the Nationals Meet?

I grabbed the phone and dialed Bryn. She could have left Ott's and just gone home. No answer. I left a message on her machine, called the dispatcher, had her ask Adam 2 to check out the house in his most official mode. If Bryn was there, she'd know the police wanted in. If she came home later, she'd find a note on the door.

Then I called Inspector Doyle.

"Can't this wait, Smith. I've been up forever and I just got home. I've got my grandchildren here from Portland. They're leaving in the morning."

"Sorry, 'Spec. I need Heling's report on Bryn Wiley's house to see if it gives me any hint about Ellen Waller's ID."

He sighed. "Smith, your assignment was to take Wiley to the morgue—"

"—to ID the body. Well, sir, Wiley's vanished and the body's still a Jane Doe."

"I know that, Smith. I knew it when I read Heling's report. It won't answer your questions. But take a look for yourself."

I could hear a small child shriek with pleasure somewhere in the Doyle house. The receiver rustled against Doyle's face or hair or maybe shirt. "Inspector, things have changed radically since Heling was in there. When Heling went through that house she was assuming Bryn Wiley was the deceased. She was figuring the murder victim's bedroom was the large one. She didn't know the true victim had no history whatsoever, that her bedroom was the small one, or that the one item she insisted on bringing to that house was the skeleton of a confessional booth."

"Wha—?"

I knew that confessional would get Doyle, the lapsed Catholic. "I—we—need to get in there and go over that confessional."

"You're going to have to do better than that, Smith."

"Ellen Waller is a Jane Doe; Bryn Wiley's in on the cover-up. What's to keep her from going home as soon as it's dark and destroying every scrap of paper relating to Ellen? These are exigent circumstances."

"What's exigence in one set of eyes can be blinked out of another, Smith. You don't have minor children in danger in that house. But you may have evidence in danger. Okay, Smith. Check Heling's report. Write up the warrant. Brucker will be back tomorrow; he'll appreciate it."

"Maybe I should just send it directly to Sacramento."

Doyle didn't say anything. He waited a moment then hung up. It was a more ominous response to my sarcasm than any words. It said Doyle knew Brucker's career goals and he was in no position to object. Brucker had that much clout. It told me to watch my mouth, and my tail.

And to move the latter. Gathering enough information to support a request for a warrant is no afternoon at the beach. It requires summarizing all the relevant reports, which requires *finding* all the relevant reports, and deciphering the handwritten notes in same. (Doyle was right about Heling's report. It didn't answer my questions.) I must have thought twenty times in the next two hours: I'm starving; I'll run downstairs for a doughnut. A Hershey's. A Snickers. By the time I picked up the phone to call the assistant DA on weekend duty, I would have chomped through my pencil if it had been coated in chocolate. Any illusion I had about being cured of my cravings was gone. For pizza maybe; it is, after all, only food. But chocolate is the nourishment of the soul.

The ADA, just back from hiking on Mount Diablo and on his way to the Warriors game, listened as I read him the papers and answered his questions for twenty minutes. My neck, my throat, my stomach were all knotted; my head pounded. I wasn't even *thinking* of chocolate; my reaction reflected a much deeper

panic. It was all I could do to concentrate on the questions and
formulate sensible answers. When I hung up, I sat staring at the
wall. It was the color of mint chocolate. Or pistachio. It was
insane to let a bet yank the stability out of my life. I had enough
real problems without creating more. If Howard couldn't see
that, well, too bad. It wasn't a question of asking Howard for an
out; I'd tell him. I picked up the phone and dialed the Fresno
police.

It rang three times before I put it down. I'd been right; it
wasn't a question of asking *Howard* for an out. I walked over to
the water fountain, took two Tylenols and then a long deep
breath before I dialed the judge. Marcus Redmon was the worst
judge for a cop in a hurry. He was impatient, and a stickler for
order. And he had just taken a lot of heat about two warrants
he'd issued for another department. I dialed.

After all that, Redmon was out. He'd be back at seven o'clock
for a few minutes. So I had a two-hour reprieve. I could make
sure this request was in Redmonian order. Or I could find out
what the story was with Tiffany Glass and Fannie Johnson. I
didn't have time for both. But I had to have both if I had any
chance at all to solve this case before it went to Brucker. I'd have
to deal with Fannie damned fast.

In most places, putting a blazer over a sweatshirt does not rate
as tie optional, but in Berkeley such a move shows intent. Some
places too much intent.

The Johnsons' house was one of those. Here a jacket was as *de
rigueur* as Spode china at McDonald's. Or a Tiffany lamp—
there or here. I left the jacket on the hook and ran up the steps.
In a navy turtleneck and jeans I was still overdressed.

The place hadn't been much last night, but without the cloak
of darkness it bared its stucco to the world. A layer of cream-
colored paint had been applied when the stucco had dried in the
1930s. Perhaps it had been advertised as "the only coat you'll
ever need"; certainly it was the only one this place had gotten.
Above the level of the stoop, stucco shone through like scabs;

below it was splattered mud from the cars that had parked on the patch of brown that stood in lieu of lawn. Definitely not a setting for Tiffany Glass.

The door inside the screen was open. I knocked.

"Come on in," a male voice called. It wasn't Sam Johnson's.

I stepped into a small foyer and left to the living room that covered the front of the house. A four-window bay revealed a bright, airy view. I'd seen this model of house with a sumptuous leather couch by those windows, an Oriental rug in front of it, and the white brick fireplace at the far end of the twelve by twenty room, a sheepskin rug tossed cozily over the sofa back. Then, the room had just about wrapped its arms around me and offered me wine.

The Johnsons' sofa was Danish modern, with thin, faded orange cushions. In front of it was a pine-veneer door cum coffee table, adorned by flyers, new and recycled into scrap paper. The room had a unity of colorlessness. Even the two middle-aged guys sprawled on the sofa dressed in the worn cloth of their outrage and the post-teenager on the edge of the table flapping a sheet of paper could have faded back into the mist here.

"Fannie here?" I asked.

"Back room," the nearer couch guy said. "Fannie! Someone here for you."

I started through the dining room cum office with the built-in china cabinet—stacked with old newspapers.

The bedroom door swung slowly open. I had to take two steps into the room to spot Fannie, on a rumpled bed behind the door. Herman Ott had called her attractive in an arty, young–Jacqueline Kennedy way. There are times when it amazes me that one so utterly devoid of perceptive discrimination survives as a private detective. There was nothing arty about the pale, square-faced woman in old and quilted bathrobe, with faded comforter drawn around her. Nothing young. It was hard to believe she was diving at Cal the same time Bryn was.

Earphones in place, she gave a last glance to a book before putting it down, cover down. The window shades were drawn.

With as little light as got into this house, how had so much managed to fade? The one attempt to break the pervasive gray was Fannie's flowered bathrobe, and that effort, clearly, had been made years ago. The room screamed—no, nothing so energetic, it moaned—of inertia.

I needed her to reveal things she didn't want to deal with. Here, in this room, in the aura of entrenched depression, she wasn't going to tell me a thing. I didn't have time to . . . but I had no choice. "Get dressed. We're going out."

"Who are you?" She pulled off the headphones.

"Jill Smith. Police. You talked to me last night."

"Are you trying to take me to jail?"

"No. To coffee."

CHAPTER 17

I HAD BEEN ONLY half surprised Fannie Johnson didn't object to breaking bread with a member of the city's finest.

I could have taken her to the Med, the original European-type coffee house—it was closer—but I wanted her away from Telegraph Avenue and Sam's colleagues. She seemed relieved when I suggested the French Hotel Café, and more relieved when I asked her to follow in her car. A good thing it was; explaining the liability issues of my driving a witness in my own car in a city that is self-insured would have taken me the entire trip across town.

The French Hotel is named for the laundry that used to occupy its space, in a long, narrow brick building. I hadn't realized how fast I'd been driving until I sat in the supermarket lot beside it, waiting for Fannie's Nova to pull up. When Fannie got out, she was dressed in wool slacks and a short, boiled wool jacket, in red. The jacket was not secondhand, and it certainly hadn't been cheap. It shouted of a stubborn inner core, or maybe just counterculture in-your-face. Her ensemble was a more stylish equivalent of her husband's button-down shirts. The Johnsons must have made quite an entrance at the anarchists' conventions.

When Fannie started toward the hotel, I almost gasped.

"Limp" didn't begin to describe her unwieldy walk. Instead of swinging one leg after the other, her two steps became parts of one great thrust that yanked up her left leg and sent the force down her right side to jerk that leg along. The force gone, the next step began anew from a cold start. The process looked as awkward and exhausting as driving in first gear with stop signs every twenty feet.

I stared, horrified. I wanted to run up and help, to say how sorry I was even though her condition had nothing to do with me. I yearned to look away, but I didn't; I just stood, staring blankly. Every step seemed agonizing. God, what was her life like? Each time she wanted a glass of water she'd have to question whether she wanted it enough to move for it. And if she took too many steps, would the stress on her joints create new pains—sharper or heavier? Was this the outcome of that trip to Alta Bates twelve years ago? Had she been limping like this for twelve long years? Most of her adult life?

She was almost to the door of the French Hotel Café when I caught up with her. "Let's go across the street."

She hesitated only momentarily. Then a smile lit her square face, and in that moment I could see where Herman Ott had gotten the notion of Jackie Onassis. "You cops must have hefty expense accounts."

"I invited you for coffee, not the prix fixe dinner." So it would cost more than the French Hotel; it was worth it to go to Chez Panisse. Fannie would be pleased—and perhaps, more forthcoming. It would also take longer than the counter service at the hotel. I glanced at my watch. It was already five forty.

I led the way in through the trumpet-vined gate, across the brick patio, to the stairs. Chez Panisse, the birthplace of California Cuisine, occupies a two-story brown shingle adorned with buffed wood railings and prairie-style sconces, and huge sprays of exotic flowers. The prix fixe rooms downstairs are quietly elegant. Fannie passed by the entrance and hoisted her weak leg onto the first step.

"Oh God, I forgot about the stairs!" I blurted out. "We can go to the French Hotel."

Fannie turned, taking a moment to catch her breath. "Not on your life. I was a high diver. I'm used to climbing to the ten-meter platform. Besides, when we get up to the café, you'll feel so guilty you'll buy me seconds. Maybe ply me with liquor. I love their Kir." She turned and maneuvered her leg to the next step and the next, awkwardly, but with speed that amazed me. Maybe it was not the woman in the boiled red jacket who was the anomaly but the one in the faded bathrobe.

"In the bar?" she said, standing by a black marble café table.

"No, it sounds like you're going to need a whole table."

If it hadn't been the middle of the afternoon, we'd have been lucky to get a spot either place without an hour's wait. But now we followed the waiter into the front room that must have been a sleeping porch when Shattuck Avenue was still a sleepy street. I ordered Fannie her promised Kir, and scanned the dessert choices: poached pears in red wine, apple crepes, chocolate decadence, Tarte Tatin, and Timbale Panisse. The last two I dismissed because I didn't know what they were. But it was really no contest—nothing, no matter how elegant, original, and superbly prepared equals chocolate.

"So, Fannie, one of each?"

"I'll take decadence for now. But I may need to keep my strength up for the trek down the stairs."

The waiter brought her Kir. I ordered us both coffees.

Strange how easy it is to forget when you want to. I was ordering two decadences before the awful truth occurred to me. This doesn't count, I quickly assured myself. I'd made an honest mistake. I could hardly open an interview with a possible suspect by describing a stupid bet I had with my boyfriend. I was so rushed, this would be my only chance at food tonight. I'd already told the waiter . . . Besides, nothing served at Chez Panisse could be classified as junk food.

Okay, so technically "junk food" meant all sweets. Even so, Howard surely would excuse this one incident.

Sure he would! He'd discount my wolfing down the epitome of chocolate cake just as quickly as I'd overlook his repainting the dining room because a friend gave him two gallons of Paris green. I raised a hand to signal the waiter. But seeing the child-like pleasure on Fannie's face as she contemplated the bourgeois indulgence, I couldn't tell her she'd have to eat alone. That would undercut the bond between us. And maybe she *could* down both decadences. I'd let one just sit in front of me while we talked. Hell, I could look temptation in the face; I was tough. I was a *cop*.

"Don't think you've bought me," Fannie said as the waiter slid the dark chocolate slices in front of us.

"I'd assume you'd cost more than this." I laughed. I hadn't expected Fannie Johnson to be fun!

She sipped the Kir, glancing at the bright oversized French posters on the wall. Her dark hair was caught at the nape of her neck like mine used to be. A satisfied smile played on her wide mouth as she leaned back in the chair, looking relaxed, healthy, and utterly at home. In that moment I could see how much she had given up for Sam Johnson. She had a good job; if she had married a man with one, drinks at Chez Panisse needn't have been rare. And medical care: Would an insured husband have bought her two good legs and painfree nights? But I didn't have time to speculate about that; I needed to find out her relation to Bryn Wiley, and get back to the station. "You were taken from Harmon Gym to Alta Bates hospital twelve years ago? Was that from a diving injury?"

She forked off a hunk of cake—dark brown, gooey, big—and opened her mouth wide to get it all in. She shut her eyes as she chewed.

It's damned lucky for perpetuity that mankind doesn't have to choose between sex and chocolate. Only when she had swallowed, sighed, and taken a sip of coffee did she answer me. "Look, I'm going to save you some time. You want to know about Bryn Wiley and me, right?"

"Right."

"No problem. Starting at the top—I didn't kill Bryn. Not that I haven't thought about it. Nor that I'd be above it. And not that I couldn't hire a hit-*person*." She grinned. "Job's become equal opportunity, and I know Bryn prides herself on creating strong women."

"Your motive would have been?"

"The perennial favorite—revenge." She forked off a hunk of cake and stuck it in her mouth, swallowing it this time before she had time to taste. "I was on the team. I had a diving scholarship. I was the only one on the team on full scholarship. Bryn Wiley carries on about how hard it was to be an adolescent recuperating for a year, to miss her high school prom and all that crap. She was lying in bed with her mother to wait on her. In college she took the easy classes, and as few of them as she could get away with. If she wanted to know about hard, she should have tried carrying a full college load plus training. My old roommates used to bitch that I didn't do my share; by the time I moved out, two of them weren't speaking to me. Of course, they weren't on athletic scholarships; they didn't really believe that I had their schedules plus four to six hours in the water or dry land training—"

"Dry land?"

"That's practicing stuff like somersaults in a harness belt. And all that's not counting the weight training or hill running I did on my own."

"For how long?"

"Three and a half years."

"And then Bryn Wiley went to the Olympics and you were injured?"

She took another bite of cake, got it halfway to her mouth, and stopped. "Yes. And did that make me bitter, you ask? What do you think? Ask me when my leg wakes me up in the middle of the night and I'm thankful if there's just throbbing instead of shooting pains."

I nodded, taken aback by her outburst. I'd already misjudged the woman twice—first as a standard-issue radical, second as life's witty skimmer in the expensive jacket—and now she showed me raw honesty. How many more unexpected levels did she possess? "Tell me about your injury."

"Smacked my back on the flexible board. Then I lost it with the dive and hit the water full out on my back. That's what the witnesses said."

"Witnesses? In court?"

"Yeah."

"So that's where you got the money for The Heat Exchange and the house?"

"Yeah." She looked up, and another grin crossed her face. "Did Sam tell you I inherited it?"

"Yes."

"It's our joke. My inheritance. I wasn't on scholarship because my family had just enough money. My parents haven't died and left me anything; they're still alive and angling to get a share of my settlement."

"The accident," I said, "it was a month before the Olympics?"

"During the National Trials in Hawaii—the Trials Bryn and Helena made it to. But all three of us were invited to compete, did you know that? They went, and I missed the plane and ended up in surgery, intensive care, rehab."

"Oh my God."

"Damned right! Why was I diving then, *after* it was too late? Because I thought it would take my mind off missing the plane. Why did I miss the most important flight of my life? Because the time was wrong on the itinerary. The plane left at three fifty-six, not six fifty-six like the itinerary said. I waited, standby, till the last flight out, but there wasn't a seat to be had. 'Well,' you're going to say 'how come Bryn and Helena found the error and you didn't?' Because the travel agent got hold of them. I had just moved; I'd given the travel agent my new number. He swears he called. I never got the call." Her mouth opened, and she smacked in a piece of cake and swallowed so fast it stuck in her throat. Her face turned red, sweat coated her forehead. I was just about to do a Heimlich when she forced the cake down.

She took a long drink, almost finishing the Kir, and when she looked over at me, her eyes were still moist, I couldn't tell whether from her gagging or her subject. "I was better than Bryn. I'd already placed third and fifth in Nationals. If I had gotten that call, I'd have beaten her. She'd have been ninth. You get what that means?" she demanded. "You have to be in the top eight in three National Trials. Bryn would have missed the cut. No Olympic Trials! No Olympics! Nothing!" She took a deep breath, never releasing my eyes. "Maybe I'd have a gold medal. Maybe not. But I'd have two good legs."

There was nothing to say. No horror I felt could match the truth. And like a well-trained athlete, I couldn't veer into emotional byways; I had to drive straight with the investigation. I sipped my coffee and placed the cup silently on the saucer. "Why should this convince me you *didn't* shoot her?"

She gave a laugh—the sophisticate shrugging off the question. "Because death is too easy. Too final." She drank the last of the Kir, closing her eyes and holding the sweet liquid in her mouth, then swallowing and running her tongue over her lips. "And, Officer, I learned a lot in those months of rehab. I hated Bryn. Every time I saw her—'the brave little girl with the scoliosis no one can even notice'—I could have shot her. In all those interviews she never once talked about me or my accident, only how the dive should be done, as if *she'd* have been flawless!"

Bryn's reaction seemed typical of any athlete's. Fannie probably would have done no differently. I didn't point that out.

"It took me a long time to figure out why Bryn Wiley couldn't face seeing me—Helena came every day after she got back from Hawaii."

"Helena wasn't going on to the Olympics?"

Fannie just glared, but it was clear that she knew Helena hadn't had to follow the athlete's training anymore. Helena could afford to be sympathetic. Still glaring, she said, "I embodied Bryn Wiley's worst nightmare: that she could lose everything and become ordinary!"

Bull's-eye! Bryn Wiley, after dreams of the gold medal and her picture on Wheaties boxes, how could she ever face being ordinary? I knew the answer as clearly as Fannie did. I shivered.

Now Fannie smiled. "See, I understand how terrified she is of losing everything. I can dangle that in front of her. Forever. Because, Officer, she's so scared, she runs every time. She'll never look at it. I can play her forever. And, Officer—Jill?—I love it. I am not about to give that up. And now that I own the house next door, I can go up there and watch her squirm from my very own window." She glanced down at her empty cake plate and my untouched one. "You saving that decadence for me?"

I pushed it across the table. I wondered how much she'd altered history to support her bitterness. Or had she created a helluva tough shell to protect an interior still too tender to touch? I guessed the latter. But as far as Bryn Wiley was concerned, the outcome would be the same. "You came up with the idea of turning that house into cheap apartments?"

She waved off the compliment. "No, I'm not that clever. The house was Sam's idea. He was so pleased when he spotted that place. He raced home like a little kid with a present for me. He was going to get Bryn where it hurt.

"Sam's a sweetie, and he's a brilliant tactician, and I love the man. But I'm not blind. And the thing with Sam is that he's been in the movement too long. And you and I know, Jill, that the movement hardly has a good record on women and equal rights, appalled as they'd be to admit it in public."

" 'The only position for a woman in the civil rights movement is prone,' " I said. "H. Rap Brown? Stokely Carmichael?" It was a quote I'd read years ago, and was waiting to hear redressed. I'm still waiting.

"Right. Sam's not like that. Hardly. If he were, he'd be missing a part he might have wanted to use again," she said, digging into the new piece of cake. By now she must have consumed enough calories to support a small village. "Even so," she said, "Sam's obsession with the movement clouds his vision. He really wants to save the masses. He can't understand that the masses don't want to be saved anymore. Hell, the masses vote Republican! But Sam still sees everything as a class issue. With Bryn he figured: Endanger her expensive neighborhood and you've got her."

Bryn's house. A place so peripheral to her soul that she didn't object when Ellen overwhelmed her living room with the confessional bench. I laughed.

"Right. You want to get Bryn Wiley, get her in the reputation, hit The Girls' Team." She grinned. "And so I have."

"So the whole point of The Heat Exchange is to get Bryn?"

"Right!"

"And you don't care if the people on the floors underneath get no heat?"

"We're not living in Maine! This is California! In a two-room apartment your gas bill is never even twenty bucks!"

"Twenty bucks means a lot to someone who doesn't have it."

"My husband has given his life to the poor!"

"And he doesn't care about this broken promise?"

"One in many for the poor. One in many many he's seen."

I wished I had this interchange on tape! "So," I said, "Sam's sold out."

"Hey! You don't just enforce the laws you believe in."

I shook my head. "Uh-uh. I don't make the laws. Sam created The Heat Exchange scam. Sam has sold out."

Automatically she reached for . . . her fork, her plate, the coffee cup, anything. But her hands remained empty. She turned to face me, any hint of amusement gone from her face. "Jill, I'm going to be straight with you, straighter than I should be with a cop. This is off the record."

It pained me to say, "Not in a murder case. Nothing's off record. But I won't bandy your confidences around the locker room." When she didn't respond, I said softly, "It's the best I can do. Honestly."

It was a minute before she said, "Sam and I met in the hospital rehab. after my accident. He had taken a bullet in the thigh. We were focused on rehab. And we were in love. I was a miserable patient, adjusting to a life I couldn't stand. I wouldn't have made it without Sam. I'd be in a wheelchair without him. To him I wasn't working twice as hard as they said I should just so I could be a cripple, I was showing up the establishment, the doctors, the therapists, Bryn Wiley! It didn't occur to us until later how different we were. The only things we had in common were injuries—and love. I don't care about politics. Sam doesn't just care; politics, the movement, is what he is. It governs who he hangs out with, the hours he keeps, it pervades every thought he has. I look at a pool and ponder if it would be good enough for a great diver; Sam demands neighborhood access. I get up to go to work, I have to step over unwashed bodies in the living room. We have no friends in common. There are only a couple places we go where I'm not bored or annoyed or Sam doesn't feel guilty. It's amazing we've stayed together this long. But things between us got rockier and more silent. You understand?" Her eyes beseeched me to understand.

"I do."

She smiled, then grinned. "I got the idea to shoot Bryn in the heart, so to speak, in The Girls' Team. It was brilliant. Sam grabbed it. He's the one who came up with The Heat Exchange. You know what a great tactician he is. We're having such a good time with it, watching her squirm. Did you see what happened at her press conference? Was that a master work or what? Sam's a genius," she said, forking off a bit more of her second dessert.

"I do understand," I said slowly. "But none of this says you wouldn't enjoy taking a brick to her Girls' Team van or shooting her car windows."

Her fork banged down on the plate. "Look, have you missed everything I said? You think I'd toss this all away so I could hack at her van with a brick? You insult me!"

I believed that—the brick attack was beneath her, and Sam would be appalled—unless that was a tactic for an even more deeply covered plan. I glanced at my watch: six ten. I had to get back to the station and get that warrant request in better shape. Keeping my voice neutral I said, "What about Ellen Waller? Did you shoot her?"

"Ellen? Why would I . . . . Omigod, you mean it's Ellen who was shot?"

"Ellen's dead." I let that sink in a moment, and added, "Her face was shot."

Fannie's eyes widened and she pressed her jaws together hard. Any color evaporated from her face. For a moment I thought she was going to faint. Now I leaned forward and repeated, "Did you shoot her?"

"No, damn it. Why would I want to harm Ellen? I liked Ellen."

The last words, *I liked Ellen*, she said in exactly the same intonation I had said them in my mind last night. It comforted me, as if this range of fondness somehow made Ellen's death less stark. But it didn't help me to track her murderer any more than it had saved her from being murdered. "Who would have had reason to shoot her?"

Slowly Fannie shook her head.

A blond woman in a blue sari stopped midbite and stared at us from the next table.

Lowering my voice, I said, "Think! Let me be real clear about this, Fannie. I don't have a lead to a single suspect. Except you and Sam. And between the two of you there are enough motives to keep Homicide busy for a year. If you want us to focus elsewhere, make it your business to tell me where."

"I can understand why you'd think I'd have it in for Bryn. But Ellen? I wouldn't hurt Ellen. I barely knew her. I only saw her a couple of times when she first got to town—the first times she was at Bootlaces, before she ever met Bryn. Omigod! Was she shot in mistake for Bryn?"

I glanced at the sari-clad woman, but she had returned to her food. "Why would you think Ellen would be mistaken for Bryn?"

"Because they looked so much alike."

"So you didn't only see her a couple of times months ago *before* she met Bryn. She didn't resemble Bryn then. You've seen her since she moved in with Bryn." But Bryn had never seen Fannie; Bryn didn't know who Johnson's wife was. So Pironnen was right; he had seen Ellen and Fannie together. "You visited Ellen, and later you waited outside her house for her. Tell me about it. *All* about it."

She sat back and said in a soft voice, "I'll tell you this much, Sam and I've been skeet shooting—it's one of the few sports where it doesn't matter if your legs don't work right. I'm a damned good shot. And if I'd planned to kill Bryn, I would have taken her out on the ten-meter board."

I liked Fannie, just as I liked Ellen. But I tend to go for the brats. Be quick, witty, pull for the underdog, and I'll give you the store. Amuse me with your quirks and I'll overlook a lot. I would have liked Fannie as a friend, but despite all she'd said, I knew two things. Number one: If I asked straight out about Ellen Waller's missing past, Fannie wouldn't tell me. Number two: I wouldn't trust her at the business end of a rifle.

I had just time to organize the warrant argument—if I left right now. I could pay the bill here and . . .

But sometimes you have to go with your gut feeling, your intuition. I picked up my coffee cup, smiled at Fannie, and asked, "How did you meet Ellen Waller?"

CHAPTER 18

BY THIS TIME, IT was nearing the hour for early Sunday dinners. Two women in jeans and sweaters settled between us and the sari-clad woman. Behind me, couples sat together by marble tables and a threesome was grouped in the corner. It was twenty after six. Allowing ten minutes for travel time, I'd have to be paid and out of here in half an hour to get back in time to call the judge at all. I'd have to reorganize the warrant request as I presented it.

Fannie Johnson glanced at the spray of dried leaves and maroon flowers at the end of the bar. She fingered the black frog on her red martinet's jacket. I had to keep myself from hurrying her. She sighed deeply and said, "I don't know when I first saw Ellen. I wouldn't have noticed her. She was just another woman at Bootlaces."

"The re-entry center?"

"Right. I'm on the board. I decided to stop bitching about protesters who were doing nothing but protesting and do something constructive, like help get people back on their feet."

"And Ellen?"

"When I first saw her at Bootlaces, I didn't realize she was one of the clients. She was better dressed than most of the board members."

In Berkeley that's not akin to saying she'd patronized a Paris couturier. Maybe she wore corduroy slacks instead of jeans.

"Then she was helping me send invitations for the Bryn Wiley event—the first one, the one Bryn didn't show for. We were chatting . . ."

"About?"

"The normal new acquaintance stuff. Why we were there. You know."

"So why were you there?"

"Because my house was full of strange men and Sam was up on Tamalpais rebuilding. But I didn't tell her all the details; I just said my husband was renovating a house on Tamalpais." She gave a small shrug. "I thought at the time how upper-middle-class I sounded. Who'd have guessed? I could have been married to a stockbroker."

"And what did Ellen say?"

"She was there to network into a job."

"What kind of job?"

"Gardening, secretarial, housework, that kind of thing."

Paid-under-the-table work, with no official references, no social security number, nothing reported to the IRS. Underground work. "Did you refer her to anything?"

"She didn't have a degree. Besides, the government hasn't been hiring for a decade; they're too busy downsizing, saving money for the high-bracket taxpayers. The rich love laying off workers, then bitching about paying unemployment. If they could lay 'em off and sell 'em by the pound, they would." She took a bite of cake, larger than those before. "Anyway, she didn't seem like someone who'd have trouble finding work. I figured she'd just go to a temp agency."

I raised an eyebrow, waiting for the "but."

"I was surprised when I saw her at the dinner Bryn missed. I figured she'd have been gone by then. But there she was. The next time was at the dinner Bryn did deign to honor. Ellen was wearing a leotard and jeans, her hair was shorter, and it was chestnut just like Bryn's."

"Did she ever tell you why she did that?"

"I could see. Bryn had barely been in the room for five minutes when she spotted Ellen. Ellen didn't approach her; she came to Ellen. Next thing I knew Ellen was living at Bryn's."

Now we were getting to the meat. "How did that next contact come about?"

Fannie wedged her finger in the loop of the frog, then looked down as if trying to get it loose.

"You called her," I suggested. "When you heard she was living at Bryn Wiley's, you saw a chance to find out about Bryn and The Girls' Team, right? You figured you'd make use of Bryn's unsuspecting companion."

She pulled loose of the frog and looked up, smug. "No. You're wrong. Maybe this surprises you, but she called me and suggested lunch."

It did more than surprise me. "Why? What did she want?"

"Lunch. You don't have to have an ulterior motive to go to lunch. Maybe when friends call *you*, your first question is why? Normal people don't think that."

But there was something in her voice that undercut her explanation.

"She did want something, though, didn't she?"

Slowly, she said, "Yes." Her voice was softer, fuzzy, her focus on the big French circus poster on the wall. I had the feeling I had asked a question which she had posed to herself many times and still hadn't answered. When she started to talk, it was as if it were as much for her own benefit as mine. "She invited me to the house. Bryn was at her cabin for the weekend. Ellen told me that; later I realized she'd been reassuring me."

"Luring you?"

"No, I don't think so. She didn't know about Bryn and me, not then. It wouldn't have occurred to her how much I'd have given for an hour alone in that house. At first I thought she was just showing off her new life. She'd bought flowers, made two big bouquets. A poor family could have eaten for a week off what she paid for them. Lunch was crab salad. And wine. And a fruit torte. She was going to eat in that macabre living room. But I'll tell you the place gave me the creeps. You seen it? That confession booth thing there with the ogling Shiva." She gave her head a shake. "I told Ellen that if Bryn wanted to sit in there and contemplate confessing her sins, that was fine with me, but the place took my appetite away. I mean all it needed was pictures of martyrs at the stake."

Why had Ellen insisted on that confessional? Was she pressuring Bryn to confess? Confess what? And why would Ellen have cared at all? "So you ate in the dining room?"

"It was bad enough in the dining room, with that thing looming in the next room. Even drinking wine and eating strawberry kiwi torte didn't lift the gloom. It just made it a little eerie, like a friar would pad through any minute, refill my glass, and remind me that life is fleeting but damnation eternal. Says something about Bryn, doesn't it, that it never penetrated."

"Why would she connect it with herself?"

Fannie looked at me out of the corner of her eye, then said lamely, "It was in her living room! Anyway, when Ellen and I had almost finished the wine, she asked me to tell her about the Nationals."

"What specifically?" I leaned forward, trying not to look too eager. "You mean how things happened?"

"No, she seemed to have an idea about that—not entirely accurate, I might add. She admitted Bryn had told her some. Some she'd found out at the library. Some she'd guessed. I'm not sure how much of each, because that didn't interest her. What she wanted to know was how I felt about it then, and over the years, and now."

That was like arriving at the Pearly Gates and asking about the oysters. "Why?"

She went on as if she'd only half heard me. "It wasn't like she was just asking to let me talk—you know, that condescending 'let it all out.' She really did want to know."

Without moving head or wrist, I glanced at my watch. Six

thirty-five. I had fifteen minutes at the outside. "What did you tell her?"

Fannie leaned forward and said softly, deliberately, "That I was so shocked when I found out, I blew my dive and ended up in the hospital. That I've thought of Bryn Wiley with every crooked step I take. And that nothing would give me more pleasure than to take away the thing that matters most to her."

I must have been visibly jolted by the force of her almost whispered words.

She laughed. "That's how Ellen reacted, too. Even more so than you. But of course, I hadn't told her about Sam and me and all. And she was a bit snockered. She kept asking me if there was anything that Bryn could do to dissipate my anger—not that Bryn was offering to do *anything*."

"Maybe Bryn was agonizing over you. Maybe she told Ellen that."

"Hardly."

"Maybe Ellen was afraid you were going to run Bryn out of business."

A smile crossed her square face. "I'd like to think that. Ellen didn't intend to, but she did let me know that Bryn's got every cent tied up in her gym. It's her shrine." She scooped up the last piece of cake.

I wondered if she always ate with this much gusto or if discussing Bryn Wiley and her potential misfortunes had stimulated her gastric juices. "But the prognosis of The Girls' Team wasn't Ellen's worry. Did she say why she was so concerned?"

"You don't ask when you're both drinking. And we'd killed the bottle of wine by then. Big emotions are normal then. It didn't seem strange. And Ellen, if you'd known her . . ." Fannie laughed again, but this time it was a friend's laugh. "The whole thing ended so ridiculously. I'm leaving and we're still talking, and suddenly I realize she has no idea I'm married to the guy next door. Well, why would she? I never go to that house. Sam doesn't bother with Bootlaces. And Johnson's one of the most common names in the country. Right up there with"—she grinned at me—"Smith. So she walks over to Sam's house with me. We're standing at the top of that staircase and Ellen's still going on, all earnest-like, about how the past is over and done with no matter what the consequences and isn't it better—for me—to just put it behind me and go on. All that kind of crap. And out of nowhere this big black dog comes bounding across the lawn next door, circles into the open gate at Sam's place, into the mud, then bounds back and leaps up on Ellen and plops her on the lawn. Her new white shirt is covered in mud and grass. Ellen was agape. She looked like a cartoon character lying there. You could watch her fury rising. I just stood there until her whole face was red and then I said 'So Ellen, you going to put the past behind you with this hound?' "

"What'd she say?"

Fannie smiled again. "It took her a minute, and I won't put money on it being spontaneous or sincere, but she said, 'Yeah, the past is past. You have to put it behind you and let it be dead. Dead is dead; forget it.' Then she got up and kissed the dog on the snout." She puckered her lips and kissed the air. "And the owner, a weird old guy, just stared, like she was coming on to his dog."

"And did you ever see her again?"

The smile faded from Fannie's face. "No. I called a couple of times. Once I got her and she made excuses. I asked her if she'd told Bryn about me and if Bryn had ordered her not to talk to me. She said no. But I didn't believe her."

"What did you think?"

"That she needed her job."

Maybe Fannie Johnson was right. Maybe Ellen Waller hadn't courted her and dropped her because Fannie bored her, or because she only wanted to show off her new digs. Maybe Bryn was the culprit. Maybe, but it was too easy an answer. I signaled the waiter.

Fannie leaned back now, her eyes half closed. She breathed in softly, slowly, as if inhaling the nectar of a rose. If I had been gazing at her across the room, I would have assumed Chez

Panisse was a regular stop on the way home from a matinee or
before a reading at Black Oak Books. Or that she lived a few
blocks up the hill in a fine Maybeck house.

I looked at the empty dessert plates on our table. Fannie had
finished every morsel possible to carry from dish to mouth. I
didn't doubt that she had cared about Ellen Waller, or been hurt
by Ellen's rejection. But not enough to put her off her food.
Fannie had already shown me more levels of herself than I had
suspected. I believed she loved Sam Johnson, and that she hated
Bryn. I could understand both. But damn it, she hated Bryn too
much. It wasn't Bryn's fault that the travel agent had screwed
up, and that she had missed her plane. Sam and Fannie were
both intelligent people. Why didn't they see that they'd gone
way overboard on this one? It wasn't like Sam to scapegoat. It
made me sad to think of them clinging to this vindictiveness
because they were afraid that without it they'd have nothing to
hold on to.

I tossed a ten and a twenty on the table, told Fannie I had to
run, and ran.

CHAPTER 19

"THE JUDGE SAID NO."

"How did you let him do that? Geez, Smith." Inspector Doyle sighed mightily into the receiver. I'd probably pulled him away from dinner. Or more likely sleep. But his sigh was for more than missing fried fish or forty winks. " 'S bad, Smith."

I leaned in toward the wall. In patrol there are no private phones. There was no one here in the report room but the dusty typewriters and me. Still I felt like I was broadcasting my failure. We'd already searched the house. We couldn't keep going in because we don't approve of the furnishings. "He said I could try him tomorrow."

I could hear Doyle's breath hitting the receiver. "What about Bryn Wiley?"

"The sticking point, Inspector, was that she disappeared. 'Do you have any evidence she was kidnapped?' That's what the judge wanted to know. Well, of course, we don't have evidence. As far as I know, she just got sick of things at Ott's office—"

"She was staying with Herman Ott?" Something metal clattered to the floor. A fork Doyle had dropped in amazement?

"Ott supported her efforts to close down Sam Johnson's gym. He was driving her around delivering press releases after her

193

rally fell apart Saturday night. She couldn't stay in her own house after the murder. At least in Ott's office she had protection."

"Protection? Penicillin is what what she'd be needing there, Smith."

"Whatever," I said, feeling oddly defensive of Ott. "The point is she walked out. And when the judge heard that, he said we can't just be bursting into a citizen's house because she stepped out for the day."

"Did you tell him she was an essential witness who'd withheld evidence?"

"Of course. And that Ellen Waller, on whom we cannot find one particle of ID, lived there, too. And I reminded him that the murder took place in the driveway. And still he said no."

Doyle sighed deeper, longer. The whoosh of it drowned out the whining voice coming from the television in his living room. Doyle doesn't sigh often. He sighed when the 49ers lost the playoff game in the bitter cold of the Jersey Meadowlands, and when he heard his daughter was planning to marry an unemployed poet, and when his doctor told him he'd never be able to eat spicy foods again. Or so I'd heard. "Smith . . ." He sighed again.

I realized I was holding my breath.

"Smith, when you're working a judge, it's not just one case you're thinking about. It's the whole strategy. Like a marriage . . ." I could picture his ruddy face stiffening, reddening slightly. He was only in his fifties, but he seemed of an older generation, a benign but uncompromising generation. It had taken him well over a year to adjust to having me in Homicide, and when he did accept me, he hedged by taking me under his wing as he would a daughter. And as with his real daughter, who had married outside the appropriate category of employment, he didn't quite approve of my "in lieu of marriage" arrangement with Howard. But living together had been common in the Bay Area for thirty years. He couldn't complain. Normally, he avoided the whole topic with me.

"I *was* married, Inspector. I've seen the connubial strategy fail and succeed."

Ignoring the reference to Howard, he focused on my ex-husband. "And did you have fights before you separated?"

"Yes."

"Escalating fights?"

"Yes."

"Fights where you said things not because they were true, but just so you'd win?"

I laughed. "I tossed a pan of runny eggs on his master's thesis. He stormed out of the house. And by that time, Inspector, I wasn't living there anymore; it was *his* house."

I expected Doyle to laugh. He didn't. "So you know where you made your mistake, Smith?"

"Yeah, marrying him."

"Maybe. But I'll tell you something. The place you made your mistake was in allowing the first argument to take place. Once you admitted your standards, your observations, your evidence could be questioned—"

"Whoa! Are we talking marriage here, or dealing with Judge Redmon?"

"When you tell the judge you need a search warrant, you're saying you are the authority on what is required in this investigation. You're not asking him, you're telling him. You're saying you wouldn't be there if this search were not only essential but justifiable. Once you let him turn you down, Smith, he starts questioning your observations, your actions, your need. He goes over everything with the idea that there is some error he ought to be finding, that he's on that bench to protect the citizens from *us*. And every request for every warrant after that is harder. We've got to get a dozen through him before we're back to where we were before."

I took a breath. Judges who checked every line, who were finicky about errors, and who defended the rights of the individual were the kind Berkeleyans voted in; ones *I* voted for. Admittedly, when the shoe was on *my* foot . . . "Inspector, when I have more supporting evidence—"

"No point. Brucker will be here tomorrow. We'll go with a fresh start."

"Wait a minute!" I swallowed to keep the panic out of my voice. "There was nothing wrong with my request. If you give this to Brucker, you're telling the judge that I'm incompetent. When he thinks of this case down the road, he won't remember that he opted for more evidence, he'll remember that he denied my petition and approved one by the guy who replaced me! I'll never get another warrant through!"

I heard three exhalations of breath through the receiver, each one an eternity. During the first of those long silences I could imagine the scuttlebutt throughout the station: even Doyle didn't support her. During the second, my jaw tightened, and my hands squeezed into fists. Then Doyle said, "Okay, Smith. I'll sign you on in Homicide for one more day. If you have evidence to take to Redmon tomorrow, fine. But Tuesday, the case is Brucker's, you got that?"

"I've got it," I said with a sigh of my own. It was the best I could do. Brucker was a decent officer, but he had never marched in a demonstration in college, he'd never set foot in Cody's or Black Oak Books, and he drank coffee from a 7-Eleven when Peet's was three blocks away. For him Berkeley was just a town to be policed. Brucker would have been happy if the sidewalks where street artists sold their tie-dye and stained glass were paved over, and the Avenue turned into a four-lane road with timed lights and limited access. Brucker would work his butt off to make Berkeley crime-free; and if he had to turn it into a mall town to do it, no problem. Then he would race back to Sacramento and the criminal justice fast track.

Sam Johnson and Herman Ott would have swallowed their tongues before admitting anything to Brucker. And he'd never understand Bryn Wiley and why to Berkeleyans she was an idol. With Fannie Johnson he wouldn't have gotten inside the screen door.

And if I didn't get this case closed tomorrow, none of that would matter. While Brucker was trying to find the right path past all those closed doors, Bryn Wiley could be killed.

I only had tomorrow.

Herman Ott, however, had no time at all. I wasn't surprised he hadn't called me. I'd told him *I* would call him. I could do that. But when you have to lay on pressure, it's best to be on hand to do it.

CHAPTER 20

TELEGRAPH AVENUE ON A Sunday night looks like Berkeley's answer to Pompeii. The craftsmen whose leather belts, pressed glass panels, silver rings, and snake bracelets had filled the street in the morning are gone. But the paper plates and empty coffee cups, the bits of pizza crust and discarded packets of sugar, the crumpled smoothie containers and wadded napkins would be an anthropologist's dream. He'd find a lost tarot card, a crystal that would not bring long life or heal the bark of the tree it had fallen against. He'd dust carefully around the edges of a rough hand-thrown mug with a whiskered face on one side. And he could wrap it all in newsprint ads for adult school classes —dealing with fear of swimming, driving, or cooking for company.

Yellow streetlights gave the littered sidewalks the look of an old photograph. On Sunday night, Cal students, dejected about Monday's imminent arrival, were in the dorms or even the library, high school kids from towns over the hills had abandoned the cool life till next weekend, shoppers were home with their bounty, and even the beggars for spare change had taken their quarters and dollars to the store. Or to the dealers. As Howard would be glad to remind me, it takes only ten bucks for a dealer to spit out a rock of coke.

Even the staircase in Herman Ott's building was empty. I
charged up, panting by the time I reached the third floor, and
knocked on Ott's door. I paused for a second, knocked again.
Ott never answers the first time.

"Who?"

"Smith. Open up!"

The door creaked open and I strode in.

"Hey, whatsamatter, Smith? I said I'd talk to you. No need to
burst in here like some TV drug squad."

"You could have told me Ellen Waller engineered her meeting with Bryn Wiley at Bootlaces."

He shrugged.

I couldn't decide whether that was his normal brush-off, or a
cover for his *not* knowing about Ellen. We'd both be more comfortable with the first interpretation. "I wasted my afternoon
and a whole interview finding that out."

"From Fannie." He settled in the cracked yellow chair behind
his desk, his narrow lips pulled into the smallest of smug smiles.

I plopped on the corner of his desk, shoving together two
piles of papers in the process. "I'm going to overlook that
breach of faith—"

"Hey, I didn't—"

"And let you remind me what you promised to give me: the
background on Ellen Waller."

"Okay, Smith. Ellen Waller is an alias."

"There's a news flash. For what?"

"Don't know."

"Ott!" The man was slippery at the best of times. But with
him a promise was a commitment. I could almost see the inter-
nal tug of honor with principle vs. commitment yanking him
back and forth. "You gave me your word," I said, hoping that
would drag principle over the line.

"She didn't tell anyone her legal name."

"So how do you know 'Ellen Waller' is fake?"

"Five months ago, she worked for a friend of mine. Cleaning
house."

I resisted the urge to glance into Ott's pigsty of a bedroom. *He* had a friend who hires outside help to clean his house? "And?"

"Well, normally he would never have contacted Social Security, not before the Zoë Baird flap in Washington. And even so, he wouldn't have bothered until Ellen had been working for him for months. She started a couple of weeks before Christmas; she probably figured she wouldn't earn enough for him to report that quarter. But he'd had a couple run-ins with bureaucracies and he was tiptoeing around like the ground was on fire. So he sent a form in. And it came back a No Match."

"The number was legit, but it belonged to someone else, right?" Social Security checked automatically for transposed numbers. Ellen Waller hadn't merely made a mistake.

"Yeah."

"And so you suspect . . . ?" I suspected too, but I didn't want to lead Ott.

"The obvious, Smith. That she's a fugitive. She was smart enough to know she'd normally have four months before an employer gets word her number's a phony—the three months of the quarter and another month before Social Security's computer gets a letter out. She quit in the middle of January. As little as he paid her, he shouldn't have reported for that period either. She should have had plenty of slack. It was just a fluke he filed last year, and that she was still in town. Even so, Smith, it's not like he ran into her on the street or tried to find out about her."

"But he contacted you."

"About something else. He just tossed that in because it struck him as weird."

I nodded. I'd guessed Ellen Waller to be in her midforties. She could have been older, but the fugitive lifestyle isn't conducive to preservation of a youthful complexion. When you move fast and travel light, it's not with a valise full of cosmetics. And the stress of being ever on the watch is likely to cause wrinkles. Ellen could have been one of the remaining antiwar fugitives from the Vietnam Era. We had run her fingerprints and come up empty. So she'd never been arrested, taught school, or worked for the government. Plenty of people go through life without ever being printed. Didn't mean she hadn't committed a crime—just that she'd managed to avoid being caught. "Ott, you're not telling me anything I don't already know." Or couldn't have figured out.

"Well, Smith"—he leaned back, his straw-colored head nowhere near the top of that leather swivel chair—"I guess you're just too smart for me."

"Come on, Ott! When you agreed to find out about Ellen Waller, that meant coming up with more than I could surmise. So she's a fugitive. You've got connections who can tell you about that."

"Not ones who talk to the cops."

"Our agreement wasn't conditional on your friend's delicate principles."

"You may think you make the rules, Smith. Ain't so."

He was still sitting smug, like a canary on the best egg in fowldom. I wanted to grab his shoulders and yell: *Fine, keep silent. See how well Brucker takes that Tuesday!* But Brucker would never hear about this deal, and I would never let Ott even *think* my word to him was so valueless. Still . . . "What about Sam Johnson? He knows everybody in the movement."

"You believe him, Smith, you might as well throw the I Ching for your answer." The smugness was gone from Ott's pudgy face. He looked like his egg had just cracked. Like Sam Johnson had cracked it.

"Johnson's busy revamping a house in the hills into flats for the poor and radical."

"They better not give notice where they're living."

I smiled. "Waiting for Sam to actually get the work done, huh?"

"He'll get it done all right. Co-opt some of the young guys who think he's a mix of Machiavelli and Marx. Wear through their idealism. When he's done, you see how many flats for the poor he's got, in a house that Fannie wants for herself." Ott shoved back from the desk and spun his chair to face the window. It should have been a statement of outrage. But the chair's battered condition turned it into a slow, bumping rotation that mirrored Ott's impotence, and left him facing the airshaft window that hadn't been washed since World War Two.

Ott and Johnson should have been allies. Ott wasn't as far left as Johnson, but if Berkeley is the retirement home of the sixties, Herman Ott is rocking on the porch. He doesn't call us pigs anymore, or view anyone over thirty as untrustworthy, but he could walk into most any counterculture meeting and not worry about being tossed out.

"Ott," I said, to his back, "what happened to Sam Johnson? There was a time when he would have lit himself on fire rather than set foot in the high-priced hills. Then, suddenly, he marries a woman with a steady job and crushed ambitions, and he's buying a house up there."

Ott rotated slowly. When he was facing the desk again, he stopped and leaned heavily forward. "I never thought it would happen to any of us," he said with a sigh, "that we, too, would become burghermasters. I thought our commitment was real, that it was different. The classic delusion, right? I was a history major; you'd think I'd have known better. But what's history: the story of all men but yourself."

"Ott, you're still pure." I grinned, but I meant what I'd said.

"Who knows, Smith, maybe I'll give up caring about the guys without enough sense to stay out of your way. Maybe I'll pack it in and take over the family business."

"Which is?"

But Ott wasn't mellow enough to divulge that. Instead he pulled a stack of papers toward him and poised his finger at the edge, ready to tap the papers into line. "Sam Johnson grew up in the kind of family that's not embarrassed to admit it has a maid, and a cook. Over the years the hardships, the disappointments of the movement, wore him down, and at some point he began to yearn for a 'normal' life." He tapped absently. "I ran into him a couple years ago when he was getting fed up with the kids in the

203

movement going off half-cocked, when he was tired of spending nights in jail for no purpose. He was reconsidering. And I'll tell you, Smith, the guy was embarrassed about it. Well, hell, who wouldn't be?" His tapping finger slowed. "But you get invited to a fund-raiser in the hills and you find those people up there aren't all bigots and money grubbers. The fund-raisers are accomplishing more in one evening than your protesting does in a month. And you reconsider some more. And you like playing with their breadmaker, and clicking the mouse on their computer, and whipping down Shasta in a Miata. 'Normalcy' starts looking good. Not to worry every time a cop comes toward you looks real good. So you make a compromise here and there, and each time you block out your friends' reactions and soon you don't see the people you've affected at all, because you can't, not and go on." His finger hit the edge of the stack and papers shot across the desk. Ott made no move to corral them.

If Ott was right about Sam Johnson having abandoned his friends and his principles for the kind of life symbolized by his house on Tamalpais, what would he do to the woman who tried to dismantle it? And Fannie, who loved him, what would she do? Strange what a conventional couple the Johnsons had become, worried about their mortgage and property like the drones Sam had so scorned, ready to compromise everything because they loved each other. Soap opera, radical style? Not *The Young and the Restless*; but *The Middle-aged and the Burned Out*! In contrast to them, Bryn Wiley was much more radical, committed to her ideals, using her house merely as a place to sleep. And Ellen Waller had been the most radical of all, with neither house, nor goal, or even a "self."

I studied Ott, needing to be reassured he was talking only about Sam Johnson, not himself. Ott's sallow cheeks looked grayer and more sunken than I'd ever seen them, and his eyes seemed almost too large for his face. It took me a moment to realize they weren't squeezed in wariness as they had been every other time I'd seen him. The man just looked dismayed. "What about misleading the poor?" I asked, partly for my own reasons and partly to snap him back on track.

"Just what I asked. But you know, Smith, I don't think he even heard me." Slowly Ott shook his head.

I could see how the drive for normalcy could blinker a man. I'd known cops who quit the force and moved to the country in search of a safety and stability that in their saner moments they knew was a fantasy. Certainly, I'd dreamed of a normalcy that excluded Howard's tenants.

Still, if Ott had objected to the creation of The Heat Exchange, he had had plenty of time and ample commissions, boards, and hearings at which to air his grievances. This was, after all, Berkeley, where only one kind of erection can be attempted without a permit. Sam Johnson might be end-running the process as he rehabbed his house in the hills, but turning a floor of apartments into a gym on Telegraph Avenue was another matter entirely. You don't take housing units off the market in this town without a very convincing argument. If Ott and his fellow tenants had complained, the city would have been only too glad to hear them.

If they'd complained, the city would *still* be hearing them.

So, Ott had *not* complained.

He had stewed, but done zilch.

Why not? What had Sam Johnson promised him?

A light went on in my brain. "Ott, you supported The Heat Exchange!"

If I'd had any questions about my conclusion, Ott's expression would have cleared it up. He shrank down in the seat, his narrow shoulders drawing in protectively. I could have asked how Sam had roped him in, but knowing Ott, it was with the promise of heat for his fellow tenants. Ott was no physicist, and the chances of his ever having set foot in a gym of any kind or seen a StairMaster or computerized stationary bicycle were as great as the Nixon Museum being moved to Telegraph Avenue.

I didn't push him. I didn't say there are worse things than making a mistake out of compassion. Sympathy from a cop, Ott wouldn't want. Nor did I add that if word of this mistake got out, Herman Ott, who counted on his reputation for seeing the truth behind the camouflage and knowing everything that went on, would be the joke of the Avenue.

I had no intention of wasting my advantage on things we both already knew. I asked the question no one had come near answering. "Who was the nude runner?"

"Which one?" A hint of a smile tried out Ott's lips. "The one on Rose Walk a week ago or the press conference guy?"

"Both. Who are they? Or do I mean who is he?"

"I can't say."

"You don't know, or you won't pass on the information?"

"They're just kids passing through town, making an easy buck. Probably in Portland or Santa Cruz by now." He sat up to his full—not great—height, unlocked the desk drawer, and handed me a business card.

Rent-a-Freak. In the lower-left-hand corner was a phone number.

I picked up Ott's phone and dialed. The message said: "This is Rent-a-Freak. Freaks for every need, party, prank, personal pleasure. Leave your name and number, I'll get back to you." No name, no address.

Keeping my face impassive, I put down the phone. "So, Ott, who is it?"

Ott shrugged.

"Not good enough, Ott. You promised me background on Ellen Waller. You didn't come through. You indicate you'll tell me about my nudists and you hand me a card that leads nowhere. You made a commitment. I expect you to honor it. Find out about Ellen Waller. Do it tonight. Call me at home."

I slid off the desk and strode out the door, only banging it softly.

I was to the staircase before I let the smile cross my face. The individual runners weren't important. If I got their names they'd mean nothing to me. The guy who was running the runners was the key. There *had* been no name on the Rent-a-Freak message, but the voice on that tape was familiar. It had cracked just the way Jed Estler's had when he reported Ellen Waller's death.

CHAPTER 21

W$_{\text{HAT WERE THE CHANCES}}$ of Brucker matching the voice on the 911 tape to the one on Rent-a-Freak's answering machine? It galled me to think how much would be lost if the case were taken over by a man who hadn't met Ellen Waller, hadn't been to Chez Panisse with Fannie, or had anything but contempt for Karl Pironnen. But there was no way Doyle would keep me on once Brucker returned tomorrow. I left Doyle a terse message about Rent-a-Freak. Then I made my call-back to Candace Upton, the 5150 with the presidential problem. The phone rang eight times.

"What do you want now?" The voice was wiry, whiny. My data listed Candace Upton's age as 48, but her voice could have been ground down by six or seven decades.

"Officer Smith, Berkeley Police. I'm returning your call, Ms. Upton. What is it you'd like the police to do?"

"Keep him away from me."

"Who?"

"The President."

"How is he bothering you now?"

"He's tying up my phone. No one else can get through. I'm missing all my calls. I have business to conduct. I can't be talking

209

to him all night. He won't take no for an answer. He's the
President. He's not used to being told no."

Which showed how little she knew about politics. "Why
don't you take your phone off the hook? That'll get the point
across to him."

"I can't! I told you, I've got business to conduct."

"What kind of business?"

"Important business."

"Right. Well, Ms. Upton, here's what's going to work. Line
up all your business calls, and as soon as I hang up, start making them. Get the second number ready before you're through
with the first call, and the third ready before you're off the line
with the second, and so on, so you don't let any time lapse
between calls. You follow?"

"Of course I follow. But it's not going to work. He'll still
push his way in, even if there's just a second. I know him."

"Well, I'll call him and keep him on the line for half an hour.
You can finish your calls by then, can't you?"

"Oh, no. It'll take a full hour. It always does."

"Okay, an hour." I could offer her two hours, even a whole
day: Ah the joy of magnanimity. "You ready? Okay, I'm poised
to dial. Hang up."

"Wait, don't you want his number?"

"Ms. Upton, this is the Berkeley Police Department. Do you
think you're the first person to call us complaining about the
President? We have the numbers for all the former Presidents."
I hung up and headed to Jed Estler's room on Tamalpais.

But as I neared Andronico's market, I realized just how long it
had been since I'd eaten. *Not* eating chocolate decadence had
hardly ameliorated the problem. I headed inside to make up to
myself for the chocolate cake sacrifice. Howard had accused me
of being addicted. Maybe he was right. A benign little addiction.
A harmless vice. Everybody has some small addiction, some
small shrine that makes their life better . . . at least when they
can get to it. How many more days was it till the end of the
month? An infinity. But when that day came . . . I'd have

Chocolate Shower ice cream for breakfast. In bed. With Howard sitting next to me, empty mouthed. I'd eat it with a tablespoon and savor every bitter chocolate flake in every mound of
milky chocolate.

I made an unfamiliar right turn toward the fruit and vegetable
section. Surely I had been here before; I couldn't believe . . .
But it didn't look familiar. All that green stuff. All those weird
fruits they didn't have in Jersey when I was growing up, fruits
with spikes, fruits with fur, fruits in colors you don't eat.

Behind the pile of fruits was a dazed woman with short dark
hair sticking out on the sides. It took a moment to realize there
was a mirror behind the fruit and the woman I was looking at
was me. The hair wasn't right, the face was shaped wrong, and
even the expression looked funny. The face in the mirror's was a
stranger's.

It shocked me more than I would have expected. I turned
away quickly, from the face, and the cold, empty feeling it
brought up, grabbed a couple of bananas, and ran to the check-
out line.

The case! Think about the case. Even if Brucker had checked the
911 tape, I silently informed the gum and candy display, he
wouldn't have made the connection to Jed Estler, because he
wouldn't have had the Rent-a-Freak card to begin with, because
Brucker was the last person on the face of Berkeley that Herman
Ott would confide in!

I wouldn't confide in Brucker. If the case were transferred to
Eggs or Jackson, I'd have no problem telling them I got my lead
from "a source they weren't privy to." They'd know who I
meant, but they would also know not to ask more. And if they
kidded me about the unnamed Ott, it would be with a smile at
the eccentricities of our city. Brucker . . . his ideal Berkeley
would be as aesthetically appealing as the county autopsy room
—all metal so it can be hosed down. He'd love to spray away
bacteria like Herman Ott.

By the time I was in the car and turning onto Tamalpais, I
realized I was almost glad it was Brucker to whom the case

would be transferred. I'd never be able to work up this much indignation for Eggs or Jackson. I could imagine calling Howard about it in the morning. Howard would agree in spades. He'd be more furious than I was. He'd . . .

In fact, maybe I wouldn't call Howard. I might forget this, but Howard would hold it like a heavy rock in his stomach. It's one thing to get over a slight to yourself, but it's so much harder to forgive a dismissal of someone you love.

I parked in front of Sam Johnson's house and called the dispatcher to let her know—1097—I'd arrived at the scene. Then I walked back to Bryn Wiley's. The dining room light that had been on last night was still on. Mail stuck out of the box at the foot of the steps. Otherwise nothing had changed. Patrol had checked it every couple of hours. I rang the bell without expecting an answer and stood listening to its echo, picturing the sound ricocheting off the walls and through the skeleton of the confessional bench. It was nine thirty; chances were if she was coming back there tonight, she'd already be inside.

Slowly I walked down the steps, across the damp dirt driveway where Ellen had been shot. It made sense that she would have been mistaken for Bryn here. And yet . . . I wondered.

The fog had rolled in and the streetlights lit it from underneath. It hung like a high flaccid tent over Bryn Wiley's empty house, Johnson's forbidding shell, the black stand of redwoods across the street, and Karl Pironnen's dirt-dimmed windows next door. Was Johnson here? He could be creeping around the crawl space or asleep on the cot under his shelf of military strategy texts in that back living room. Or setting up the next great—final—move in the game he and Fannie lusted over?

I was tempted to check out the house. But there were no new questions for Sam Johnson. And I had so little time left. Still, as I walked down the cement staircase, noting once again the damp slippery leaves on its steep, shallow, irregular steps, I checked Johnson's window for flickers of light within. If Sam was in there, he was hiding his light under a bushel.

I pulled my tweed jacket tighter around me. For the first time since I'd been transferred from plain clothes and back, I wished I was wearing a uniform. Or at least, that I had my big flashlight to shine on the steps as I made my way down. The night wind gusted up the stairs, ruffling my short hair, flicking the collar of the cotton turtleneck that was now too light. Goose bumps covered my arms and the cold wrapped around my spine. In the dark I was virtually feeling along the wood fence for the door. It would be embarrassing to go out on disability from splinters.

The door, when I found it, was one of those that opened by pulling a string you have to feel around for on the back. But when I opened it, it was like going from midnight to noon. The wind stopped within the walls of the protected yard. Jed Estler's manicured lawn stood perkily in the beams from crossing lights. The white plastic lawn chair looked like he might bound out any minute, lather himself in suntan lotion, and plop on it. I could imagine him sprawled there, reflector to face, beer at hand, as he hatched the various scenarios for Rent-a-Freak, a minor league middle-of-the-road Sam Johnson.

Or could I? The truth was I could imagine *myself* creating the hit-and-run farces. I could see myself living Estler's life in the small white Sheetrocked room, with the very part-time job of caring for Karl Pironnen and the dogs, knowing that he could move on anytime, that the road unfurled before him and this was merely a rest stop. It was one of the Berkeley archetypes, where the season is forever spring, the year forever the one after college.

Inside his room the lights were off. No muted sound of music or TV chatter came through the door. Without much hope I knocked. It had been only last night that I'd stood inside there watching him move around like a windup toy, bitch about the cold in his little Sheetrocked room, and demand "Omigod, you don't think that I did that to her?" And when I'd ordered him to take the towel off his head, had he known I'd figured him for the bald nudist? Had he laughed himself silly after I left?

Estler seemed too flighty to concentrate on anything, or anyone. But he'd quoted Karl Pironnen word for word: "If you throw the pebble, you should feel the splash," and he hadn't laughed about that. As with Sam and Fannie, there seemed to be a bond between the two utterly different characters. Jed might move on, but I doubted it would be with the ease of scuttling a temp job. Jed earned only his rent, so his responsibilities to Karl couldn't be much more than dog walking and runs to the grocery. Certainly not cleaning! That was about all that seemed feasible for the antsy kid who had changed position on the bed three times in as many sentences.

I couldn't imagine how he'd pulled himself together to organize Rent-a-Freak. The events, sure, but getting the business cards printed, distributing them, coordinating the actors with the events; Jed Estler wouldn't make it through the second event.

But it was definitely his voice on the machine. I knocked again. No answer.

I wrote *Call me as soon as you get in* on my card, added my beeper number, and stuck the card in his door. Then I made my way through the sea of grass beside the house to the front. It wasn't so unusual, the arrangement Karl Pironnen and Jed Estler had; two men marking time at different eras of their lives. Going nowhere, Brucker would say. But in Berkeleyese, they were just doing their thing.

Maybe contrasting myself with Brucker had nudged me into the more-Berkeley-than-cop mode. I emerged from the underbrush into the front yard and spotted Ocean, the shepherd-springer mix. His thick gray and brown fur was flecked with leaves and twigs and bits of grass, and he ran a zigzagged trail of all-consuming smells. I gave his rump a rub as he bustled past, and grinned at Karl Pironnen as Nora, the Dane-setter, trotted up and waited for a scratch. "The queen, huh?"

A smile played on his thin lips. "She's got all the moves."

It took me a moment to make the connection between the regal aloofness of the tall, sleek black dog to the chess piece. "And Pablo, he's your protector, huh?"

Pironnen patted the nondescript brown dog who stood so

close to his owner's baggy brown chinos he could have been part of the fabric.

"I've heard some rescued dogs seem to understand what you've saved them from. And they never get over their gratitude."

Pironnen smiled, pulling the pi dog against his leg and scratching his side. "He knows he'll always be safe with me."

I gave the gray dog another scratch and stood a moment watching tall, lean, gray-haired Karl Pironnen bending over the shivering Pablo. Pablo would probably quiver nervously for the rest of his life, even if he could keep Pironnen in view every minute. I pushed away the question of what trauma had left him that way. I dealt enough with people's misery; I didn't have to imagine dogs'. As Karl Pironnen stood up, I could almost see his resemblance to his pet, down to the sharp features and the oh-so-hesitant trust.

I followed the other dogs to the door. "I'm Jill Smith," I said. "From last night."

He opened the door and let the dogs jostle in.

"Is Jed around? Could he be inside?"

"Could be." Holding the door, he looked at me questioningly. Pironnen was a relic of a more gracious era. Inside, I'd be his guest. He wouldn't want to be rude. Brucker wouldn't understand that either. To him Karl Pironnen would be just another Berkeley weirdo.

But, I thought as I walked into the hair-carpeted room, understanding Pironnen cut two ways. I could see how Jed Estler felt defensive about him. I was feeling a bit protective myself.

The dogs circled around the downstairs room stirring up enough dust and dirt for the Indianapolis 500. "Jed's not here. If he was upstairs, they'd be up there checking in with him."

Quickly I asked, "Is he out on one of the Rent-a-Freak things?"

If Pironnen was surprised I knew about Rent-a-Freak, he gave no sign. "Could be."

I smiled. "I'll bet he has a ball planning them."

But that was beyond his sphere of interest. Without the dogs in reach, he'd stiffened back into himself. I followed him into the kitchen and stood while he poured kibble into three bowls and topped it with scoops of tuna, dripping the oil over the kibble. The dogs crowded around him, stretching their heads up toward the counter. He nudged them away as he lowered the bowls to the floor and ordered affectionately, and utterly ineffectively, "Back off, you pigs!"

It always amazes me how mealtime bares the souls of animals. The fear of loss overwhelms every moment of camaraderie among dogs who've lived their lives together. They can't trust "their" person to protect them. Once activated, the salivary glands seem to draw them beneath the level of civilization back to the wild.

Pironnen carried the nearly empty kibble bag across the kitchen and glanced into the pantry before putting it down. "Should have more." It was as close to a grumble as I could imagine him coming.

"Organization's not Jed's strong suit," I said.

"I'll have to remind him. Dogs don't wait for breakfast." He shook a kettle coated with fur and grease and, finding it full, turned on the burner under it. "You want tea?"

"That'd be nice." Great, actually. In interviews, you get ten times more from a man who is taking tea with you.

As he extricated two mugs, stained brown inside, I didn't allow myself to think about bacteria. Nor did I look too closely at the wooden chair before I sat. "Jed doesn't do the day-to-day work for Rent-a-Freak, does he? I mean the mailings and billings and dull stuff like that."

"Umm."

"I just can't picture him, well, staying *still* long enough to keep a financial log, or thinking to call and remind the players the day before they had to go on. Can you?" I was hedging so much to blend into his consciousness I was almost not asking at all.

"Oh no, she did that."

"She?"

"Ellen."

"Of course." I smiled, warmed with an unexpected flush of relief. It pleased me to think that Ellen's life wasn't all sneaking around to ingratiate herself with Bryn. I liked the picture of Ellen and Jed sitting cross-legged on either end of his bed downstairs hatching guerrilla theater. I could see Jed jumping off the bed to pace around and plopping himself back on, while Ellen sat with that wry grin on her wide mouth, flicking in ideas like water droplets to sizzle on a fire. And if Rent-a-Freak made any money, running it would be the perfect job for a fugitive— no social security number, no taxes withheld, in fact no one but Jed to know she was involved at all. "Did Ellen tell you about that on your drives to the vet or the bank?" I asked as Pironnen sat down and slid a cup across to me.

"No."

You can't win them all. "What did she talk about?" I lifted the cup of plain black tea and forced myself to sip.

He held his cup near his mouth, breathing in the fragrant steam, then slowly, carefully, as if each movement were a project in itself, he brought it to his lips and took one quick slurp. The dogs had finished eating and lay on the floor around him; Pablo, the protective one, was stationed between his master and me. Pironnen reached down and gave each one an affectionate scratch.

I almost had to bite my lip to keep from repeating my question, embellishing it with suggestions. I took another sip of tea, using it to wash down a hair that had gotten in my mouth.

"Ellen talked about being invisible," he said as if there had been no gap of time since I'd asked.

I looked away to cover my excitement. "Why invisible?"

"She knew I wouldn't be frightened; I'd understand. If I could be really invisible, I would. Saves hassle."

"You've gotten it pretty close."

He nodded.

"But Ellen didn't *choose* to become invisible, did she?"

"No. She had to. Hard, she said. Moving every three or four months, more if people are nosy. No forwarding address, ever. Friends she missed, she'd never see again. She said"—he lifted the cup and took a quicker drink—"her parents must think she died. And of course, she did."

"You mean years ago."

He looked up at me and nodded as if I'd gotten the point. "She lost herself in one of the moves."

I nodded back, imagining Ellen Waller's life, abandoning cities and friends, changing identities every couple of months, answering to a new name, ever alert so she didn't miss that name when it was called, so she didn't draw attention to herself. She'd have been alone in strange cities, unable even to swim if she was a swimmer, or to work out if she had belonged to a gym before; she must have known those were the places detectives on her trail would target. She'd have looked in the mirror and seen clothes that weren't "her," her hair a different color or an unfamiliar style. And the more she felt at home in a place, the more she clicked with a friend, the more tantalizing she found a lover, the harder it would have been to move on. She must have learned that lesson over and over. She'd come home from the kind of manual job she could get without references, with muscles she'd never given a thought to, now aching. And after a while those muscles would toughen, they'd pull more firmly on her bones, they'd alter her stance, broaden her shoulders, shift the hang of her arms. Her body would change. And whoever Ellen Waller had been would indeed have been lost in the moves.

My chest felt cold and empty. My hand stiffened on the tea mug. I don't know that I could have moved it even if I had wanted to.

Moments passed, and then suddenly, I realized the chair slats were biting into my back, my feet were pressed against the floor, the mug was burning my fingers. "Ellen must have really trusted you to reveal herself."

Pironnen wasn't moving; he was watching me like a scientist

observing the contents of a petri dish. I had that odd sense that he could see my thoughts—you do with some people on the edge—and that he knew I had experienced a flash of what Ellen had lived. Or in a way, what he had lived.

"Come," he said, standing up.

I followed him through the swinging door that led from the kitchen to the entry hall. The dogs threaded between us, Nora, the setter, bounding eagerly to the front door. When Pironnen started up the stairs, Pablo, the pi dog, moved in behind, keeping me at a distance, as if giving his owner time to reconsider. I wondered how long it had been since Pironnen had taken anyone other than Jed Estler to the second floor. Nora bounded past me, kicking up dust and hair. Behind Pironnen's back I covered my nose.

The house was a cube and the top of the staircase emerged in the middle of the south side. Across the dark wood landing was the bathroom, probably original to the house, pre-Depression. At the rear of the house, two stained oak doors stood open to two small rooms. One was a bedroom with a single bed, with the sheets and blankets pulled up over the pillow, closer to madeup than I would have guessed for Pironnen. The other must once have been an office—file cabinet, desk with phone, and now nothing else but the ubiquitous dust and hair. The floor was covered with three amoebalike dog beds. The life the rooms revealed was bare of luxuries, or interest. It was what I would have expected.

I noted all this in quick glances. Pironnen walked to the front, to the entrance to the master bedroom. The door was closed. He waited until I was beside him, stared down at me with that same wary expression, as if reassessing his decision, then he turned the knob and let the door swing open.

The room wasn't clean—nothing could be clean here—but otherwise it looked like a normal room in a normal house. It was easily twice the size of either of the others, extending across the entire front of the house. A double bed—just box springs and mattress—held a faded red and blue plaid spread. The paperback book jackets, too, had faded, witness to the movement of the sun from season to season, year to year. Between the windows was a stereo and tape deck, and at the far end sat a Danish modern love seat, a scratched oak coffee table holding an opened envelope, a knobby black orb the size of a half dollar, and a rumpled Penn State T-shirt. It could have been the room of any guy a year or two out of college. "Your brother's room?"

Pironnen nodded and walked over to the love seat, hung up a navy blazer that had been sprawled over a corner, and sat down.

When I hesitated, he said, "It's not a shrine. I didn't leave it as it was the day Dan died. That's not the day I want to remember. You can sit here; it's still just furniture."

I sat next to him on the love seat. But of course, it wasn't just any room, it *was* a shrine.

Pironnen picked up a Penn State T-shirt that Dan could have dropped on the floor there last night, or two and a half decades ago. He held it between thumb and fingers with exquisite care. Touching without touching. "I come in here to be with Dan. To bring him alive from my memory. I left the room unchanged for a year after he died. One day I realized that nothing I saw made me *feel* anything anymore. So, I put away the clothes Dan left out. I cleaned the place up. Then I tossed a sweater he wore a lot on the sofa, and changed the book he was reading. In a few days I changed things again, just like he'd have done." He wasn't looking at me—he was staring into infinity—but I could read in the tenseness of his face how essential it was to him that I truly understand what he was maintaining here.

"Like he might come in any moment?" I waited until he nodded, then asked, "What do you think of in here?"

"Think of? Nothing. Sometimes incidents I'd forgotten for thirty years pop up. But mostly nothing. I just feel like . . ."

"I know." He meant how the house feels different when someone else is home. Even if I'm sitting cross-legged on the bed reading the paper on one of those fogged-in gray mornings, if Howard is downstairs spackling, the air is charged. And with Pironnen's brother, the outgoing one, the one who made Karl brave enough to go to the chess tournaments—that charge would be stronger, hold longer, and its light would cut through the gray of his reclusive brother's soul.

Pironnen continued to look out into space. "When Dan died, it was such a shock. He was the younger brother. I never thought he'd *die*. He was so good at things, made friends so easily, he bought this house as easily as he'd pick up a newspaper. Life was the Southern Pacific tracks and he was the San Francisco Zephyr. But he did die. And then"—he swallowed—"he was gone. He ceased to exist. He wasn't married. His friends had other friends."

I nodded. Pironnen didn't react, but I sensed that he felt me listening.

"Dan only exists in here now. If it weren't for this room, he wouldn't exist at all." Pironnen turned to face me. "The neighbors think I've gone wacko here alone with the dogs all these years. They cross the street when they see me. Some try to chat, and then they're *sure* I'm crazy. I never had much chat, even when Dan was alive. He was the talker. I just followed along. Now I can't. But I'm not crazy."

"No."

"Dan was twenty-five when he died. Made no mark, as they say, anywhere. If I forget him"—he looked up, his face white with intensity, hands quivering on Dan's T-shirt—"he'll be rubbed out, erased. Nothing left of those years but an old hermit in a dirty house with dogs."

I wanted to contradict him, comfort him, tell him no one exhales without affecting everyone who breathes. But that was all too amorphous even for me, and any view of life and death I had would be an insult to a man who had spent the last twenty years of his life as keeper of the flame.

I waited until he dropped his gaze and shifted his legs, then said, "After Dan died, what did you do?"

"Nothing. Literally. It was like I was wrapped in rolls of cotton. I couldn't move. Everything was awkward, hard, worthless." A sad smile flickered and died. "They say I was depressed.

Depressed is so much better than I was. I didn't tell them that. I just filled the prescriptions I was given, took the medication home, and flushed it down the toilet."

"But you're not still wrapped in cotton. What happened?" Even as I spoke, I suspected the answer.

"I saw Adam's picture in the paper."

Adam. I smiled. "What kind of dog was he?"

"A mutt. They would have gassed him the next day."

The door to Dan's room was open, but the dogs hadn't followed us in. They came from a different era in Pironnen's life, and they seemed to know it. I sat there, feeling like I'd been transported back twenty years in time. Outside, the fog had grown dense and blocked the view from the windows. Like Pironnen had been blocked after his brother's death. When Dan died, he died.

Or perhaps he merely ceased contributing the way he had before. I said, "You keep alive someone you loved by honoring his memory. You save animals who would be killed for no reason and you give them lives most dogs would envy. And you play a mean game of chess. You could do worse."

He didn't say anything, just rested his hands on the old cloth of the T-shirt.

I had thought before that I understood Jed Estler's protectiveness. Now I realized that I'd just skimmed the surface. Being allowed into this room was like stepping into Karl Pironnen's soul. I shrank back from it as if it were a gift I couldn't swear to honor, and I felt a wave of fear for him. He never should have trusted *me*, never should have allowed a virtual stranger to touch his soul. Perhaps he had been so isolated that he couldn't judge people, and so mistook the facade of interest for trustworthiness. I looked around the room and felt the same eerie sense I had felt standing before Bryn Wiley's confessional bench. "Karl," I said softly, "have you brought anyone else here?"

He nodded.

"Ellen?"

"Yes."

On a hunch I said, "You don't feel guilty about Ellen, do you?"

"No!" he snapped, flinging the T-shirt away.

I must have jumped. He stared directly at me, insisting, "They're not the same. If I had been a normal man, Dan would have been home and I would have been at the bank like I should have been. But I never asked Ellen to take me places. She insisted, like it mattered to her."

I made my face blank, so it wouldn't reveal my reaction. The confessional bench was the one thing Ellen had chosen and forced into Bryn's house. Maybe Bryn was not the intended penitent. Maybe Ellen had been quietly obsessed with making amends for something in that hidden life of hers. Was part of her penance the trips to the vet and the bank with a dusty hermit and his dogs?

"Karl," I said, realizing the import of my question, "did you invite Ellen up here like you did with me? Or did she ask you to bring her here?"

The air seemed stiller than ever. It was almost as if the air of the past hardened around him, not permitting him to answer. "I mentioned I had Dan's things. She asked . . . three times . . . before I let her in."

I could almost see her genuflecting at the door and kneeling before the shrine of the room. Dan's room. Dan who had died in the Golden State robbery. The driver of the getaway car was Mary *Something* Nash. Mary *Ellen* Nash. "And she confessed?"

His body tightened. Now the air seemed to explode with the energy Karl had spent two decades holding in. "She said she was sorry. She said they shouldn't have picked Golden State Savings. They didn't mean for anyone to die; they couldn't know Dan would step wrong off the curb and crack his skull. She would never have done it if she had known he would die. She said she had regretted it every day since. There was never a day she didn't think of Dan. She gave me this." He picked up the dried black ball.

"What is it?"

"An orange. Dan's. He was holding it. It flew out of his hand when he fell. She had the car door open, waiting. It landed in the car."

"And she saved it all these years?" I said, amazed.

He nodded. I could tell the gesture seemed not at all bizarre to him. It was the only offering worthy of the shrine. Suddenly I felt the enormity of Pironnen's loss with Ellen's death. The only person who had shared the intensity of his obsession was dead. The chance to talk about Dan to someone who cared was snatched away. The promise of bringing Dan to life anew had been killed, shot down.

"Coming face to face with a woman involved in Dan's death; did you want to kill her?" I asked, careful not to change the tone of my voice.

He shook his head. "Revenge is a fool's game. I'm a chess player; I know that. I don't want the case all over the papers again, photographers taking my picture, asking about Dan, asking about her. Every time I'd turn on the news, they'd be interviewing her. I don't want that. What I want is what I have here."

I knew the answer to the next question before I spoke, but I had to ask. "Did you think of turning her in? The law—"

"The law! Society! Justice? Why should I care about all that? Dan never mattered to them. The columnist back then referred to Dan as 'just some poor schmuck in the wrong place.' He didn't even call him by name." He stood up, clasping the desiccated piece of fruit so hard I was afraid it would break in his hand. Anyone else would have thrown me out of the room. But he only closed me out of himself. His tense stare told me I had stomped on his trust. And the next time he was tempted to trust, he would be more cautious for having made a mistake with me.

All I could do was leave him alone in the room. "I'll find my own way down," I offered as I left.

The dogs circled me at a distance as I made my way down the stairs. At the door they stood three abreast behind me. I walked slowly to my car.

Mary Ellen Nash.

She'd been deep enough in the antiwar movement to rob a bank, or at least to be the driver (and back then, radicals wouldn't have let a woman do anything more than that). She had to know Sam Johnson, or at least know of him. But she probably hadn't suspected he was Fannie's husband. No wonder she'd steered clear of Fannie after that revelation.

Mary Ellen—*Ellen*—had altered her appearance to attract Bryn Wiley's attention, to get access to Karl Pironnen. Bryn was a fluke. If Bryn hadn't existed, perhaps Ellen would have managed to get Jed's job, or have gotten access to Karl through Jed and Rent-a-Freak. Ellen Waller was a determined woman; somehow she'd have made her way into Dan Pironnen's room.

And once she'd accomplished her reconciliation with Karl, once she completed her penance, who did that unsettle? Did it free her to goad Bryn about her past? Or during all those years underground, had she learned things about Sam Johnson he and Fannie had no intention of revealing?

CHAPTER 22

THERE WERE BODIES ON Howard's couch when I made my way through the barely lit living room. The tenants had come home to roost for another week. I was so exhausted I just trudged upstairs and flopped into bed.

And lay there for what seemed an hour but was probably only fifteen minutes, my arms and legs turned to cement, my mind abuzz with thoughts of the case. At ten to two I turned the light on, picked up the phone, and dialed the Fresno Police Department.

By the time Howard called back, I had gone down to the kitchen—startling the sofa contingent into a flurry of gasps and a flutter of cloth—started water for hot cocoa, caught myself, and poured a glass of merlot instead, and settled back under the covers.

"Jill?"

"Ah. You. I just passed the scene on the sofa. It was like when your Maserati's been in the shop so long a clunker spewing fumes begins to look like a great ride. You've been gone too long. And your junk food bet is driving me to drink." I could picture the grin settling on Howard's face. He'd be in plain clothes, jeans and maybe the forest green turtleneck I'd given

him for his birthday. He did look fine in jeans. His brown
bomber jacket would be hanging over the back of his chair. He'd
be slouched in the chair, his long legs stretched out in front.
Maybe he'd be wearing a billed cap, and beneath it, those red
curls of his would peek out.

"Miss you, too. Think of you in the wild Fresnan nights."

"How are those wild nights?"

Howard laughed. "I'll tell you, you don't need to worry about
overestimating the intelligence of the local drug dealer. I
targeted this guy, Lyle. Lyle fancies himself quite the slick operator. He's suspicious. So what does he do when I drive up to
make my buy? He says to me, 'Hey, man, you a cop?' Like I'm
going to pull out my badge, confess, and skulk away!"

"He's leaning in your van, right? You're getting this all on
camera?"

"Yeah. Got him full face. So I say, 'Forget it. You insult me,
I'm outa here.' I shift into first. Lyle reconsiders. He didn't
really mean it, he says, 'but like I gotta be careful, you know,
man?' "

" 'You gotta solve your problems before you deal with me,' I
say. So we go back and forth and I end up telling him I'm not
dealing with him, not here, not on this street corner. We've
been here too long, and now I've got my own suspicions that
maybe *he's* the narc setting *me* up. So then what do you think he
does, Jill?"

"What?"

"He tells me to meet him in an hour—at his apartment! I
mean, at that point I really did wonder if ol' Lyle was a narc and
we'd gotten our lines crossed with the feds. But no, Lyle was just
a dummy. A brain may be a terrible thing to waste, but Lyle's in
no danger."

I laughed. God, it was good to hear Howard enjoying himself.
I took a swallow of wine and slid over toward Howard's side of
the bed. Suddenly I ached for his skin against my skin, the ruffle
of the soft hairs on his chest, the mustache stubble that scraped
my mouth when he kissed me—and rasped against my finger

when I ran it across there afterward to remind him he might have shaved before. (Once he'd brought a windup razor to bed.) I yearned to feel his long arms pressing me against him, to feel so intensely that I lost myself in the sensation, and for a wonderful moment I just existed beyond the separation of thoughts.

Some lovers smoke; we talk shop, the nicotine of the cop world. I snuggled against Howard's pillow, with telephone in hand, half pretending I wasn't alone. Pretending Ellen Waller would not be merely a footnote to a failed bank robbery in which a bystander happened to die.

"So how's your one eighty-seven, Jill?"

"Hit the wall."

"Umm?"

"I can't remember how much I told you about the case—Bryn Wiley and her lookalike, Ellen Waller, who she said was her cousin but turned out to be a stranger. She shared a general physical similarity with Bryn, and she dyed and styled her hair and bought clothes to look like her. She did all that not to get closer to Bryn, but to get into Bryn's house, so she could get nearer to Karl Pironnen, the hermit with the dogs. Wait, Howard, there's more. She was the driver in the Golden State S and L robbery twenty-five years ago and the guy who jumped out of the way when the robbers ran for the car—the guy who stumbled off the curb and died—was Pironnen's brother."

"And she *wanted* to get closer to Pironnen? Sounds like she's a match for my man Lyle." Howard chuckled. If he'd been there, he'd have been draping his arm over my shoulder, pulling me against him.

I would be struggling not to lose my train of thought—which, in fact, I was from the *thought* of what might have been distracting me. "Ellen was really committed, Howard. Before she glommed on to Bryn, she had buddied up to Fannie Johnson, who, she assumed, was married to some klutz trying to rehab his decrepit house on Tamalpais. I don't know just how Ellen was intending to get an entrée from Sam Johnson—"

"This Ellen is hiding out from an antiwar heist and maybe a

felony murder rap, and she decides to cozy up to Sam Johnson's wife? Lyle may be too bright for her."

"Johnson's a very common name. Probably Fannie never mentioned his first name. Anyway, once Ellen realized who he was, she dropped Fannie pronto. But the point is, Howard, that she did all of this so she could get to Pironnen and tell him she's sorry. The woman even saved the desiccated orange his brother dropped when he fell; she gave it to Pironnen."

Howard chortled. "God, I miss Berkeley!"

"Okay, sure, it sounds ridiculous. But if you'd seen Pironnen . . . His brother's room is a shrine. It's all the guy's got, Howard. Sorry. I don't mean to drive you down Eccentricity Road, then ticket you for laughing. Anyway, that's where I am: I finally discover who Ellen Waller–Jane Doe is. She's a fugitive with reason to be worried about a felony murder rap. It's a gray area, with him not being touched but stumbling and hitting his head. One of the robbers died before he ever got picked up and the other went up for a double murder one before they connected him to the Golden State case. So the case never really figured in a trial. But the possibility of felony murder was enough to keep Ellen under cover for a quarter of a century. She spent her whole adult life hiding out."

"Sad." For Howard, who cherished home and stability, the idea of being on the run was hell. If he were here now he'd be glancing around the room—his room—at the walls he'd lovingly covered with three coats of forest green, and the trim so white it shone. Unconsciously, he'd pull the comforter higher up on his bare chest, and cup his hand around my arm. I'd rest a hand on his thigh, trail my fingers up the soft inner flesh . . .

I took another sip of the merlot. "But here's the thing, Howard. So she gets to Pironnen. She apologizes. He says he's not into revenge; he doesn't care about the criminal justice system. She's confessed, she's absolved, she's ready to go on with her life. And then, *then*, she gets killed. Before, when she had this big secret, I could've understood her getting killed—or killing.

But now her cupboard's empty. She's got nothing to protect. No one's got reason to kill her. And she's gone."

"No one?"

"Unless now that she's pure, she's after someone else's secret. Or unless the shot really was meant for Bryn."

"You ran a background on Ellen with her real identity?"

"Yeah. Then I made a few calls. You want to guess?"

"Catholic school?"

"Good try. Well, *average* try, what with the confessional bench and all. But she was the only child of 'free thinkers.' Parents were artists of sorts, but with money—"

"Landed eccentrics? As opposed to . . . fifty-one fifties."

"Right. The Nashes lived in the same town for a couple of generations. They were the accepted educated eccentrics, you know, sort of in the British sense?"

"Umm. Lived in the ancestral manse, behind their name trees."

"Name trees?" That was something we didn't have in Jersey.

"A tree their parents planted when they were born. You know —in their name? I went to school with a guy, Tim, who had a name tree. It was like losing a friend when it fell down in a storm."

I smiled. At gut level, I would never really understand Howard's need for his house and the normalcy it represented, but its hold on him was almost mythic. And for Ellen, whose family must have had its own eccentric brand of normalcy, albeit different from the community, the lure of being normal *and* accepted by the community must have grown with each year she spent hiding out. And now she'd made peace. With no one committed to pursuing her (the statute of limitations on the S and L heist had run out long ago and no one had filed a warrant for her before that) chances were she could have gotten off with little or no time for the felony murder, and gone on to live openly in say, Normal, Pennsylvania. "Howard," I said, "there's got to be something I'm missing."

"Ahhh. Need some possibilities, huh? Well, you've come to

the right man. Me, I like the Rent-a-Freak angle. Maybe they really freaked someone out. Or Fannie and Sam, maybe they took offense at her snub. Or in all those years in the underground she'd heard something about Sam, and they panicked at the idea of her passing it on to Bryn."

"Like?"

"Like Sam was involved in a murder of his own. Or maybe the key is in a slip Fannie made, like there was something fishy about the title to the house, or their mortgage, or well . . . something. I'll tell you, Jill, if I'd put as much work into my house as Sam has, and then someone I hated tried to take it away from me . . ."

I laughed. "Howard, you have put in that much work." But it sent a chill down my back. After all, the person who could take Howard's house away was me. I pulled the comforter—*his* comforter—up to my neck, leaving it loose over my left shoulder like it was when he was next to me. "So when'll you be home?"

"Might be the end of the week. More likely as early as Tuesday."

"Tuesday," I said, brightening. "I'll keep your side of the bed warm."

"So, Jill," he said before I could hang up, "how is life without chocolate?"

"About like sex with your hands in your pockets—your *back* pockets."

CHAPTER 23

Monday MORNING WAS THE beginning of a typical Berkeley day. The wind off the Bay flowed through the branches of the jacaranda, rustling leaves against my window. Above it the Pacific fog sat thin and dull. I had slept fitfully again, waking up every hour or so to worry about how few hours I had left on this case. Now, at 7 A.M. I was up too early for what I needed to do. The only thing I could manage at that hour was the warrant request. And I wasn't about to tackle that without a trip to Peet's. By seven thirty I was sipping an alto doppio latte and was halfway through an oatmeal scone from the Walnut Square Bakery when it occurred to me that I hadn't bemoaned the lack of a chocolate doughnut. I chewed slowly, tasting the nutty accent of the oatmeal, the sweet of the raisins, the vague saltiness. Were my taste buds reincarnating into *healthy* buds? If this kept up, I'd be ordering tofu in public.

I got another latte, drove to the station, and spent an hour on the report. Herman Ott hadn't returned my call. Big surprise.

I dialed Raksen in the lab. "Any word from the FBI on the fingerprints from Bryn Wiley's car?"

Raksen, a man not given to humor about his work, laughed. "Smith, you know what your chances are of getting word back in a day and a half from the feebies?"

233

I didn't ask. "Call me."

I had barely pushed the Off button when the phone rang again.

"Smith?" It was Inspector Doyle.

"Morning."

"How's it going?"

I summarized my interview with Fannie Johnson, told him about the lead on the nudist and Rent-a-Freak, not mentioning Ott's name but emphasizing that the information was from a personal source. Even though I hadn't come up with Jed Estler, I explained, Karl Pironnen had admitted that Estler had worked not alone but with Ellen Waller. "And Inspector, you probably know by now that Ellen Waller was actually Mary Ellen Nash, the Golden State S and L driver."

"Good work, Smith."

"Thanks. So, I stay on the case?"

"That's what I was calling about."

I knew that tone. I was holding my breath.

"Brucker's got a confession on his two forty-five."

Assault with a deadly weapon.

"He's finishing up the essentials now. He'll be ready for the Wiley case after lunch."

"Inspector, I haven't gotten the search warrant yet."

"Brucker can do that."

"He won't know what he's looking for in Wiley's house."

"Then, Smith, you can tell him."

"He'll never understand the people involved. He doesn't know Berkeley!"

A moment passed before Doyle said, "Smith, you're good. I wish I had you back here in Homicide." He paused just long enough for me to note that he'd never made that kind of admission before; I would have felt pleased and justified if I hadn't known a "but" would be leading his next phrase. "But Smith, you're not in Homicide. You are in patrol. Brucker is in Homicide. Got it? Whatever his failings, it's his case. Already been announced to the press. Get it transferred by twelve o'clock."

"He'll be back from lunch at noon?"

"Okay, one o'clock." Doyle hung up.

Four hours. Less than four hours!

I dialed the Telegraph Travel Service and got the manager. "Yeah, I remember Tiffany Glass, the diver. Wasn't my client. Change of time and flight number. We reissued the tickets. Guy next to me handled it. Felt awful. Wasn't his fault, poor devil. He tried every way he could to get ahold of her. Called and called. Left messages. Got the other two girls. Bryn Wiley and the other one. Wiley came in and picked up her new ticket. But he dropped off the other girls' tickets. You can't do more than that, can you?"

"What happened to him afterwards?"

"Oh, you mean was he fired? No. No reason. Like I say, he did over and beyond. But the Glass girl's boyfriend burst in here and scared the shit out of him."

"What did he do?"

"Threatened to smash him into the wall. Said he'd bang him up just the way his girlfriend was. Dave's a little guy; he was here alone. Then the thug demanded to look at the Glass file. He grilled Dave like a co— Sorry, I didn't mean to—"

"Forget it. Go on."

"He made Dave go through every contact he'd had about the flight. Like I said, he scared the shit out of him. Dave was sure the guy was going to kill him. He quit. I think he went back to school. In art, or something."

"Where can I contact him?"

"Dave? Got me; I can't even remember his last name. The school he went to, it was somewhere back East."

A few more questions and answers made it clear I wasn't going to find Dave, not in three hours and forty-seven minutes.

What had Sam Johnson found out? Was it really something that implicated Bryn? If so, why hadn't he exposed her in all these years? If not, why had he and Fannie hung on to her until she became the focus of their marriage?

I could have called Herman Ott. I didn't bother. I ran for my car and headed to Telegraph. It was nine thirty, very early for the likes of Ott. But I was sure Ott would understand.

I had underestimated him.

When I got to his building, he was on his way out. I caught him flying across the lobby, tan chinos clinging to his spindly legs, ocher down jacket zipped up to his almost nonexistent neck, and gold beaked cap pulled down low. "Expecting me, were you?" I asked, blocking the exit.

"I was getting a bagel and coffee. Want some?"

"Your mother must have drilled you on protecting against a chill." Noah's bagels was half a block away.

Ott shifted from foot to foot. "Okay. I admit it, I was skipping out. Look, Smith, the thing is, I can't find a whisper about Ellen Waller. Nothing."

He hadn't heard! I'd known Ellen's identity so long now I'd forgotten it was still a question for him. Any other time I'd have played my advantage to the max. Now I shrugged. "Forget it."

But Ott wasn't about to do that. "You mean *you* know?" The man's tone was almost insulting.

"We police officers are not like you wise and crafty private eyes but occasionally, as we plod along we do stumble, flat-footedly, into an answer."

In way of response, he pulled out a key, unlocked the old cage elevator, hopped inside, and perched on the pull-down operator's seat. "Come on, Smith."

"Come where? That thing hasn't operated in forty years."

"Does now. You can thank Sam Johnson for that." He shut the door after me and rotated the gear lever up. The mechanism was so old there were no floor numbers on the gear box, just Up and Down, meant for post–World War One operators who signed on for lifetime employment and learned every inch of their building's elevator shaft. Blindfolded, one of them could have brought the car to a stop level with every floor. Ott jerked the box up fifteen feet and stopped it, leaving us hanging in the open shaft between floors.

From someone else I would have taken this as a power play. But Ott? He didn't want to bother climbing the two flights back to his office. Here, Ott could wheedle and barter in a soft enough voice that no one would hear him dealing with a cop. If I wasn't satisfied, I could shout again and blow his cover.

"Ott, I've got less than three hours left on this case. No time for our usual pleasantries. What did Sam Johnson find out at the Telegraph Travel Agency?"

He tapped a finger on the gear lever.

"Today, Ott!"

Letting his finger come to rest, he said, "Waller for Johnson, eh? Fair enough."

"Okay. When the case is closed, you'll be the first to know about her."

"Oh no, Smith. I *want*. But you *need*. So give, or down we go." He reached for the gear lever.

I grabbed his hand. "Ott, let me tell you the lay of the land here, just between us pals."

An expression of such horror crossed his face I almost laughed. He would stuff his mouth with rusty Nixon buttons before he'd ever admit that he was on such close terms with a cop.

"I have to turn the case over at one o'clock. To Brucker. Sam and Fannie Johnson can take care of themselves. But Karl Pironnen . . ."

Color faded from Ott's sallow face. His hand lay limp on the gear lever. Clearly our game was over. "Brucker'll grind Pironnen into dust. Smith, even if you don't charge him, the harassing, the interrogation'll turn him into a vegetable."

"I know, Ott. I know."

We stood there a moment hanging high above the lobby, his hand still on the gear lever, mine halfway between us. I wasn't surprised that Ott knew Pironnen; or that he cared what happened to him. His tiny eyes were almost closed, his forehead squeezed in anguish as ethics battled concern. But even if he had something that would save an outcast and damn the man who had defrauded the poor, I wasn't sure he could bring himself to give it, free, to a police officer.

I hadn't been conning Ott when I said I knew. Standing here in the old elevator watching his pale eyes shift as he considered his unconscionable options, I realized I was at my own crossroad. Ott or Brucker? If I gave a civilian—a pain-in-the-ass civilian—vital, undisclosed case data without checking with the incoming officer in charge, I'd be facing a reprimand. But beyond that, I'd never again be trusted with protected information. And Telegraph Avenue would be under three feet of snow before I ever got back to Homicide. Howard and I had a bet on which one of us would make chief. We'd spent long lovely hours contemplating a suitable prize. And now, instead of chief I'd be what? Searching the civil service ads? Driving an airport van? Opening up an office down the hall from the only one who still trusted me—Ott?

I could push down the lever and walk out of here. Brucker would get the case as is. He'd spot Mary Ellen Nash and the Golden State S and L robbery, and zero in on Sam Johnson and the old rads. If the answer didn't lie there, he'd never solve the case. The chasm between the rads and us would deepen; Ellen Waller would fade away as nothing more than a footnote in an unclosed case. And Karl Pironnen? Ott had been dead right in his prognosis. Momentarily I shut my eyes against the no-win choice, then said, "Okay. You repeat this, the only cop you can tolerate will be off the force, you understand."

I expected him to protest or up the ante, or at least gloat at his enormous victory, but he said, "You've got my word."

"Right. Ellen Waller is Mary Ellen Nash."

"No kidding?"

"Right. Now tell me what Sam Johnson found out at the Telegraph Travel Agency?"

"I don't know."

"Ott! You lied to—"

"Keep your pants on, Smith. I'm giving you all I've got. I don't know what Sam discovered there, if anything. But here's the thing. Sam and Fannie are sure Bryn was behind her missing that plane. They don't know how, but they *know* it's true."

"And is it?"

Ott hesitated. We were on new ground, he and I, and his feet shook with every step he took.

I didn't have time to wait him out. I went with my hunch. "That's what you asked Bryn yesterday morning, isn't it? That's what made her decide to leave." I took his silence for a yes. "And you promised her you wouldn't reveal what she said, right? Come on, Ott, I'm trusting you with my entire future here. Tell me."

He pressed the lever. The car jolted. It began to descend. "She swore she wasn't involved."

The car stopped. Ott reached for the gate.

I caught his hand. "You didn't believe her, did you?"

"No."

"Wow. If you don't believe her—and you wanted to, didn't you?—no wonder Fannie and Sam don't. All these years to *know* she's guilty and not be able to find proof. No wonder they are so frustrated, so vindictive. It explains," I said with a shiver, "why they feel perfectly justified in taking the law into their own hands."

Ott nodded. "It's like Karl Pironnen said: When you toss a pebble in the water, you should be willing to get splashed. Sam would see Bryn drown."

I stood thinking of the ripples of vengeance that rolled ever outward, wider, farther from the source, till they became a force unto themselves, impossible to stop.

I fingered the abbreviated ends of my hair, my *perky* hair, and felt like the strangeness of it had seeped down into my skull. I'd made a choice that meant this could be my last day as a police officer.

But till 1 P.M. I was still the acting detective in charge. I ran full out for my car.

I was almost there when my pager went off.

Bryn Wiley's house was on fire.

CHAPTER 24

FLAMES WERE SHOOTING OUT the front door. A fire truck was in the driveway, another in the street. Hoses stretched toward the house; firefighters, masked and shielded, yanked them forward. The windows in Bryn Wiley's living room glowed red against the white stucco walls. Black smoke swirled up into the redwoods. The crackling sounded as loud as if I'd been caught in the middle of the flames.

Glass crashed—a firefighter axing a window. Flames climbed stalks of new air, pricking at the nether branches of a redwood. Water poured in the window and sluiced off the house, hissing violently. Sirens from another engine howled in the distance. Automatically I glanced at the two trucks already here—one of ours, one from Kensington to the north. The third was coming east—from Albany.

Clumps of neighbors stood well away from the action, silently watching, making no attempt to cross the lines or question the officers as they had at Ellen's murder scene. Their drawn faces showed not so much curiosity as fear. They shifted from foot to foot, alert for the flames to spread, ready to throw their photo albums and computer disks in their cars and get out. The Oakland Hills Firestorm had been only a few years ago and hill dwellers had learned that second thoughts can be last thoughts.

Three patrol cars pulled up, spitting out old-timers who'd been around long enough to get the coveted Monday–Thursday day shift. The distant siren shrieked and broke and wound itself up again.

I spotted Jed Estler and Karl Pironnen on their lawn. They were both staring silently, but Estler's eyes were wide with interest, shifting as his attention jerked from one action spot to the next. Pironnen's gaunt, gray face was blank.

"Who reported the fire?" I asked them.

Jed shrank back. "Me. I just saw it, I mean, I wasn't involved, I was just throwing a ball for Nora." His high, brittle voice seemed on the verge of cracking.

"It's okay." *Suspicious*, but okay for the moment. "Did you see anyone inside?"

"No. I told the firemen that."

"Anyone around the house before?"

He shook his head.

"It wouldn't have to have been right before, Jed. Fires can smolder a long time before they're big enough to be spotted."

"No. Look, I'd just come out to relieve Karl. Nora would chase her ball all day and all night if we'd keep throwing it."

I turned to Karl. "Did you see anything there?"

The siren shrieked; Pironnen threw his hands over his ears. The engine came around the lower corner, straining at the hill. Inside the house the dogs wailed.

When the siren broke, Pironnen lowered his hands.

I repeated my question. "Did you see anything there?"

"Nothing unusual."

Not a no.

Following the engine was a television news camera truck with the satellite dish on top. Soon there would be reporters from all the papers and television stations. One of them would spot me. Dealing with them was the last thing I needed; the department would front up their own spokesman, not me. In an hour the case connected to this wouldn't even be mine. I didn't have time— "Mr. Pironnen, what did you see? Who?"

"Only the neighbors."

"Sam Johnson?"

"Well, yes."

"What was he doing?"

He stepped back and I had to strain to hear his thin voice over the noise. "Just walking."

"Where?"

"Down the street."

"From Bryn's house."

He shrugged. "He was past it when I saw him."

"Anyone else?"

"No . . . except Bryn."

"You saw Bryn here today?"

"Yes."

"When did she get here?"

"Don't know. Late night? The van was in the driveway this morning."

"No," Estler said, "it was early this morning. She was just pulling in when I . . . around five."

"When you?"

Estler winced, then grinned boyishly. "I got back from a job," he tossed out, testing my reaction.

Finding out the exact nature of that job—what freaks had been rented for until dawn—I'd leave for later, when I might need it for leverage. "When did she leave?"

"Just when I came out for Nora. I ran into Bryn coming up the stairs, you know, from Codornices Path. I was surprised. She must have been down in the park, maybe jogging around the reservoir."

"Didn't she see the flames when she got to the house?"

"I didn't spot them then."

"Didn't she go in the house?"

"No, she got in the van and left."

"Where did she go?"

I should have known that finding that out was too much to

hope for. I backtracked, "Jed, why were you surprised to see her on the staircase?"

His tan forehead crinkled in thought. "Well, see, she'd come in so late, it never occurred to me she'd be up and jogging. I figured she'd still be sacked out in bed."

Pironnen shook his head slowly, staring at the burning house. "Poor Ellen. It really is Bryn they're after. Ellen was just a mistake, just the wrong face in the car window. An anonymous corpse."

I looked over at him and was surprised by the comfortable expression on his face. Karl Pironnen, of all people, understood the emptiness left by the death of an incidental person.

I checked in with the patrol officer, and told him for form's sake to keep an eye on Sam Johnson's house. I started my car just as the first TV truck pulled up.

The man who answered Fannie Johnson's door was the young guy who'd been sitting on the table the last time I'd been there.

"I'm looking for Fannie and Sam."

"Not here."

"Where are they?"

"Not here."

"Where!"

He let a smug grin grow on his face. "Gone. And cop, you don't need to waste your precious time looking. We all heard the call on the scanner—*another* of Bryn Wiley's many enemies taking care of her. Fannie and Sam got better things to do than hassle with you. Lady, they are gone."

"You're late, Smith." Inspector Doyle busied himself with the papers on his desk. His face sagged beneath a fall of faded red hair. He looked like he'd had a lot less sleep than I had the last two nights. "You have the paperwork for Brucker?"

"Inspector, you got word on Bryn Wiley's fire, didn't you? This case is escalating. It's—"

"It's Brucker's case, Smith."

"Give me one more day."

"Smith . . ." He looked up, with the kind of controlled annoyance you see on the face of a parent. His silence was an opening, a minute one, but if I shoved the narrow end of the wedge in it, I could force it open.

The strength of that wedge was this: Herman Ott supported Bryn against Sam and even Ott didn't believe she was innocent. He believed Bryn caused Fannie to miss the Nationals and wreck her body. I could tell all this to Doyle, that I had to hunt down Sam and Fannie; that I had to protect Bryn. But that was what I'd promised Ott I wouldn't repeat. "Inspector, there isn't time for someone new to familiarize himself with the case, the witnesses, the secondary motives. This is a very high profile case—"

"Just get Brucker the papers, Smith. Then you've got a day off before your patrol shift. Use it to get some distance."

Brucker was sitting in my former chair in my former office when I brought in the Waller/Nash case.

"Where do you want it?" I asked, glancing over the tidy piles on a desk that had never before known neat.

Brucker held out a hand. I placed the case between his stubby thumb and square palm and turned to leave before—again—I said things that weren't going to do me any good. Before I had to deal with him talking about "scumbags like Herman Ott."

"Wait a minute, Smith." He opened the case and began paging through.

"I'm on my own time."

"Mmm. Lot of reports missing."

"Mmm. 'Swhat happens when you pick up a case in the middle. I'm sure you'll round them up."

He ran a square finger down a form, his forehead crinkled like part of a box that's been wadded for the trash.

I could have left. I *was* on my own time. Nothing I say is going to make a difference, I assured myself. But in the end I couldn't *not* try. "Brucker, this case isn't letting up. After the murder it seemed like it would, but now there's the fire. I'm worried about Bryn Wiley." I hesitated. So far I hadn't revealed anything.

Brucker looked up, finger tapping on the file almost imperceptibly—almost, but not quite.

"Brucker, Bryn Wiley was at the scene today. She lit out right before the neighbor spotted the flames."

"*Lit* out, huh?"

"Wherever she is, she needs protection."

"And where is that, Smith?"

"Don't know."

"Well, when you find out, you tell me."

I started to the door, then stopped. "Bryn Wiley got to her house very late last night, at almost dawn. She could still have been sleeping in the house when the arsonist torched it. Brucker, we have to assume this is another homicide attempt."

He smacked the folder shut. "*I* will decide what *I* have to assume, Smith." He flipped open the file with the finger he'd had inside, marking his place. "Now Smith, you can tell me this: The neighbor who saw the flames, who was that? The kid or the old weirdo?"

"I thought we respected all our citizens."

"No, Smith, you coddle the crazies. And there are lots of them here. That's why up in Sacramento they call this place Berzerkeley." He leaned back in my—his—chair and said, "Smith, you got such respect for the weirdos and scumbags, you must've had a tête-à-tête with your scumbag PI. What'd he tell you?"

I stiffened. Up until now I had only kept quiet about Ott. I hadn't impeded the investigation aloud, in a word that could be recalled and used against me. "Nothing," I said quickly, and walked out the door, careful not to slam it. As I strode down the hall to the parking lot door, I wondered if this was the last time I would walk through this hall.

I could have gone home, or driven across San Francisco to Ocean Beach and walked along the dunes halfway to Pacifica. I wasn't due on patrol until Wednesday morning. There were a lot of things I could have done.

Instinctively, I headed back to Telegraph Avenue, heart of "Berzerkeley."

I walked along the Avenue trying to decide what to do with my newfound free time. The buildings like Ott's had thrown the west side of the street into deep shade by now. I passed the pizza place where I had spent many chunks of discretionary cash on the way to Ott's heart and information. The street was relatively empty midafternoon on a Monday. Only a few diehard street artists were on duty, sitting behind tables of crystals or arrays of painted candles that hadn't changed since before Bryn Wiley was in college. There was a time when half of Berkeley had big round candles hanging from leather harnesses, dangerously near their ferns, coleus plants, and wandering Jews. Were there really people who still bought them? Or were the sellers caught in a time warp, as if their futures had retired in Berkeley with the sixties? I glanced at the woman behind the crystals. Her dress was faded, worn, so far out of style I couldn't have placed which decade it belonged to.

"The candles, they have fragrances, you know," she said without hope.

I wondered where she lived, *how* she lived, when she had made the decision to close off other opportunities, or if those doors had been inched shut by things too small to remember. I wouldn't have chosen her limited life any more than she'd have been willing to put in forty hours in uniform, give orders, take orders, turn over cases before they were ready, like candles not quite set. It was an odd bond we had, her job to keep alive the fragile hope of a bygone era, mine to protect her right not to be pushed aside.

I bought a round candle, not quite the size of a bowling ball. Who knew when the next earthquake would come and we'd need auxiliary light for a week?

Half an hour later from Noah's, I got a poppy seed bagel with a chive cream cheese schmear and sat on a windowsill near Ott's building. I should go home, I told myself. I'd handed over the case. But I hadn't handed over my fears that Brucker would crush Karl Pironnen, that Bryn Wiley guarded secrets I hadn't been able to uncover, and that the killer would track her down. I thought of the confessional bench. Had it burned to stakes of charcoal by now? I wondered if the arsonist had started the fire there.

I chewed slowly on the bagel, thinking of Ellen Waller with her life ready to start anew, and how Karl Pironnen had described her: "The wrong face in the car window. An anonymous corpse." I'd been sure she was the intended victim, but now the fire screamed to the world that it was Bryn. Ellen had been just a mistake.

"Spare change?" asked a college-aged kid in matted street clothes.

I handed him my untouched half bagel and headed inside Ott's building.

It took me five instead of the usual ten minutes to get into his office.

Herman Ott was clothed in the last garb on earth I could have imagined on him—sweat clothes. A gold sweatshirt and khaki shorts. The former spanned his little round paunch. The latter bagged in back like he'd gotten up so fast he'd forgotten his butt. Extending from the shorts were spindly legs a color I had not heretofore associated with the living. "What?" Ott demanded.

I walked in and waited until he'd shut the door. "I need to find Bryn Wiley."

"Out of town would be the smart guess."

"Out of town, where?"

Ott shrugged his sloping golden shoulders.

"At her cabin, right?"

His right eyebrow lifted a scintilla.

"Of course I know about that," I insisted. The man could be downright insulting. "What I need from you is directions."

"Well, Smith," he said, propping a hand on the spot where

his hip might have been. "You've got the entire Berkeley Police Department. Hunt her down."

In my head, I composed a smart-ass retort: Not anymore, Ott, not since I lied to Brucker to protect you. But I caught myself before the words were out. It wasn't that I feared he would expose me to the department or the press. He would be proud of me; he'd think much, much better of me than he ever had. And there was just a minute chance that the next time one of Sam Johnson's buddies castigated me, Ott would leap to my defense with the tale of my glorious deed. "You leave me in an untenable position. We're talking murder here. You know where the intended victim is and you won't tell me. What do you expect me to do, Ott, sit around while the killer trots from cabin to cabin, tapping on the door, asking for directions to divers?"

Ott fingered his wispy mustache. He was considering. "Smith, you give me up to the cops, I won't ever, under any circumstances, no matter what you offer or threaten, tell you as much as the time of day."

"Ott—"

"And that's because, Smith, I will be dead."

The corner of the desk was poking into my leg. I didn't move.

"Because, Smith, my clients will hear that I turned over information told to me in confidence by the only person who had that information, and my clients will start to tote up what I know about them and what would make me spill that, too. And soon, Smith, you'll find my remains up in Strawberry Canyon, or floating in the Bay, or maybe in the lobby of the police station and you'll be real sorry. Because . . . you will have so many viable suspects it will take you the rest of your career to close the case."

I boosted up onto the desk. Ott wasn't kidding. *Lips zipped* was not only his motto, it was his safety. When you deal with guys who live on the edge, it doesn't take much for them to push you over. He was being straight with me, all right, but the interesting thing was that he didn't have to bother. He could just have stonewalled. He'd done it often enough. But despite the finality of his statements, the fact that he was making them at all, and that I was here instead of stomping down the stairs empty-handed, meant that there was some give in his position.

"I just need to know Bryn's address. Tell me that and you have my promise that I will not repeat it, not if the entire police force and every sheriff in Sonoma County begs me one by one."

"No circumstances whatever will make you repeat this? Even if it means you can't get enough to charge the killer?"

He was raising the ante a thousandfold. This meant not merely denying what I knew about his opinion on Bryn Wiley. This meant withholding tangible, possibly life-or-death evidence. Evidence I wasn't going to get any other way. If I agreed, that meant I couldn't reveal the location of Bryn's cabin. I would have to go alone, unauthorized, to track down a witness in a case that had been taken away from me. There should have been a better way. There wasn't. "Okay."

Ott caught my eye again. "You break your word, I die. But not before I tell every guy on the Avenue you're responsible."

"*Okay*, Ott. You're on the verge of overkill."

A hint of a smile lifted Ott's narrow lips. He walked behind his desk and settled into his torn leather chair, forcing me to give up my perch on his desk and settle for the latest of his miserable client chairs. Ott didn't need to worry about my betraying him into the hands of a killer client. Sooner or later these chairs would make one of his clients mad enough to kill him. "So?" I prodded.

He gave me directions for the hour's walk from the Cazadero road to Bryn's cabin.

I headed back to my car. Dusk was already clearing out the Avenue. The wind slapped my short hairs against my face. Cazadero was a two-hour drive. It was too late to start out now. I drove home.

Before dawn I got up, showered, changed into hiking boots, lined jeans, a heavy wool paid shirt, and a fanny pack for my semi-automatic, and headed north to Cazadero.

CHAPTER 25

Rain splatted on the windshield just north of San Rafael. March is the wettest month in this area, as if the rain gods know this is their last chance until November. The windshield fogged; I had the defrost on, pouring all the hot air onto the glass and leaving the skin between the top of my socks and my jeans icy. I'd thought about the dirt roads outside Cazadero and the rickety condition of my VW and opted for Howard's new truck. It drove stiff and required a firm hand to remind it who was in charge when it came time to shift gears. And with the two-step-up cab I felt like I was driving on stilts. I'd only driven it three or four times before, and each time I'd had a big reaction to it. I had loved it . . . I had hated it . . . but now I had no reaction at all. The big tank of a truck was just one more strangeness in a week where I had stepped out of my skin and left my familiar world behind with it.

I turned on the radio and half listened to the news as I drove over the shining green hills of spring. I almost missed the last story—a highway patrol officer shot in a routine car stop. I cringed, as I did every time I stopped a car for running a red light, for speeding, for an expired license plate. Each time I stood behind the driver's door, keeping my eyes on his hands.

I knew he could have a weapon hidden under his jacket, beside the seat, in the door pocket. He could blow me away.

When I hit Santa Rita, I had the wipers on high. I opened the window to clear the windshield and the rain splatted my face. Cazadero is west of Route 101, along the River Road beyond Guerneville. The road is two-lane, the Russian River on the left, thickly wooded rain forest hills on the right. Redwoods grow over three hundred feet tall, as wide as the length of the truck I was driving. Branches hung over the road, slapping water on interloping cars. In spring the runoff can turn the shallow river into a torrent that rushes over banks and sweeps away buildings. The river wasn't going to flood this year, but it was running fast and brown and I could make out branches being tossed and twisted by its currents.

I stopped for lunch in Guerneville, bought a couple of apples and oranges in case the traipse to Bryn's cabin took longer than I expected. I wasn't dropping in as an invited friend. She might not ask me to dinner.

If she was in any condition to ask at all. She had left the questionable safety of the city for a secluded spot with danger on every side.

The redwoods closed in around the road to Cazadero, making the rainy morning as dark as dusk. According to Ott, Bryn's turnoff was just past an abandoned ranch house. "Not paved," he'd said, "but she told me the surface is good for a couple of miles. Then, she said, the road peters out and you've got another hour's walk." If I came on the Girls' Team van, I would know where to leave my truck. Ott, himself, never traveled unless in emergency, and even then never off asphalt.

Already I was glad I'd opted for Howard's truck.

The ranch house huddled on the right, its withered boards bowed inward and its roof collapsed. I turned off onto the bumpy, unpaved road. I hadn't gone twenty-five yards before the trees closed in, sheltering me from the rain, muting the light. The truck jostled from rut to rut. I opened the window and let the clean smell of wet redwood flow in.

The road rose, coming to a clearing, then descended the far side of the mountain. Here on the north side, the land got the full brunt of Pacific storms. Dirt had soaked to mud. I downshifted into first. When the road flattened, in the crack between mountains I could see tracks from another vehicle. There was no way of telling how long they'd been there. The trees were two feet from the sides of the truck. What would happen if Bryn Wiley drove out? Would one of us have to back up for miles on this hilly, deeply rutted lane?

The road curved sharply to the left. I yanked the wheel; the truck skidded in the mud before it responded, and I almost hit Bryn's van parked halfway into the road. I slammed on the brakes, sending out a wave of mud. Then I spent the next ten minutes maneuvering a seventeen-point turn so the truck would be facing out.

Ahead there was little more than a path. The redwood branches formed a thatched roof over it. With each step, the fanny pack with my semi-automatic in it tapped my stomach; I found it comforting. I slipped the hood of my anorak off and walked along the soggy ground inhaling the strong, clean aroma of the trees. Like walking through a giant cedar chest. I laughed silently. I might be a stranger to myself, but that stranger was still a total city woman.

My mouth was still slightly open from the laugh when the wind snapped the smaller branches and a sheet of water slapped my face and doused my hair, and started slowly seeping down my back. I had forgotten just how well wool holds water.

Doubtless native Americans of old could differentiate the flap of dozens of birds' wings, tell by the snapping of a twig at a hundred yards whether they walked with deer or bear or raccoon. To me the forest seemed totally silent except for my feet on the soggy leaves, and the rhythm of my breath. I glanced to the sides, and every few minutes behind me, but in the dim light and the rain a stealthy bear could have had me for a snack before I spotted him.

As thoroughly as the thatch of trees kept out the light, it held in the cold. My hands were fisted in my side pockets, pulling my jacket tighter around me, and its wet collar stuck against my bare neck.

About half an hour into the walk it struck me all at once how totally exposed I was. I might as well have been standing at Seawall and University with a thousand-dollar bill hanging out of my pocket. No, there I'd be better off. There, the patrol would come rolling by sometime soon. There, I could turn on an attacker and yell, "Police, get your hands where I can see them! Do it!" I'd done it often enough; I *expected* suspects to obey me. Here there was no patrol, no car parked outside with the flashers on so backup knew where to find me; no comforting city smells of Chinese food, gasoline, newsprint; no solid ground under my feet in case I needed to push off to pursue.

I felt like I was walking in a dream. The heavy anorak dragged on my shoulders, and the gun smacked harder against my stomach. My newly shorn wet hair clung to my head and neck. Three times I reached back to cover it with the ponytail that was no longer there. I didn't feel merely out of place; I felt like I no longer had a place. I was the short-haired woman with the different-shaped face; the driver of trucks and buyer of oranges, the woman who had tossed aside her career and the chance of making a Berkeley safe for people like Karl Pironnen. The ground was no longer solid under my feet. I looked down, and saw mud; that made me smile at last. But when the smile faded, I still felt hollow.

I walked more quickly, checking around me with my antennae up. I heard birds, of course, and rustling leaves, but when I crossed the last rise, I heard something unexpected: the sound of an unattended door creaking on its hinges. I slowed, circling away from the path.

The clearing around the cabin ran from grasses near the house to underbrush, to scrawny trees before it disappeared into forest. Stealthily, I moved around the side of the house. The cabin was just that, a twenty-foot wooden square with a peaked roof. From the untended looks of the grounds, Bryn used her visits here to do absolutely nothing.

I moved toward the back, stepping carefully, keeping behind the trees. A back stoop led down two steps to the ground. The door was slightly ajar, like someone had stepped out for a moment. Or perhaps someone else had walked in.

Taking pains not to snap twigs or rustle leaves, I approached the house, squinting to see in the dark windows. The one by the back door—probably a kitchen window—was propped open, but I couldn't see whether anyone was inside.

I stepped beyond the trees into the underbrush.

And a bullet whizzed by my head.

CHAPTER 26

I HIT THE GROUND and rolled. Brambles scraped my hands and snagged my jacket. My gun cut into my ribs. I scrambled behind a tree and pulled my gun free. On patrol in a situation like this I would have been behind the car door, and wearing a protective vest. "Police," I would call out, "Put down your weapon." I'd be calling in 10-99: Officer needs help. Patrol cars would be speeding in. All I'd have to do would be stay down and wait.

Here I could wait until I died.

Another shot snagged the tree in front of me. So much for concealment. Whoever was in the cabin knew exactly where I was, and probably that I was alone. But he, she, or they probably did not know *who* I was. I didn't intend to point out to them that they were dealing with a cop. "Bryn," I called, hoping it was she in there, "it's Jill. Why are you shooting at me?"

"Jill who?"

It *was* Bryn. "Jill Smith, from Berkeley."

"What the hell are you doing creeping around my grounds here?"

"I've come to warn you. Step outside where I can see you."

"Hey, this is my house. I don't—"

257

"You tried to kill me!"

"Okay, okay. I'm coming out the front door."

She almost jumped out, banging the door behind her, then stopped abruptly, like she had been jerked back on a leash. Her hands were empty. She was a ghost of the woman I'd seen days before, a ghost who'd been through a terrifying death. Her short chestnut hair stood out in clumps, weary hollows turned her angular face gaunt, and her blue eyes had an eerie shine. Her sweater was struck through with brambles and twigs. I'd have put money on the fact that she hadn't slept in days. But for all that, she could still aim and come within a hand span of killing me.

"Are you alone, Bryn?"

"Uh, yes."

I glanced at the windows again. No sign of a companion or captor. No way to be sure, though. I could keep my gun out, ready to shoot. Or I could put it in my fanny pack, with the safety on, and be dead before I could get it out. There was no middle ground.

My gut feeling was to trust Bryn. I stashed the gun and walked toward her.

Under the thick maroon sweater those strong swimmer's shoulders of hers were hunched in fear. Her hands were shaking. Those unnaturally shining eyes jerked around like they were on overload. She was on the verge of mental collapse. I shepherded her back inside.

The house was the size of a two-car garage and looked like it had been built in a week. Plain pine walls. A wood stove for heat, a line of bottles to be carted to a stream somewhere, a paper garbage bag by the door. Open shelves and a closet rod for clothes. The only accommodation to visitors was the extra director's chair by the round wood table. A futon sofa, ready to take up the rest of the floor space, was still folded on its frame. No doubt sleep had been so far from Bryn's mind she hadn't thought to stretch it out.

I motioned her into a chair, pulled out an orange—the worse

from my rolling over it—and handed it to her. "Eat." Before taking the other chair, I closed and locked the back door. Then, fanny pack still on, gun still by my stomach, I took the untouched orange from her hands and began peeling. "Bryn, I'm here to protect you, you understand that?"

She nodded mutely. Sitting there, warily fingering the orange sections I handed to her, she looked more like Ellen Waller than she did herself. This was the woman who had done triple back flips forty feet above the water. She had pushed aside the terrifying possibilities that loomed in the air above and the hard water below her. Now those possibilities had caught her.

"If you want me to help you, Bryn, you're going to have to be straight with me. Okay?"

She nodded obediently.

"*Okay?*"

"Yes." Her voice was almost a whisper. The cables on her sweater were brown with dirt. She must have fallen outside, in the mud. Her shoulders were hunched, this time against the cold. I glanced at the wood stove—no fire. Two blankets were wadded on the futon. She probably hadn't thought to make a fire all night. I wanted to heat water for tea, to check outside for wood, but there was no time. I needed to be sure who the killer was. Wrapping one of the blankets around her I asked, "The National Diving Trials? Why wasn't Fannie on the plane to Hawaii?"

She dropped the orange section she was holding as she shrank inside the blanket. "Tiff—Fannie—missed it."

"Why, Bryn? You didn't miss it."

"The travel agent gave us the wrong time on the itinerary. The flight left three hours earlier. He couldn't reach Tiff in time."

"Right. Because she had moved. But Bryn, you and Tiff trained together every day. You spent hours in the water, and hours out of the pool doing dry land training. You two talked. You knew what a hard time she had with her former roommates. How many times did she tell you about those girls who didn't understand what it was like to be on athletic scholarship? Those girls who thought Tiff was just weaseling out of her share of the work? You knew about them. And you knew she moved."

"So?" She was shivering inside the thick blanket.

"So, you knew where she moved. When the travel agent told you about the mix-up in flight times, you could have told Tiff."

"*If* I'd thought of it. I was rushing around; I was all caught up, getting ready . . . I . . ." She was staring blankly out the window into the gray. Then she gave her head a sharp shake. "Look, the Nationals were do or die for me. I just didn't think." Her words had the ring of an explanation well used. But not true.

"No, Bryn. There's more to it than that. The travel agent said he called Tiff. She never got the call."

"It was a shame."

She wasn't accusing the travel agent of incompetence.

"Bryn, I called the travel company. The agent didn't get fired over this. His boss swears he tried everything to get hold of Tiff. He took Helena's ticket out to her. He even went out to Tiff's address."

She nodded. She'd heard all this before.

"But he went to the wrong address. Her old address. The one where she lived with roommates who weren't speaking to her. Why did he go there, Bryn? Because you told him that address was current?"

"No. He never asked me. He never said he asked me, never, not to his boss, or Tiff or anyone." She picked up the orange section.

So I hadn't gotten the mechanics right. The itinerary listed the flight leaving at 6:56 instead of the correct 3:56. What had happened when the agent realized his mistake that noon? He had called Bryn and Helena. He'd left a message for Tiff. When she didn't respond, he hadn't called Bryn or Helena back. He had tried too hard to reach Tiff; why hadn't he bothered to ask her teammates where else to find her? "You went into the travel office to pick up the new ticket. You saw the travel agent there."

Her fingers closed around the orange.

"And while you were there, he asked you about Tiff. You looked at the address and phone number he had in her file. He must have lost the new address he'd written on something, a scrap of paper, a message sheet. You realized the address was the old one. And yet you said nothing."

"That's crazy. Why would I do something like that to a . . . friend."

"Because Tiff was better than you were. You had to make the cut in the Nationals. You'd only been in the top eight twice, seventh once, eighth the other time. This was your last chance to get the three 'top eights' you needed to make the Olympic Qualifying Trials. With Tiff there your chances were minimal. Then, suddenly, the universe offered you a gift, right? All you needed to do was keep quiet. So tempting; so easy. A panicked decision made by a nineteen-year-old. A decision that makes a mockery of everything you stand for, everything you've done since. If word got out, your reputation would be ruined. The very name 'The Girls' Team' would be a joke. You'd be like Ellen—you'd have to hide out."

The wind stopped and there was no sound but the odd settlings of the cabin, board against board, squeaking futilely. Her face was ashen, her eyes unseeing. Her tight throat turned her words gravelly. "Tiff could have . . . checked with the agent. She didn't. She could have . . . called the airline. No. She didn't do anything. It was her fault the flight was at the last minute. She had an exam that day. Helena and I, we put off our flight for her. We should have gone a day early. But we didn't; we waited for her . . ."

I shook my head. "That doesn't change anything."

The wind rattled the windows, scraping branches against the panes. It chilled my fingers. I looked down at Bryn's hand; she had mashed the orange section to pulp.

"It just happened. I didn't plan to do it. It was split second. I was there picking up my new ticket. The agent had the file open on his desk. There were two sheets of memo paper with Fannie's

name, her address, her phone number. Both places, the old and
the new. I just picked up the new one and stuck it in my pocket.
Nothing more than that."

"On impulse."

"I didn't know it would keep her from getting to the Nationals. He could have called; her old roommates could have given
him the new number. She could have called him to confirm. He
could have called Information . . ."

Tiff wouldn't have bothered to list her name with Information in her new place with only a couple weeks left in the term,
but I didn't want to interrupt Bryn. She was just throwing out
excuses she'd tried on herself and rejected over the last twelve
years, hoping desperately that this time they wouldn't be too
slippery to stick.

Her shallow breath caught, she breathed in deep and glared at
me. "Okay! Okay, it was wrong, but I didn't force her to go up
on the platform and crack her spine. She could have just gotten
drunk and come up with nothing more than a hangover. She
didn't have to dive."

"But she did dive. And you do feel guilty," I said softly.

"Guilt?" She looked puzzled. I wondered if she had walled
herself off from emotion so completely that she had never even
named the emotion she was hiding from. No wonder she had
never been able to face Tiff. But she had allowed Ellen Waller to
bring her confessional bench into her living room.

For the first time I could see the bond that had kept her and
Ellen together, the pain of living with unmentionable guilt.
Guilt that could never be voiced, never atoned, never forgiven.
Ellen had agreed only to drive a getaway car; she had never
dreamed she'd cause a death. Bryn had made a snap decision
expecting to delay and disconcert her rival, not to maim her.
Youthful, self-absorbed, ill-conceived decisions, pebbles tossed
with no thought of the water. One killed, one injured. How
many other lives corroded? Not the least of them Ellen and
Bryn.

Now Bryn's charge up to the microphones in the Olympics

shone in a different light. "Could you have allowed yourself to win a medal?" I asked. Or had she been so obsessed with injustice at the Olympics she couldn't have concentrated on diving?

She looked blankly at me. I wasn't surprised, only disappointed. Bryn was not an introspective person and she'd had years of practice blocking out thoughts of error. "But Ellen did bring in the confessional bench. And she did start to talk about the benefits of confession, right?"

Bryn laughed, a weak sound, but still startling. "She tried. God, she tried. I told her if I'd wanted a therapist there were probably six within spitting distance—from *every* person in Berkeley!"

A gust of wind shook the house. For a moment I thought it was an earthquake. The rain smacked down on the roof. The windows rattled in their frames. Branches scraped across their panes like giant claws. Bryn Wiley sat rock still, braced as if against lashes of retribution.

I wondered if she was as maimed as Fannie Johnson, as dead emotionally as Karl Pironnen. But of course, emotionally dead is hardly the same as having a tag on your toe.

Outside, the rain was as thick as plastic sheets. In here, it was dark as dusk. I could have used that bowling ball of a candle I'd bought on the Avenue. But I didn't dare light a candle. If anyone had followed me, he or she could trot up within spitting distance of the house and I'd neither see nor hear. Right now the killer could be out there.

Or in here.

Bryn was a good enough shot to have taken out Ellen. And setting her house on fire after Ellen was dead neatly turned the focus back to herself. Everyone assumed that Bryn was the intended victim. She could go on being Bryn Wiley, the Olympic Hero. Eventually she would get another secretary, and people would forget she'd ever had this one.

Bryn had snatched Tiff's address impulsively. A quick, sure movement, the way she walked, sat, drove. I remembered her the night she shot out of the driveway and nearly hit the nudist.

But not everyone was this impulsive. Some killers needed time to prepare. I had a thought. "Bryn, Ellen wasn't comfortable driving, right?" I asked.

"She hated it. She drove like a snail and stopped dead if she saw a squirrel."

"So anyone who had observed the two of you pulling into the driveway would know the difference?"

"I should hope," she said, sarcasm dripping from her voice.

I was amazed how quickly she could regroup. Were the wheels already turning to push today's disclosure behind her? "If you had called her to pick you up, would Ellen have gotten back in the car and driven to get you?"

"At night? Maybe if I were bleeding on the sidewalk, if I could pluck her heart strings enough. But I don't know that I had enough emotional pull to do that."

But Ellen took the car home after the rally. And then three hours later she went out again, and got in the car, ready to drive. The key was in the ignition. There was only one "bleeding" that could have made her do that.

There was a sudden shattering of glass. Bryn screamed.

I shoved her to the floor.

CHAPTER 27

"GET DOWN!" I YELLED again.

Bryn jolted up, ran to the window.

A second shot cracked through the air. She staggered back a step, staring down at the blood coming from her shoulder.

I grabbed her and pulled her to the futon. Blood oozed on her sweater. A few inches southwest and that bullet would have killed her. "We need to stanch the blood! Towels? Where do you keep your towels?"

She stared at the wound. Athlete's shock, I'd seen it before. Bryn couldn't believe that her shoulder, a key part of her dive, could be mangled like this, away from competition.

I yanked open the curtain in front of the closet, pulled out a sheet, tore it into wide strips, and wrapped them tight around her shoulder. "Press it hard against the wound. Don't let up."

She complied without comment, pressing down with her right hand.

Squatting, I moved to the window and leaned against the wall beneath it, listening. Rain still smacked the roof; the casement windows had burst open and banged against the house. Nose to sill, I peered outside. But the rain was like one of those old hippie beaded curtains; it blocked out everything but its own shimmer. In the time I'd spent settling Bryn, the shooter could have moved anywhere.

Keeping down, I moved to the back window and repeated the procedure with the same results. There were three more windows, one on the other end of the back wall, a high one at the end, and another on the front wall. On the futon, Bryn was beginning to moan.

"Bryn! Quiet!" But I might as well have kept still. I didn't know how long shock would mask the pain of her wound. Or how many hours before blood poisoning set in or she would bleed to death. Damn it, why hadn't I studied the first aid manuals? Why had I always counted on having an ambulance at the ready?

With one eye on her, I squatted by the front window, listening. The rain shielded us from view, but it blocked any chance of my spotting our assailant outside. It was late afternoon, already dark. In a couple of hours there would be no light at all. If we survived until morning, Bryn would be delirious with pain or gangrene or loss of blood. *If* we survived, we'd face another day like today, only worse.

I thought of Ellen Waller, sitting safe in Bryn's house when the phone rang. The last thing she had wanted was to drive Bryn's station wagon again, in the dark. Volvos shift hard, even for drivers used to manual transmission. I'd driven my friend Mary's old Volvo once and stalled out six times going across town. I'd been furious and humiliated. What could have drawn Ellen into the car?

I recalled the Volvo wagon as I'd last seen it, with the punctured window, and the Victorian house comforter that covered the backseat.

"Bryn, did you keep a comforter on the backseat of your car?"

She looked at me as if I'd lost my mind, then turned back to her wound.

"When Ellen was shot, there was a comforter covering the backseat. Victorian houses on it, etched in black on white."

Still staring at her shoulder she said, "That's Ellen's."

266

"Was it there when you drove the Volvo to People's Park?"

"No. Of course not." She drew in a deep breath and looked up. "I keep my car clean. I don't have crap on the dashboard or debris on the floor. I was only taking a box of flyers with me and they fit on the floor. Why would I pull the comforter off Ellen's bed and stick it in the car?"

"To protect the backseat?"

"From what?"

"From a dog."

Suddenly I understood what the comforter meant. There was only one person whose opinion mattered enough to Ellen for her to drive the Volvo at night—Karl Pironnen.

What had Pironnen said when he called her? "Nora's cut her paw; she's bleeding. She's got to get to the vet. My car won't start. Please help me! Meet me in your car; I'll carry her over there." Something like that.

And Ellen, anxious to help, worried about a sick or bleeding dog lying on Bryn's leather seat, would have grabbed her comforter—the only thing she owned that was big enough—and spread it over the backseat.

"Bryn, when Ellen took Pironnen's dogs to the vet, did she ever miss an appointment?"

There was no answer from her; but the sadness and the horror hit me hard. Karl Pironnen. I didn't want the killer to be him.

When I had pounded on his door a week ago, I was in uniform, patrol car pulsar lights still flashing, a dozen armed cops behind me. Now reality had flipped over and it was he out there, backed up by his knowledge of the woods, a force greater than a score of police officers. At the door that night I had hidden beneath his view and waited until he peeked through the leaded glass window in his door. Then I'd leapt up and got him. Like he could get us.

I knew now how he'd felt, an alien in a friendless place where lights mean only danger. I understood why he'd backed away when I came near. And I realized how long a leap of faith it had been for him to take me into his brother's room. He had brought Ellen there, exposed the core of his life to her, and then she had kicked it aside so she could get on with her own life. If his brother Dan was forgotten, that was fine with her; that's what she *wanted*.

His attack on Bryn's van, on her look-alike in her car, and then the fire would assure the world that Bryn Wiley had been the intended victim all along. Like Dan Pironnen, Ellen Waller would be merely a nameless footnote. The pebble she had tossed when she drove the getaway car splashed Dan Pironnen not only with death but anonymity. Now Karl had sent that karma back at her. Now she would be dead and forgotten. Bryn had agreed with Ellen—the past is past. Bryn could die.

There would be no reasoning with him; there was nothing left that he cared about saving.

I shivered. As he had shivered that first night. After he had shot Ellen. Automatically I reached for my radio, the radio I didn't have, on which I could not call in 10-99. Out here I wasn't a cop. I was just a city person with the odds stacked against me. He was out there with his dogs, and we were cornered like foxes. City foxes. Out here I had nothing to grab on to, no backup, no experience, no knowledge. I could feel panic rising, overwhelming me.

Bryn moaned louder.

No time! I had to move. If I waited until dark, I'd never find my way out of the forest. I had to make my move now.

Keeping low, I hurried across the room, put a pot of water on the burner, and dumped in all the coffee in the tin. When it came to a boil, I brought the whole pot over to Bryn.

"Bryn! Listen! We can't both just sit here and wait. I'm going out there. And you're going to have to give me cover."

Her eyes widened.

I repeated the instruction.

The third time, she nodded. But how long would she remember? How long would she have the strength to care?

"Here's a cup. Dip it in the pan; keep drinking coffee. You have to stay awake. Do you understand?"

Her head bobbed. Her normally hooded eyes were almost closed.

I grabbed her good shoulder. "Bryn! If he kills you, only Fannie—Tiff—and Sam will be left. When reporters ask them about how you got in the Olympics, what do you think they're going to say? You will be dead, and all people will remember of you is that you were a cheat!"

She dropped the bloody sheet and backhanded me across the face.

It startled more than stung. This was one woman who would keep herself alert until she dropped. "Bryn, if we get out of here, then this case will focus on Dan Pironnen and Ellen Waller. Sam and Fannie and the Olympics won't even be part of it. I'm leaving you your rifle."

She nodded, propping the rifle on the back of the futon. I put the coffee beside her, and then, with a longing look at my warm, waterproof anorak, I spread it over her legs. "I'm going out the back. Give me a cover shot." I started to add, "If I'm not back in an hour . . ." but the logical end of that sentence was "you'll bleed to death or Pironnen will shoot you."

She looked up at me. Her breathing was so shallow it seemed that she was afraid to exhale, afraid she would fall to dust. She cranked up a shadow of a smile and said, "The coffee, it's not Peet's; but I'll drink it anyway."

I grinned and in that moment liked her more than I had anytime since I'd met her.

I opened the front fireplace window, shot toward the woods, and pulled the window shut. "Okay, Bryn."

She fired just as I opened the back door.

I ran full out. A shot came from the far side of the house. Glass shattered, but no scream followed. He hadn't hit Bryn. He was firing at the house.

Another shot cut the air, closer. I kept moving, slower now, stepping carefully, back toward the cover of the redwoods. Rain smacked my head, my shoulders, my back. When I made it to the trees, my sweater was sodden and my hair was streaming. I turned to face the cabin. It wasn't fifty yards away but I couldn't make out more than a dark blob. And Pironnen could be anywhere.

I stood listening. The gunfire had stopped. The only sound was the rain and wind, and that so steady it was like cotton jammed in my ears blocking out any warning.

If I could circle around to the path, I could run. Maybe Bryn's cellular phone was still in Pironnen's car. I could get the sheriff out here in . . . in two hours, one and a half at best. Too long, much too long.

My hand tightened on my gun. I had never shot a man. I'd pulled the trigger in training but never in real life. Pironnen was a good shot; probably a better shot than I was.

Lifting each foot carefully, I made my way to my right, away from the sound of the shot. I counted twenty steps and stopped, surveyed 360 degrees around me. Branches waved; dark clumps squatted thigh high. But there were no sharp movements; he wasn't there. Probably.

I moved on, another twenty-five steps. Checked again. And moved on. The drenched sweater felt leaden on my shoulders. My feet squished with each step. Twenty-four, twenty-five. I turned slowly.

Behind me a twig snapped. I spun toward the house.

Underbrush rustled.

Both hands on the automatic, I braced my legs, moving the gun in a side-to-side arc.

The rustling was closer. He wasn't even making an attempt at stealth. Too cocky? Too desperate? Carefully, silently I shifted behind a tree. The trunk wasn't wide enough for protection, but in the semidark it gave some cover.

Leaves rustled. He was moving in, like he knew where I was. I slid my finger from the ready position to the trigger.

And then he barked.

I gasped, with shock. Then with relief. Then with fear.

Pablo, the pi dog. The dog who had kept himself between
Pironnen and me. The rescued dog who would protect his master to the death.

He was a blur between the trees to my right, barking, point-
ing me out for the kill. I aimed my gun at the center of the blur.
Rain ran down my forehead into my eyes. I shook it off. The
dog had inched closer. I could see him clearly now, his ears
cocked, mouth open panting, his short black and brown coat
slick against his body, his ribs lifting and giving way with each
tense breath. I sighted between his eyes, tightened my finger on
the trigger. My finger was stiff; I wasn't breathing. I couldn't
. . . shoot this trusting dog. I couldn't . . .

Pablo barked again. He jostled the tree beside him. Pironnen
could be back there, part of the noise, or coming up behind me,
his movement covered by it. I had no option to run; all I could
do was shoot the dog. My whole body felt frozen . . .

But I was a police officer, for Chrissakes, I had a duty. I
couldn't be paralyzed by sentiment.

I sighted him one last time.

Then I realized that once again reality had reversed. We were
on Pironnen's playing field, but now I made the rules. My hand
eased on the trigger. "Pironnen," I yelled, "I've got your dog in
my sights. Walk over here slowly, hands on your head, or I will
shoot Pablo."

The barking stopped, the rustling ceased. Only the pounding
of the rain held steady. And my heart thumping in my rock-
tense chest.

"Now, Karl! Don't call him. He moves, I shoot! Walk over
here, out in the clearing, hands where I can see them. I'm counting to three. If you're not here by then, *you*'ve killed Pablo!
One!"

There was a rustling of leaves, but I couldn't tell where it
came from. It could be Pironnen; it could be the storm. The dog
barked.

"Two!"

Pablo barked and kept barking, as if he knew his danger. My

hands were shaking on the gun. The trees, the wind, the dog, the rain mixed into one great well of sound. I waited another beat, watching, hoping.

On three I would shoot and run like hell.

CHAPTER 28

"WAIT! DON'T SHOOT PABLO! I'm here! Pablo, stay, boy!" Pironnen shrilled in panic as he ran into the clear.

"Place your gun down on the ground in front of you where I can see it," I yelled. "Do it now!"

Tall, thin, charcoal gray in the dim light, he lifted something —a rifle?—from his shoulder and dropped it on the ground.

Still barking, Pablo ran toward him, stopped in front, and stood barking at me.

"Hands above your head! Now!"

A tear ran down my cheek. "Karl, make the dog sit! I don't want to have to hurt him!"

Pironnen reached forward, his hand shaking so hard it looked like a fan. For an instant I thought he was going for the rifle, to protect his remaining companion. But he dug his fingers into the dog's fur. Then he murmured something and the dog lay warily down, leaving Pironnen's hand empty and quivering.

"Okay," I forced out.

Pironnen fell to his knees and pulled the pi dog to him. I thought I heard a sob but I couldn't be sure.

I knew then that the possibility of Pablo dying was much more real to Pironnen than the deaths of Ellen or Bryn. We, people, couldn't squeeze through his protective grate. For Pablo it was no barrier at all.

I suppose I would have shot Pablo—logic assures me I would have, but God, I'm glad I didn't find out. I couldn't have borne taking the friend Karl Pironnen loved more than his own life.

If I had had second thoughts about this single-handed excursion to a cabin an hour's walk up and down hill from the end of the road, the events of the next two hours made clear I should have had third thoughts, fourth, however many it took till I came to No.

I handcuffed Pironnen to a tree and went to check on Bryn. After the half hour of terror and loss of blood, she was barely lucid and too weak to walk. I didn't dare leave her. I found a wheelbarrow behind the house, rigged a support across the handles, and made it as comfortable for her as possible. Maybe it was from the relief that Pablo was okay—more likely it came from the overload of emotion so foreign to him—but Pironnen clearly wanted to help out. I warned him against fleeing, reminded him I was armed, and unlocked the cuffs. He took the handles of the wheelbarrow and steered as carefully as if Pablo had been the injured passenger. And so our odd little parade headed off over hill and dale to the cars.

I'd been afraid the trek would be too much for Bryn, but the air or the coffee or the prospect of safety actually revived her. When we lifted her from the barrow, she was coherent.

I didn't even bother to question Pironnen. He was the prime suspect, and I was about to arrest him. If I asked anything about the murder, I would have to read him his rights and offer him a lawyer, which I couldn't produce. And when he did get a lawyer, that officer of the court would say I had single-handedly scuttled the state's case. So I did what any wise police officer does in these situations. The law does not preclude our listening to statements freely offered by a suspect. I moved Pironnen to the back of Bryn's van and cuffed him out of reach of her. Then I kept my ears open as I drove out.

His first question was what I would have guessed. "My dogs, what'll happen to them?"

"Your dogs!" Bryn demanded. Her voice was soft but it didn't waver, and only someone from another planet would have misconstrued her anger. "You're worried about your dogs! You could have killed *me*. You shot a woman who looked like me when she was sitting in my car!"

The outburst seemed to have gone over his head. In the same slightly confused voice he said, "Ellen killed Dan."

"She wasn't the gunman, only the driver. And she went out of her way to tell you how sorry she was."

"Sorry?" he said as if contemplating a strange substance. "What difference does *sorry* make? Does it give Dan life? Or me Dan?"

Bryn started to protest. "No!" Pironnen shouted. "The only thing sorry would change would have been how *she* felt. She killed my brother as an aside! An inconvenient incidental! Dan died and no one cared. No one *noticed*. They didn't even remember his name!" He sucked in his lips. "And then she comes around my neighborhood saying the past is over and you should forget it and go on with your life. I heard her tell Fannie Johnson that! On the lawn, right in front of me!"

"But—"

Out of Pironnen's sight I waved my hand at Bryn and put a finger to my lips.

"She killed him. Then she used my dogs to get to me. And she used me, dragged me to that bank where he died. She sat in his room! She didn't care about Dan, she didn't care about me; it was all so *she* would feel better. She wanted me to absolve her, to say Dan's death didn't matter. That Dan's life was nothing."

"That's why you killed her?" Bryn's voice was stilted and barely audible. "I don't believe that. You thought you were shooting me."

I glanced in the rearview mirror; Pironnen was smiling. He didn't explain. Bryn gave a weak snort. She may have taken his silence for agreement.

But it was a smile of victory. I wondered how long he waited for just the right moment. Chess players are patient planners. And this was one well-thought-out murder. Ellen had thrown the pebble in the water; the ripples had splashed on Dan, and on Karl. It must have taken her years to realize that she'd been drenched too.

Victory meant in death Ellen would receive as little notice as Dan had. In Berkeley, where we have twenty or fewer murders a year, each one gets noticed. It's hard to murder a woman and have no one eulogize her. But Pironnen had set up this one so everyone, including Bryn, focused on Bryn. He'd made it seem as if Ellen Waller was just the pawn in Bryn's place.

We reached the road before Bryn demanded, "This cabin is my hideaway. I bought land as inconvenient as I could get, so I wouldn't have people dropping in, and then you . . ." Her voice trailed off as she must have realized the irony of her first visitor. "How the hell did you find it?"

"Ellen looked in your papers for me. Once I understood her game, I knew she wouldn't chance refusing me."

I pulled over at a phone booth and called the sheriff. In twenty minutes the medics took Bryn and the sheriff guided Pironnen into the back of his car.

To me the sheriff said, "We'll get animal control for the dog."

"No!" Karl Pironnen's scream filled the air. "Pablo, no." Palms against the window, eyes fathomless with grief, he stared not at the sheriff, or even at the dog, but at me. "They'll kill him. No. Don't let them. Please!"

An eye for an eye? I thought of Ellen and how much she'd risked to recapture her name, her life. Too much. Once you lose hold of who you are, you never get it back. I shook off the thought, rested my hand on the dog's back. "I'll find him a home, Karl."

CHAPTER 29

"YOU COULD HAVE BEEN in a lot of trouble," Howard said as we sat on the sofa in the living room.

"So Eggs told me, and Jackson, and Pereira just about fell off the desk confiding that bit of information. All before Doyle called me into his office and just about sent me to my room without dinner."

It was now three in the morning on Friday. Between the Sonoma County Sheriff's Department and our department the aftermath of the case had taken well into Wednesday morning. I'd missed the Wednesday patrol shift altogether, leaving the team short. Howard had arrived home sometime Wednesday night when the end of the world wouldn't have woken me. And when I finally did drag myself out of bed Thursday afternoon, I barely had time to get to team meeting at 4 P.M.

I don't know what I had expected when I got to the station. Everything was, of course, the same. And yet it was different, as if the colors were slightly off, or the wall and the tables against it were not metal and masonry but made of something very different. Or maybe it was all the same and it was me that wasn't quite all there under my uniform. I had trusted Ott and withheld information from Brucker. I had endangered my life and that of a witness to protect a murderer from a fellow police officer. But the case was closed, the media happy, and no one was on my back.

It's a myth about walking through the sand and leaving no footprints. There might be hints of prints in Doyle's view of me, and Chief Larkin's. And Brucker wasn't likely to forget. Since this high-profile collar wouldn't go on his record, he wouldn't be as choice material for Sacramento. There were footprints, indeed, and they traipsed over me. I had cared too much about Karl Pironnen. Police officers have to trust each other; they have to mesh into a team, interdependent to the death. I knew now that I could pull my weight, do my share, protect my buddies. But there would never be a point when I would take an order automatically. And if I were asked tomorrow to give Pironnen to Brucker, I wouldn't do it. Ott, of course, would understand. And Murakawa and Leonard and Pereira. And, I expected, in the privacy of his home, Inspector Doyle might, too. No one would admit it publicly. But that's why we worked in the city that resented authority and spent a year considering whether it was legal or *fair* to prevent people lying on the sidewalk or walking nude down Telegraph Avenue. I was glad to be with *this* department. The room hadn't changed; it was still solid. It was I who had become more porous.

Now a fire worthy of Brian Boru, the Celtic king, crackled, and leapt wildly in the great hearth. Smoke rejected by the inadequate flue seasoned the air. On the disc player a guitar and a cello keened, the sound drifting off into the smoke. I nestled back into the sofa cushions and smiled at Howard. He wrapped his long arm around my shoulder, pulled me closer against him. "I didn't pay enough attention to those cute little ears when they were covered with hair," he said, and nuzzled one. "And I did think that by the time I got back, you'd have collared my nudist."

"Gone. The nudists were just cogs in the wheels of private enterprise."

"Very private enterprise." He laughed. "Maybe someone will sue over Rent-a-Freak. That'd be a show."

When he settled back, I grinned at him—in time to see his blue eyes narrow covetously. But his gaze was no longer on me, it was at the wall beside the fireplace, specifically at the cracks and gouges therein.

"Howard," I said, reaching for my wineglass, "you've gotten off very easy on this bet of ours. You've been away from your temptation. Me, on the other hand—well, chocolate didn't leave town."

Howard laughed delightedly. The man really loved to win.

"But now," I said, running my finger under the edge of his collar, "you've got the whole weekend here."

"Hmm. And just what is it you have in mind?" he asked as suspiciously as I'd ever heard him.

"The month runs another eleven days."

He was figuring, I could tell. He was concluding that he was about to lose not one but two weekends of the joy of spackling, the satisfaction of sanding, the pristine pleasure of painting. "So?"

"So, we're adults. In our time we've made mistakes, done stupid things, misjudged effects. But we are mature adults. Let's scrap the bet."

"Now?"

"Now."

"And hit a twenty-four-hour grocery for ice cream, is that what you mean?"

"No. I can go on without sweets. It's no big thing."

Howard was laughing.

"No, really. I could shift into fruits, and uh, stuff."

He threw his head back and roared. "I was just picturing you whipping up carrots and yams."

"Howard, I've just single-handedly corralled a murderer. I'm sure I could do whatever it is you do to a yam." Ignoring his hoots of laughter, I went on. "I could go either way on junk food. But like I said, I'm a sensible adult. Why should I fill my

279

mouth with orange tuber when I could have chocolate? I mean, people have been committed for less than that."

Howard's laugh eased off, but he was still smiling. He lifted the skewer of the last chicken brochette out of the Da Nang Restaurant carton. "You know, Jill, you really are lucky that Doyle likes you. Brucker's got a lot of ties in Sacramento. The guy is pissed. You could have been in a lot of trouble."

"I may have closed another case today."

"Changing the subject?"

"Not totally."

"Okay, which case?"

"Candace Upton."

"The one who's getting the phantom calls from former Presidents?"

"Right. First thing I got on shift today was another call back for her. By now half of patrol has dealt with her. But I don't think she'll be bothering patrol again."

"Who will she be after?"

I leaned back, propped my feet on the coffee table, and took a bite of Howard's brochette. "Well, Howard, you remember that framed photo Brucker displays so proudly on his office wall? I photocopied it, affixed Brucker's card, and slipped it under Candace Upton's door."

It took Howard a moment to recall the picture of Brucker shaking the hand of Ronald Reagan.